GRANTS PASS

A Post-Apocalyptic Anthology

Published by Morrígan Books
Östra Promenaden 43
602 29 Norrköping,
Sweden
www.morriganbooks.com

Editors: Jennifer Brozek & Amanda Pillar
Editorial Assistance: Mark S. Deniz

ISBN 978-91-977605-6-0

Cover art by Reece Notley © 2008

First Published August 2009

Morrígan Books
Available titles from Morrígan Books:

The Even
by T. A. Moore

How to Make Monsters
by Gary McMahon

Voices
Edited by Mark S. Deniz & Amanda Pillar

Dead Souls
Edited by Mark S. Deniz

Coming soon from Morrígan Books:

The Phantom Queen
Edited by Mark S. Deniz & Amanda Pillar

GRANTS PASS

A Post-Apocalyptic Anthology

Edited by
Jennifer Brozek & Amanda Pillar

DEDICATIONS

AMANDA:
To my friends and family,
May we stand together.

JENNIFER:
For my parents, John and Sigrid,
For their support and encouragement

For my husband, Jeff,
Who has his own hut on the island and always will.

JENNIFER WOULD ALSO LIKE TO THANK:
Rick Silva and Rory Clark, for being there at the start and sticking with me through thick and thin. Montgomery Mullen, for indulging my flights of fancy and not laughing at me when I presented you with the idea of Grants Pass as a place of sanctuary.

Thank you, Mom, for enduring years of fiction and editing each piece with firm tact and support.

Finally, thank you, Amanda Pillar, for being an excellent co-editor and Mark Deniz of Morrígan Books for making some hard decisions and taking a chance on both me and the *Grants Pass* anthology.

AMANDA WOULD ALSO LIKE TO THANK:
Thomas G. Bicknell for proofing and offering his journalism skills in preparing the news articles for *Grants Pass*. Maria-Luisa Rodriguez for translating three of the news articles into French and Spanish.

And of course, Jennifer Brozek for letting me make *Grants Pass* my baby too.

FOREWORD

What makes Grants Pass, Oregon, in the USA so special? It is a small city of 23,000 people in the middle of the Rogue River Valley. It also happens to be almost exactly halfway between Redmond, Washington and Mountain View, California. This is important because I drive between these two cities twice a year on average. Grants Pass has become the turning point for my road trips. It has also sunk itself deep into my subconscious.

It may amuse some readers to know that the journal entry written by Kayley in the prelude is based on one I wrote online back in May 2004. After receiving a number of responses from my friends saying that, yes, they would be there or no, they would not be there and why, the idea for the anthology was born.

I spent the next four years advertising the anthology, collecting stories, editing stories and shopping the manuscript around. The most common response I got from publishers was, "This is a great idea but you don't have enough big-name authors. Let me know if you ever get it published". It was both encouraging and heartbreaking at the same time. All the while, my apocalyptic minions would send me story after story of every natural disaster, every possible plague and every great catastrophe that occurred around the world, proving to me that this anthology was relevant to what was happening in today's society.

In early 2008, I had a heart-to-heart conversation with Mark Deniz, who had a story in *Grants Pass*. I knew he was succeeding with his independent press, Morrígan Books, and I asked if he would be interested in publishing the anthology. He told me that he would on two conditions:

First, his editor, Amanda Pillar, had to approve the anthology. Second, he would have to pull his story from it for integrity's sake. I agreed to both conditions. Though, I was sad at the loss of his story. I thought it was one of the strongest in the book.

Long story short, Amanda approved the anthology with a few caveats. The first was that the guidelines had to be tightened up and that all of the stories would need to be re-evaluated to go with the new guidelines. Not all of the stories would make it. This was difficult for me. Some of these stories had been with me for four years, but, I understood why it was necessary.

The *Grants Pass* anthology of today is different than the one I started in 2004 and, yet, the spirit of what I created is still there. Only better. I have learned much working with Amanda and Morrígan Books as we brought *Grants Pass* to life, and I appreciate the effort that goes into creating and publishing a quality anthology.

Five years from conception to publication is a long time. It was hard work but, in the end, I believe it was worth it. This book represents many of my own hopes and dreams for the future, just as the stories within speak of trials overcome, strength of wisdom, hopes, dreams, and sacrifice in a post apocalyptic world that has not yet come to pass.

But what if it did?

Where would your *Grants Pass* sanctuary be?

Jennifer Brozek
August 2009

FOREWORD

CONCLUSION

When Jennifer approached Morrígan Books with *Grants Pass*, Mark asked me to read the collection. He gave me a rundown of its concept, told me he had a story in the anthology and emailed the MS over.

I scanned the contents page and hunkered down with a can of Pepsi, my personal addiction. I read the journal entry and was hooked on the concept. I had to finish the whole thing.

I knew some stories weren't going to make the final cut, and emailed Mark my thoughts immediately: We had to have the anthology, but we had to make some changes. I also emailed Jennifer with the same information, and naturally, she was reserved. Mark read the anthology and agreed.

I arranged an IM meeting with Jennifer and revisited the Destruction of Humankind. Since I have a background in science, I was harsh with the former guidelines. I emailed Russell Kirkpatrick — a fellow author and lecturer — for advice on global warming, and set about restructuring the apocalypse. It had to be as realistic as possible. After a few hours, and Jennifer probably wanting to commit murder a few dozen times, the guidelines were updated. We then made the final cut as some stories no longer worked with the anthology.

I emailed all the authors to update them. I felt horrible, but knew the anthology needed the change. We took on new authors with new stories with the request: We want stories set outside the USA.

And we got them.

Why outside the US of A? This was my fault. I thought that Jennifer's story, 'The Chateau de Mons' was great, and

Mark's tale, 'Russian Roulette', also set in Europe, gave a new sense of desperation and hope to the anthology. But we couldn't use Mark's, so that reduced the number of non-USA stories. So I asked for more, as their tales made me ponder the concept that everyone would have an individual version of Grants Pass, if the real Grants Pass was inaccessible.

Would I travel to Grants Pass? No, I can't say that I would. But that's because I live on the other side of the world, in a remote country, with an extremely harsh climate that is completely surrounded by sea.

Australia.

Would I have my own, personal Grants Pass? Yes. But you will have to read the anthology to find out where that might be.

Amanda Pillar
August 2009

TABLE OF CONTENTS

PROLOGUE: Online Journal Entry:

KAYLEY ALLARD

MAY 26
GRANTS PASS

This post is semi-in-cheek and semi-not. Occasionally, it amuses me to think about these things. The short version of my thought is this: When the end of the world comes, meet me in Grants Pass, Oregon.

I'm not saying that the end of the world is coming. I don't know if it will happen in my lifetime or if at all. But, as a writer, I often ask "What if...?" What if something like Skippy the Super flu virus happens? What if something like "The Day After Tomorrow" happens? What if we are invaded or World War III happens? Better yet, what if, for some reason, the government and known society collapses due to a great loss of life and/or immense structural damage...and I survive it?

Then what?

Well, my plan, as of now, is to meet Monte in Grants Pass. Why Grants Pass? Because I have dreamt of the coming of the end of the world several times. In my dreams, as the End comes, I always wind up in Grants Pass and that's good enough for me. Why Monte? Because he's a good friend, and he indulges my whims when I present him with these mental exercises. And because he has become one of my dream symbols representing Survival. Just like the few times I dreamt of Ice, who represented Leadership and Yony, who represented Desire.

Recently, I mentioned this to Ice and invited him to meet us. If anyone is going to survive the end of the world, it would be him. Then, James jumped in and said it sounded like a plan and he would meet us there, hauling fuel. Suddenly, it occurred to me that maybe I should just let others in on this little plan of mine.

Obviously, not everyone who reads this would survive an apocalypse. Maybe I would not survive it. My desire for immortality says I would, but that's just me. In any case, if the apocalypse comes, and you're a good person who wants to survive with other good people, meet us in Grants Pass. Think about what you would bring. Think about joining a surviving band of people from all walks of life.

I know. I know. This is a silly mental exercise but there is no harm in thinking about it. Which leads to more questions: How would I get there? Would I go by car, more secure and sheltered, but meaning that I have to travel ruined roads? Or a motorcycle for maneuverability? Bicycle for the lack of dependence on fuel and ability to easily bypass obstacles...but with more exposure and slower travel time?

What would I bring with me? Fuel? Food? Water? Weapons? Probably all of the above. I think REI would be the first place I would raid. Wouldn't you raid a giant sporting good store for camping and survivalist gear first?

I know I would try to contact friends by cell phone or IM as long as the electricity lasted. Mostly to see if they were still alive and coming to Grants Pass. Of course, if the end of the world is like "The Stand" and Mother Abigail is saying we should come to Colorado, well, I guess Grants Pass would be the meeting and staging point for it. It is better to travel in groups, I think. Especially if you have both human and animal predators out there, which I think would be the case.

You can't tell me that some survivor (probably male), wouldn't get it in their head to become some sort of warlord and try to rule their own little bit of land. You know it would happen. Personally, I'd rather band together with people I already know than some random tough guy who has figured out how to rule through strength and fear. Though, I admit, not all warlords would be bad. Generally, things go better when there is a clear leader in a group; someone with the ability to make decisions quickly.

Still, coming up with a way to protect and feed a group of people during and after some sort of apocalypse brings to mind some interesting ideas. Some of it goes back to my parents' lessons on wants versus needs. Needs would be paramount — food, shelter, protection. Wants would have to be indulged when it was possible and safe to do so. But, one person's need could be another person's want. It can be very subjective. That's where we come back to the importance of leadership. Someone must be the parent and the bad guy for your own good.

Now, I'm randomly babbling. In a time of crisis, having a plan can make the difference between life and death. If an apocalypse comes and you survive, think of me and then head to Grants Pass.

My whimsy could save your life.

PLAGUE

Hospital Quarantine Declared

The Sydney Morning Herald
Wednesday, June 20th

SYDNEY -- Authorities have imposed quarantine in a wing of the Prince of Wales Hospital, following an outbreak of Ebola on Monday.

The hospital's Albion Street Centre was closed late last night following the fifth confirmed case of the disease, which doctors believe is the Zaïre strain of the Ebola virus.

"At this stage we don't think there's any significant risk to the general public," said Professor David Rawlinson of the Prince of Wales' virology department. "The disease requires contact for transmission, and the outbreak has been isolated, so there's very little chance of it spreading."

No other cases have been confirmed since the quarantine was declared, but hospitals throughout Sydney have been put on alert for early symptoms of the disease, which include vomiting, joint pain and fever.

Hospital staff members have been unable to trace the origin of the first reported infection, but are investigating whether the disease was carried by a passenger on a flight from Africa.

"Ebola has historically originated in Africa, although it has appeared in the past in the Philippines and the US," said Professor Rawlinson. "We're looking at the possibility it crossed from one of those regions via plane."

The Ebola virus typically has a mortality rate of 50-90 per cent, and is transmitted via skin and mucous membrane contact.

The Price of Wales quarantine coincides with three other cases of rare disease outbreaks that occurred early last week in Paris, Tokyo and Austin in the US state of Texas.

Diagnosed as bubonic plague, the other outbreaks are also suspected to have been spread by airline passengers, and have already led to several deaths. The US Centers for Disease Control has declared the outbreak contained, echoing statements from authorities in France and Japan.

Ogawa Calls Black Death Emergency

The Japan Times
Friday, June 25th

TOKYO (Honshū) -- Prime Minister Taro Ogawa has declared a state of emergency in the Adachi, Kawaguchi and Hatogaya metropolis wards in order to contain the spread of what has become Japan's worst disease outbreak on record.

"We cannot ignore the fact that there is a humanitarian crisis underway," Ogawa said at a news conference on Friday in Tokyo. "We have acted to contain the spread of the disease, and we are evacuating neighbouring wards."

Cases of the Black Death have risen to the hundreds since the original diagnosis of the virus almost two weeks ago, and the body count hit 90 early this morning.

Coinciding outbreaks of bubonic plague in the United States and France have already quarantined sections of Austin, Texas and Paris, France and health authorities have estimated cases at 220 and 312 respectively.

Scientists are still struggling to isolate the exact strain of the disease, which has exhibited significantly higher fatality rates than other known forms of bubonic plague and has so far proven resistant to antibiotics.

The carrier for the disease has also yet to be found, with the historic transmission via fleas having already been discounted.

Meanwhile, efforts to control the spread of the Ebola strain dubbed Severe Viral Hemorrhagic Fever (SVHF) in Sydney, Hollywood, Cape Town and São Paulo have stalled as...

Peruvian Army Begins Lockdown

Agence France-Presse
(AFP)

...said General Muñoz.

Army trucks have begun ferrying bodies to mass graves on the outskirts of the city as improvised morgues have become overwhelmed, according to local media reports.

The flood of refugees to neighboring states, many wearing the white surgical masks already proven so ineffective, have had to contend with police roadblocks and bridges washed away by heavy rains.

Peru's government remained optimistic that the international research coalition formed yesterday under the aegis of the World Health Organization would yield a vaccine quickly, despite the WHO's declaration on Tuesday that the three diseases ravaging the globe had been deliberately engineered.

"We have determined that the Severe Viral Hemorrhagic Fever and the new strains of bubonic plague and the Super Flu were intentionally created — designed to become more transmissible and fatal than their original forms," WHO Director General Dr Paula Chernoff said in a statement.

"It seems obvious from the breadth and speed of the outbreaks that they were also released deliberately, although no terrorist groups have so far claimed responsibility."

Walton Makes Address on California Earthquake

The Washington Times

President Walton made an address to the nation early this morning, rallying the public to increase relief efforts across the country.

In the President's address, he said the earthquake that hit California yesterday would serve to stiffen the spine of all Americans in their effort to overcome the challenges placed before them.

"While Los Angeles may not be part of the continental United States any more, the city and its people will live on in the hearts and minds of all Americans, for all time," the President said.

"In this darkest of hours, it is our duty to rise up against the massive difficulties placed in our path."

The death toll from the earthquake may never be confirmed, but local disaster relief authorities have estimated it in the hundreds of thousands.

"Most of the city has been flattened. Parts of it are just gone. Just...gone into the ocean. I can't even begin to describe it," an unnamed spokesman from the Los Angeles Fire Department said.

Thankfully, large numbers of the city's population had already been evacuated in the effort to contain the Super Flu and SVHF outbreaks in the metro area...

La Super Influenza

La Vanguardia

El Servicio Nacional de la Salud emitió algunas cifras hoy confirmando la muerte del número de muertos producidos por la Super influenza en Barcelona. Esta cifra en Barcelona ha llegado a 100 000.

El caso inicial en Barcelona se reportó durante los últimos días de la semana pasada.

La cuota de muertos en Madrid, donde se cree que fue el inicio donde esto comenzó, se reporta en los miles ya.

Se considera que el virus llegó al país a través del Aeropuerto Internacional de Barajas de Madrid.

El Rey Felipe ha tomado control, después de que las muertes el Vice-Presidente y del Presidente fueron publicadas.

Radio Announcement

This is the BBC World Service.

Fighting has broken out across Northern Ireland following the British army's declaration of a total quarantine yesterday afternoon.

Elements of the New IRA along with groups of armed civilians attempted to storm army blockades at ports and airports in Derry and Belfast, but military sources say the attacks were turned back.

The Prime Minister is due to enact further emergency powers tomorrow, which will include full martial law over the British Isles and a suspension of parliament.

In other news...

Invasion du Canada

Quebec Post

Tous les contacts ont été perdus avec les stations de control de la frontière de Edmunston ā Cornwell. Le gouvernement a admis que un grand nombre de refuges (lesquels sont armés) ont inondé les frontières.

La police a calculé que le nombre de refuges ont contribué avec l'épuisement du systēme de la Santé de l'Ámérique avec 1.2 millions.

L'armée a envoyé 3 bataillons ā la frontière, mais les troupes ne vont pas arriver jusqu'à demain...

Radio Announcement

This is...this is the BBC World Service.

Following the death of the Prime Minister, Deputy Prime Minister and head of the opposition, the Queen has announced the dissolution of parliament, and urged all healthy Britons to coordin- [Sound of coughing.] To coordinate...

I can't do this anymore. God, forgive me. No James, I can't. Just turn it off.

[Quiet, rough-voiced singing]

God save our gracious Queen,
Long live our noble Queen,
God save the Queen.
Send her victorious,
Happy and glorious,
Long to reign over us...

[Coughing.]

Oh Lucy. Oh Lucy...

[Broadcast fades out into static].

Ham Radio

"And the Lord spoke unto Moses; say unto Aaron, take thy rod, and stretch out thine hand upon the waters of Egypt, upon their streams, upon their rivers, and upon their ponds, and upon all their pools of water, that they may become blood; and that there may be blood throughout all the land of Egypt."

And Aaron did so as the Lord commanded, and so he has done again! The judgement of the Lord has fallen upon this world of sinners, and the unclean shall be washed away; the adulterers, the homosexuals, the heathens, the worshipers of false idols.

All across this land, the three plagues are performing the will of God as the sword of Azrael. Repent, sinners, for the time of the Lord's judgement is at hand! For too long you have mocked the word of the Lord. Repent, sinners! The wrath of a vengeful God is upon your backs!

Reverend Robert Whitlock

Radio Announcement

Todos están muertos.
Todos están muertos.
Todos …. En el río.
Todos están muertos.
¿Qué puedo hacer?
¿Qué puedo hacer?
Lucía dijo, vamos al norte
Antes de morir, dijo que deberían ir al norte.
Hay un pueblo, dijo en el pasado de Grant. La gente iba ahí.
¿Hay alguien más vivo?...Por favor… ¿Hay alguien ahí? Por favor.

THE SURVIVORS

14 months since Kayley's post…

AN UNKINDNESS OF RAVENS

STEPHANIE GUNN

Ravens mourn their dead. I didn't know that, before. I always thought that ravens were solitary animals. I don't know where I got that idea. Maybe in school. I'll never get to find out now. Now, there is no school, no New York, no world.

Now all I hear is the mourning song of the ravens, and in my head is the line from Poe's poem: *Quoth the raven, nevermore.*

Back in June, when it started, we thought they were just aberrations, the effects of global warming. The hurricanes, the droughts. The earth gone crazy. But then the plagues came, the Black Death, the hemorrhagic fever. And then the super flu. Rob told us that it was the end of days, thrusting a moldy New Age tome in our faces. We laughed at him, of course.

We stopped laughing when the plagues hit New York.

This is my city, for all that I was born on the other side of the country. I came here ten years ago, drawn by Broadway, the television shows and movies. I was going to be a model, an actress, a star.

I think you can guess where I ended up, even if you can't see my thigh-high boots and miniskirts.

I'm not ashamed of it. I made good money, sharing an apartment in a good building with another one of Rob's girls, Renee. Life was easy.

I was working the night it started here. A Japanese businessman. He'd been a customer of Renee's, but she had called in sick. I'd been happy to step in for her, borrowing one of her Versace gowns for the night.

The dress had been discarded on the floor, the champagne popped when he started to cough. This deep, rasping cough that went on and on until he was coughing ropey strands of mucus and blood.

It was at this point that I blanked out. It's something I've done for as long as I can remember. When I'm with a particularly repulsive client, my brain just switches off, and I go through the motions on autopilot.

When I came back to myself it was to find the bed littered with the pillaged remains of the mini-bar. Even the chocolate bars had fallen prey, and a crumpled cigarette packet was on the nightstand, for all that I had given up years ago.

It seems so insane now that I thought that renewed habit was the worst of my problems.

I returned home to find Renee gone, and Rob seated in the living room. I had blanked out again on the trip, but found myself unlocking the door with a bottle of bourbon and carton of cigarettes under one arm.

Rob fixed me with bleary eyes as I entered. "Renee's dead," he said, his voice flat.

I dropped the bottle of bourbon, the cigarettes following to splash into the puddle. "What?"

He rubbed a hand over his eyes. "It was the flu. Just the flu," he said. "But, at the hospital, there were people everywhere. With the flu. *Dying* from the flu. There were bodies in the corridor, on the lawn out front."

I pulled the cigarettes from the bourbon puddle. "People don't die from the flu."

He strode across the room and seized my arms. "They do from this flu," he said, his eyes wild. "People are dying. There are corpses out in the street. They're dying of the flu." His fingers tightened on me hard enough to bruise. "The goddamn flu."

He began to cough.

That's when I tuned out again. I don't know how much time passed in that fugue state, but I know that when I came back to myself again, Rob was dead. It must have been days. He lay on Renee's bed, fetid fluids staining the silk coverlet. His eyes were still open, bloodshot and staring.

That's when I got really scared. I ran from the apartment to the elevators, and punched the button hard enough to crack the plastic face. The first doors to open revealed a group of elderly people clustered on the floor of the cab, all dead. A rat was gnawing leisurely on the neck of the closest woman, whiskers beaded with blood.

My stomach heaved, but nothing came up but thin, acrid bile that tasted of ash. Thankfully, the next elevator was empty.

The electricity flickered halfway to the street, bringing the elevator to a screeching halt. It swayed from side to side in the shaft, metal clanging on metal like the ringing of a church bell. After a long moment it started again, shuddering its way down.

The lobby of the building was empty, but someone had covered the walls with hundreds of pages of paper. When I moved closer, I saw that each page was identical. As I took one down, the electricity flickered again, the hole I had created suddenly an abyss. I turned and fled from the building, holding the paper like a talisman.

The area immediately outside was empty, a small pool of captured sunlight; the warmth baking into my shoulders bared by the thin straps of the tank top I wore. I was also wearing an ancient pair of jeans, the fabric little more than threads at the knees. On my feet were Renee's black stiletto Gucci heels.

The paper I had taken from the lobby wall was crammed with tiny print. Several pieces were on the flu, as well as newspaper clippings on the plagues worldwide. At the bottom was a journal article, written by a girl named Kayley the previous May. In it she outlined a sketchy plan to meet in Grants Pass if the end of the world ever eventuated.

I folded the paper carefully and tucked it into the pocket of my jeans. It was then that I noticed the complete and utter silence.

For me, New York has always meant noise. The ever-present music of traffic, yelling voices, the thump of bass from the clubs. Today, there was none of that. Just the eerie, flat silence that crowded at my ears, pressing against the hollow of my throat, close as a lover.

I ran then, heedless of the stiff leather scraping at my heels, the screaming of my calf muscles. I blanked in and out as I ran.

Lines of cabs still neatly parked in their lanes as though waiting for a change of lights, their drivers still behind the wheel, faces swollen with the putrid gases of death.

Black.

A woman sprawled on the sidewalk, her hands reaching out for a nearby newspaper stand, now empty. Her fingers were heavy with gold rings; her lacquered nails the color of blood.

Black.

A group of children huddled around the still form of a dog. Their limbs were locked over the matted fur, stiff and blue. I tried not to see the ragged holes in the dog's sides where the children's teeth had been.

Black. Black. Black.

I stopped at an abandoned newsstand and helped myself to a chocolate bar, digging change out of my pocket to leave on the counter. No newspapers were left. I walked down the street, looking upwards at the buildings to try to orient myself. I didn't want to look down at the sidewalk or street anymore. When my feet nudged against something solid, I felt my way around without looking. I focused instead on the taste of the chocolate, the rich creamy sweetness. It was warm, half melting in the packet.

It hit me then that it was summer; that the dead would putrefy rapidly in the heat. Suddenly the chocolate tasted rancid, and I tossed it away half eaten in a trashcan.

My sense of direction clicked in then. I was only a few blocks away from Central Park. I walked them quickly, eager for the refuge of the park. I passed a hot dog vendor on the way. A hot dog, complete with mustard and ketchup, sat on top of the stand. Next to the food, a large black bird eyed me before dipping its beak to the sausage, tearing away a shred of pink, gristly meat. I shooed the bird and took a bottle of water from the cart. I didn't leave any change this time.

Strangely, the park was almost empty. I passed only a few corpses, splayed out as though sunbathing. Their eyes had dried to opalescent pools in the bright sunlight, lending them the aspect of surprise, as though death had snuck up behind them. Gotcha.

I swigged from the already warm water as I walked, feeling a thin sweat break out on my forehead. The sky above was completely clear, a gorgeous summer day. A month ago, there would have been dozens of people sunbathing here.

I came across another of the black birds after a few more minutes of walking. This one was perched on a small rise in the lawn, gazing steadily at me as I approached. It didn't move when I moved close, not even when I attempted to shoo it. When I looked over the rise, I saw why.

They were a family, united by rigor mortis into a single unit. The baby was wearing denim overalls, unsexed. The father was dressed in full army regalia, camouflage useless against death. Letters embroidered on his breast spelled his name: Brown. Their eyes were all gone, ragged crimson holes left in their place.

21

It hit me like a soft blow to the midsection, standing there looking down at the Browns. This was it. The world was at an end, and I was left, somehow immune to the plagues. And except for the bird still staring at me, I was alone.

I lay down on the grass next to Mrs. Brown, curled an arm around her waist. Her flesh was hard beneath my touch, feeling more like stone than muscle and skin. I closed my eyes. Prayed the lord my soul to take.

When I woke again, the air was cooler, the sun a dim orange eye sinking beneath the buildings. The bird was still there, watching. But now it had been joined by three others, all arrayed in a neat line along the ridge, all gazing down on me. Were they ravens? Crows? I didn't recall ever seeing anything but the ubiquitous pigeons in the park before. The pigeons were all gone, leaving only these black birds. The lines from Poe's poem rolled through my head, and I knew. They were ravens.

A series of shots echoed across the park, unnaturally loud in the stillness. I scrambled to my feet and was running towards the sound when another volley of shots sounded. I didn't care if it was a madman. It was someone alive.

I found him near the edge of the park, blood still pumping in arcs from the hideous wound that had consumed most of his face. Surrounding him were at least a dozen ravens, all dead. The closest was still bleeding, its thick blood blending with that of its murderer.

As I watched, a group of ravens spiraled down from the sky to form a circle around the fallen birds. As one, they began to vocalize, the noises coming from their throats rising and falling like song. Were they mourning?

"A group of them is called an unkindness," a voice said from behind me.

I whirled around, blood hammering in my ears. Sitting on a park bench was a man who appeared kin to the mourning birds. His hair was long, as black and glossy as their feathers. He had skin paler than anyone I had ever seen, tracings of blue veins mapping his life. His eyes were fixed on me as intently as the raven's had been, a deep sapphire; the color of the sky at dusk.

He lifted himself off the bench with a dangerous, feral grace, his steps eating up the distance between us with disconcerting rapidity. He was wearing brand new combat boots and a pair of black jeans slung low on his slim hips. His chest was bare but for a tattoo, its ink faded, obscuring what it had originally been.

"He was going around shooting the ravens," he said, gesturing to the corpse in the middle of the circle of mourning birds. "He must have reached his target or something, because he turned his gun on himself." He slipped through the ravens, who shifted slightly to allow him passage, though they didn't break their song. He knelt down and began to pry the gun from the dead man's fingers.

"You can't do that!" I protested.

He worked the gun free and wiped it on the man's shirt, tucking it into his waistband before pillaging the corpse's pockets for ammunition. "Why not? He doesn't need it anymore." He slipped back through the circle of ravens again. "There's no law that says only the good guys survived."

I found that I couldn't look away from the gun, this murder pressed against his pale flesh. "Have you seen anyone else alive?" I asked.

He shrugged, muscles sliding smoothly under his skin. "There was a baby in the building I was in, crying. But the door to the apartment was locked and reinforced, and I couldn't break in." He was quiet for a moment, rubbing his fingers against the stubble on his chin. "There must be others, but I haven't seen them."

His accent was strange to my ears. "Where are you from?"

His lips curved in a half-smile. "That obvious, is it?" He laughed. It was a harsh noise when juxtaposed against the song of the still-mourning ravens. "I'm Australian. I saved up my money for a few years to be able to come here. I'm a songwriter, thought I could make it here."

"Well," I said, arching one eyebrow in a practiced coy smile. "There's a lot less competition here now, sugar."

He stared at me for a moment before laughing. "That's true, I guess. You're from here?"

I nodded. "For the last decade, anyway."

"What did you do for a living?"

I looked down at my shoes, the leather now scratched. "Oh, this and that," I said. I don't know why I didn't tell him. As I said, I wasn't ashamed. "Nothing now." As the words left my lips, the ravens abruptly fell silent, turning as one to gaze at us.

"Quoth the raven, nevermore," he said, lips curving into a half-smile again. "I'm Lucas."

I noted the lack of a last name and decided to follow suit. "Sarah."

He held out his hand, and feeling slightly ridiculous, I shook it. His fingers were cool and dry. "I have a place that I've set up," he said. "You want to come back there with me?"

I shrugged, my hand still in his. "Why not? It's not like I have anywhere else to go." As we left the park, we heard the ravens begin their mourning song again.

His place consisted of the lobby of a tiny hotel, the neon sign gone to darkness. One of the glass entry doors had been smashed; he put a piece of cardboard up in its place after we entered. The lights in the dusty chandelier were glowing reluctantly, flickering as the electricity waxed and waned.

I felt a surge of hope at the sight of those lights. "The electricity is still on. That means that there must be someone still alive."

"I think the plants can keep running for a while unmanned," Lucas said. "It's been cutting in and out for a while, and I guess it'll go out for good soon. I have plenty of candles and torches and stuff."

In the dim light, I saw boxes and plastic bags stacked up around the sides of the room. Lucas led me past them to a small office at the back of the lobby. There were no lights on inside, and it took me a moment to recognize the black chitinous items piled within. Guns. He pulled the weapon from his trousers and added it to the pile before closing the door firmly again, locking it with a key that he pulled from the pocket of his jeans.

"What are you going to do with all of those?" I asked.

He turned to me, the dim lights flickering like flames in his eyes. "Like I said, who knows who's left out there? There are people like the raven killer, gone insane. I'd rather have them here. Protection." He began opening some of the boxes lined up against the wall. "You like Spam? I hope so, because I have cartons of it."

"I'll eat it."

He gathered up a few cans, placing them on top of the teetering boxes before turning to a pile of plastic bags. "It's lucky that I found a camping store," he said, his voice muffled. He came up with two sleeping bags, still rolled in their cases. "We're gonna need these when night sets in." He threw one to me; I was glad to see that it was a single. "I have some air mattresses here as well. I'll set them up after we eat." He ducked down again, coming up this time with a loaf of bread and six-pack of beer.

We made rough sandwiches with the bread and Spam, pulling chunks from the loaf with our fingers. Though Lucas had managed to amass many essentials, it seemed that he had neglected cutlery. I ate slowly, forcing the greasy mass down my throat with swigs of beer.

Lucas finished his food quickly, and was starting on his third warm beer when I finished eating. "You usually wear shoes like that?"

I looked down at the Guccis. "Yeah, why?"

"You're not going to be able to run around for long in them. They're already blistering your heels."

Easing one shoe away from my foot, I saw that he was right. A row of angry red blisters dotted my heel.

"It's okay," Lucas said. "We'll get you some more tomorrow. I'll buy you some," he added, laughing, the sound slightly blurred from the beer.

I retired to sleep as soon as possible, inflating my air mattress with difficulty. Lucas watched me, but didn't offer to help, methodically finishing the six-pack of beer. I deliberately set up my mattress on the far side of the lobby. When he set up his mattress, he placed it directly next to mine.

When I woke it was dark, and Lucas was gone, his sleeping bag shucked like a snake's skin. I lay there for a moment, disoriented by the silence before the pressure in my bladder forced me to rise and seek a bathroom. I performed my ablutions rapidly, the chemical smell of the water heavy in the still air.

The girl in the mirror was a stranger, her face bare of makeup and dyed red hair limp around her shoulders. Automatically I dug in my pockets and retrieved a tube of lipstick. I got as far as rolling the tube up and placing it to my lower lip before dropping it in the empty sink.

I dug into my pockets again, finding loose change, a Metro card, credit card, my pager. Each item I dropped in the sink, the change rattling against the porcelain like chains against bone. Last of all, I drew out the piece of paper I had taken from the lobby of my apartment building. This alone I replaced in my pocket.

I found Lucas out on the sidewalk, smoking. He held out the packet to me wordlessly; I took one. When I inhaled the smoke it tasted stale. He nodded towards the horizon. "You see that?"

A faint glow lit the sky. "The sunrise?"

Lucas smiled. "The sun rises in the other direction. That's a fire. New York is burning."

I shivered, cold despite the warmth of the air.

Lucas threw the butt of his cigarette to the pavement, where it smoldered balefully. "It'll take the whole city if no one stops it." He pressed the heel of one boot onto the butt. "We should get you some shoes. There's a lot of broken glass around."

We walked three blocks, me limping in my heels. There we found a small discount store, the kind of place that I would never have set foot in before. Lucas vanished upstairs, waving me towards the women's department where I picked out a pair of cheap trainers and thick socks.

Lucas reappeared while I was lacing up the new shoes, the Gucci heels discarded among a pile of dollar rubber sandals. "Look what I found!" He brandished a plastic bag filled to the brim with apples. All were perfect, identical and shining deep red. I took one and bit into it.

The sweetness exploded in my mouth, more delicious, it seemed, than anything I had tasted before. The second bite revealed only twisted bitterness. I spat the bite out, Snow White in cheap plastic shoes. The apple was black at the core, rotten. I lobbed it into the midst of a display of cheap jewelry.

"Bad luck," Lucas said. "Want another?"

I shook my head, nausea thick in my throat. He shrugged, and polished off his own apple in quick bites, throwing the core after my rotten one.

We walked back to the lobby, a task made much easier by my new shoes. "So, what's your plan?" Lucas asked.

"My plan?" I found myself looking towards the fire, turning back to see where the sun was beginning to rise, staining the sky blood red. "I don't know. Get out of New York, go somewhere else."

Outside the lobby, Lucas sat down on the hood of a stalled cab, blithely ignoring the dead driver who leered at him through the cracked windscreen. He reached into his bag and selected another apple. "I was thinking of heading out to one of the military bases. If anyone's left alive, or has a cure, it'll be there." He bit into the apple, a wet tearing sound. "You know, it's entirely possible that they bred this thing, and released it." He took another bite, and spoke with his mouth full. "They did that with AIDS, you know."

I restrained myself from correcting him. Most people might think that I'm just a dumb hooker, but even I knew that what Lucas was saying was unfounded. "I have another idea," I said, reaching into my pocket and handing the journal entry to him.

He scanned it quickly, gulping down the last of his apple and flinging the core over his shoulder. It landed in the lap of a woman seated in a pink convertible, her blond hair still perfectly coiffed around her withered face.

"Grants Pass?" Lucas asked. "You want to go clear across the country on the basis of some girl's diary?"

"Someone put these up in the lobby of my apartment building. Someone is going there at least," I said.

He twisted the paper in his hands before folding it up and thrusting it into the pocket of his jeans. "Maybe it's part of the whole conspiracy. Maybe Grants Pass is a testing area."

He leapt off the car, landing heavily on the pavement. "Why the hell not? It's as good as anywhere else."

I watched him vanish into the gloom of the lobby, restraining the urge to run after him and snatch the paper from his pocket. As he vanished completely, a raven swooped down, air from its passage lifting my hair. I looked up to watch it as it wove through the buildings. In the distance, the raven's mourning song began again.

Despite Lucas' initial enthusiasm for making the trip to Grants Pass, he didn't make any plans to move. The passing of days was measured with the waxing and waning of fires in different parts of the city. It seemed that there was always an eerie glow on the horizon, sometimes brighter than the sun itself. And always, there were ravens in the sky, mourning.

I began collecting supplies for a move, haunting army surplus and camping stores. I assembled my cache in an old restaurant several streets away from the lobby in which Lucas and I spent nights. This wasn't by conscious choice. The first day I gathered a shopping cart full of supplies, a raven swooped me as I tried to return it to the lobby. It kept on swooping me, its beak eventually carving a thin strip of flesh from my scalp until I turned away.

Lucas took to vanishing for days at a time, returning with guns and ammunition, and eventually also maps. One day when he returned to the lobby, he was dressed in army fatigues, the shirt open, revealing a thin slice of pale skin. I shuddered when I saw him, afraid that the name patch would read "Brown", but instead it read "Singer". Two guns were holstered at his hips and he had shaved off his long dark locks, the tender skin of his scalp strangely vulnerable.

To cover up my expeditions to gather supplies, I had taken to raiding bookstores, returning to the lobby at night with armfuls of reading material. I was reading *MacBeth*, propped up on a pile of cushions on the sidewalk. Lucas tore the book from my hands without a word before dragging me into the lobby.

Inside it was dark, the air rank. Lucas had taken to hoarding what fresh produce he could find, and most of it languished uneaten and rotting. Added to that was the sickly stench of human effluvia; the toilets had blocked and overflowed.

Lucas threw me down on his mattress, standing over me. The sleeping bag was thick with the sour scent of his sweat. "It's time you paid your debts," he said, one hand curling around a gun. "I fed you, let you stay here. You owe me."

I didn't argue at first. I didn't even protest when he pressed himself down against me, the acrid scent of his unwashed body smothering.

But when his fingers fumbled at my jeans, I screamed. I don't know why I reacted how I did. I had done this many times before with men far more repulsive. All it would take would be to blank out, and when I woke it would be over. But I didn't blank out. I fought. I scratched at him, aiming for his eyes, stomach, groin. My bare feet were poor weapons, my nails too short to be claws. He slapped away my blows as though they were flies.

He managed to unclasp my jeans, pulling them roughly away from my legs. My underwear followed suit, and I was naked against the rough cloth of his stolen uniform. His flesh beneath it was heated, almost feverish. His breath steamed at my throat, his chin heavy with stubble.

His fingers worked at his own fly, and I screamed again. In that moment, I heard the mourning song of the ravens again, and it was as though something possessed me. This thing twisted my body against him, pressing my mouth against his and twined my free arm around his waist, pulling him close.

Something other than me gripped the gun still holstered at his waist, turned the gun up and pulled the trigger.

The sound exploded like a bomb, and in its wake the ravens fell to silence.

I left him there, bleeding from his belly. I took nothing with me but the journal entry that I retrieved from his pocket, miraculously unstained by blood. The clothes he had torn from me I left there, walking naked into the street.

There, an unkindness of ravens waited. I nodded to them as I passed, and as one they rose and flew into the darkness of the lobby. To Lucas' credit, he didn't scream once.

I began my pilgrimage to Grants Pass naked, baptized in blood. The sky above was heavy with smoke, the sun a tarnished disc. The concrete beneath my feet was cool, almost clammy, like the skin of one of the corpses rotting in the street. The city was dead, decaying. And I was dead, a ghost walking through the afterworld.

There would be others, waiting in Grants Pass. There, my ghost would take form again.

The ravens flew above me, beside me, their voices rising in their song of mourning.

BIOGRAPHY

STEPHANIE GUNN

Stephanie was born and raised in Perth, Western Australia. While her formal education is in microbiology ʾand immunology, she has discovered the worlds in her mind to be far more interesting than any seen down a microscope. She is an associate editor for *Horrorscope* and a reviewer for *Black Magazine*, and has had short stories published in the likes of *Shadowed Realms*. She is currently at work on several urban fantasy novels.

AFTERWORD

I've long been fascinated by cities and the way that our urban society would crumble in the wake of an apocalypse. New York, for me, is the quintessential city, and the perfect setting for this story. Ravens are a motif that feature in a lot of my work, and it was natural for me to include them here, as both carrion eaters and heralds of the future.

I'd like to hope that even in the event of a series of global catastrophes, humanity would find their way through to something better.

BOUDHA

K.V. TAYLOR

A low buzz trickled through the wet evening — those few who weren't sick were taking advantage of the momentary lull in the storms to find supplies. The buzz used to be the sound of mantras or prayer wheels, shopkeepers playing their Tibetan chant CDs at top volume to attract business. Now the shops were shuttered and abandoned, the only sounds left were low, frantic snatches of gossip from the rest of the Valley.

Pema didn't need to listen to it to know what it said. Most of Kathmandu was dying, and those who weren't would be dead soon. The circle of shops and monasteries around the stupa had gone from a busy spiritual and commercial center to a soggy, spare hub in mere days. The relative handful of people still healthy enough congregated here when the weather allowed, maybe so they could pretend they weren't the only ones left.

She hefted the pack on her shoulder and led her brother home through the too-thin crowd, sparing a glance here and there for some of the beggars — the ones who were still alive. She pressed a few rupees into a hand here, a bottle of water there, and she knew Sonam did the same behind her.

Water was more precious than rupees. The Bagmati was swollen with monsoon waters, even more so than usual, but this year it was poisoned and overflowing with bodies. Cartfuls of them were left at the ghats, so that everyone had to abandon the Pashupati temple-town there, except the most devoted sadhus.

Which figured. When you devoted your existence to a god who danced in a cremation ground, it was probably second nature to do it yourself. Especially when you smoked as much hash as the sadhus did.

A thicker-than-usual knot in front of one of the monasteries blocked Pema's progress, and she was forced to stop. She was in a hurry to get back to Tenzin, but they were near their apartment now — she could see their curtains fluttering in the open window above. Sonam bumped into her from behind. "What's happening?"

She shook her head and went up on her toes.

Sonam turned and looked over the heads in front of him, taking it all in with eyes even more intense than usual. "There's a monk on his knees, and another one with a stone."

Someone near her muttered in Nepali, "It will come to us all."

Pema almost asked the speaker, an older woman in a black-and-red Newari sari with her wrap over her head, what would come. But just then a tall man who'd been standing in front of her moved, and she saw for herself.

The monk on his knees was fully prostrate, his forehead pressed to the marble entryway, a small, adolescent figure in saffron and red. Another monk, older, kneeled over him, wielding a large, smooth stone two or three times the size of his head. He raised the rock and brought it down, pretending to smash the smaller monk's brains out.

Pema furrowed her brow. Some of the Nepalis around them muttered, beginning to understand. But the other Tibetans seemed to grasp what was happening immediately — or at least, they didn't question it.

"Like sky burial," Sonam said quietly, into her ear. He sounded sad — he had for days now.

She nodded, unable to tear her eyes off the spectacle. It wasn't something that belonged here, so it struck her as odd. This was for pilgrims who traveled to the sites behind Ganden and Sera, the other sacred places. But she knew what was happening, and why it was significant now, as all anyone could talk about was the third plague; the one that had finally reached them here. Where everyone had desperately hoped they'd be safe.

The young monk on the ground was meditating on his own death, and it was definitely a sky burial. He would be thinking of his body being taken apart piece by piece and fed to vultures on one of the high plateaus of their homeland. The stone was for crushing his skull, so the vultures could have what was inside. It would all be eaten, gone to the sky — food for the gods.

Returned to the circle.

The Nepalis weren't squeamish about death — their beliefs were similar, especially the Buddhists, even if their death rituals were different. They all understood the most basic message of this meditation.

Existence is impermanent. Don't become attached to this world. It's not real. It won't last.

Pema chewed on her lower lip, watching the young monk hold his position after the symbolic crushing. She could barely see his lips moving against the marble under them, praying, meditating. Reminding himself that this was what they would all get, and that it was...all right.

She took a deep breath, subconsciously missing the smells that used to linger there. Frying samosas and nag champa incense, replaced now by sickly sweet death. But watching the monk whispering his mantras into the ground, she felt a little better.

But she had to get back to Tenzin and make him as comfortable as she could.

Pema turned away for a moment and reached for another wet cloth for Tenzin. Sonam was on his own bed in the corner, under a wall covered in his own fantastic drawings and paintings. Cities he'd never seen and creatures that had never existed, pictures of deities and myths from Greece to South America, sensitive portraits of friends, spread over his head. His legs were propped up in front of him, one of his elbows resting on a knee. His hand hung low, holding a string of beads, his mala, and he pushed them through his fingers, one after the other. Staring straight ahead, he didn't seem to realize what he was doing. His lips moved, but no words came out.

She didn't blame him. Even the incense couldn't cover the smell of sickness in their one-room flat, all sour and *wrong*. The storms had started again, and the sky hung heavy and gray over the Boudhanath Stupa outside. Thunder rolled now and then, and bucketfuls of rain slammed against the roof. They couldn't even open the window to let in some air.

New cloth retrieved from the cool bowl beside her, she took the old one from Tenzin's forehead and replaced it. He made a face, like her touch hurt him. Pema winced because she knew it did. It had started three days ago. Now Tenzin's normally sun-brown skin looked like pale wax, wet from sweats that came out of nowhere. He'd sleep for a few minutes, then wake up and twitch in some awful unspoken pain, then sleep again.

She hoped he'd sleep forever soon. When he did, she wouldn't leave him at the ghats with all the others. Sonam wouldn't want to either.

Cloth replaced, she stood and wiped her hands on her jeans and went to the desk, flicking on the computer screen. The Internet connection had gone down last week, but she still opened up her inbox and went through her old mail now and then. They hadn't seen anything from their oldest brother, Thinley, who had been in Chicago, for weeks. The last she'd heard, the sickness and devastation was worse there.

Here, they'd had landslides in the mountains, disasters along the roads to Tibet and floods on the roads to the Terai. The monsoons had begun early for the last two years, the rivers had been flushed with too much runoff from the Himalayas, but the Valley and her people had mostly survived. Pilgrims had still come from the villages, Hindus for the temples, and Buddhists for the stupas and monasteries. Shopkeepers had opened their doors in spite of the fact that there were no tourists, and hadn't been in over a year. It was an act calculated to ward off their own despair, but it spread to the rest of the city — or at least the neighborhoods like Boudha that used to thrive on tourism.

Pema wished she could find out about Chicago — whether things were better or worse there. Thinley's emails used to be so funny, full of stories about the city, how different the clubs were there, the jokes people told him, and the strange Inji couple who owned the restaurant where he worked. But she didn't open any of those; instead, she opened his last mail, scanning it again, even though she had it memorized.

It still didn't make any more sense than it had the first time. He must've been sick when he'd written it — Tenzin sounded the same, fevered and confused. There was something pasted into the text — a journal entry, maybe from someone he knew there, but definitely an American.

When the end of the world comes, meet me in Grants Pass, Oregon.

That, at least, made a little *more* sense, these days. But still, not much.

As she had the thought, there was a sudden popping sound from the computer, from inside the walls, and the screen went black. The sound of the tower's fan stopped short. The light overhead flickered and went out.

A hard knot formed in Pema's stomach, as she sat there in the gray-almost-dark, listening to the suddenly deafening sound of the storm outside. She looked over her shoulder at Sonam.

He sat in the exact same position: Staring at nothing, fingering his mala thoughtlessly. He hadn't even noticed.

"It's not Thursday, is it?" she asked, because she wanted to hear him say something. Thursday was Boudha's scheduled evening for blackouts, to save power…but she knew it wasn't Thursday.

"No. Saturday." His expression never changed.

He could've at least smiled at her, she thought. He was the oldest here — he used to smile at them when things got bad. He used to at least *try*.

She stood and went to the window, looking through the torrents of rain down to the circle below. The tiny crowd in front of the monastery had cleared when the storms started again, but a few monks were still there, meditating on their mortality. She looked to the stupa, the center of their world — its seven-foot high outer walls a stark white in the growing darkness. There were three levels of platforms up, a walkway of a mandala, to the whitewashed dome. She tried to see it as it used to look, with saffron lotus petal shapes sprayed across it every new moon; the eyes on the tower above still bright and blue, the fringe of material shielding them; and the strings of prayer flags above, bright red, green, yellow, and blue.

But it was all faded and frayed now, endless rain and shortened manpower taking their toll. Her eyes started to burn, and a loud clap of thunder struck, rolling over them. It shook the walls.

She returned to the desk and opened a drawer, looking for candles and a torch. She didn't figure the power would be coming back. Not ever.

♦

A sudden crack of lightning forced its way behind her eyes, tearing her out of a deep sleep. Pema sat up in bed, breathing hard. She glanced over to the next bed quickly, saw Tenzin there, silent and pale. She watched carefully in the dark and...yeah. His chest rose and fell.

She started to take a deep breath and reached for a bottle of water on the desk—

Another crash, though, this one from inside the room. Her eyes darted through the shadows, her entire body tensed. There had been so many lootings this past week, with everyone falling sick one after the other. Anyone could be inside, and Sonam slept like the dead. What if?

He stepped out of the shadows on the far side of the room — a tall, broad-shouldered figure. Familiar.

She took a deep breath, finally. Just Sonam.

But Sonam was in his jacket, with his Adidas Sambas laced up. A backpack hanging from one hand, a small purse, the kind the Indian beggar-kids tried to sell to tourists for twenty times their value, from the other.

The purse they kept all their money in.

"What are you doing?" she asked. Her body began to tense again, although she wasn't sure why.

He stepped closer, skirting the edge of Tenzin's bed until he came to the foot of hers. He looked down at her, biting his lip, his fingers clutching at the Indian purse fitfully. Like he was trying to strangle it, but couldn't quite bring himself to.

"Sonam," she said through her teeth. A command.

He shook his head. Sadly, she thought. "We have to go."

Her heart began to race, and a sick feeling rose in the back of her throat. "Go where?"

"Lumbini—"

"Lumbini flooded last summer, they barely saved the pillar. Do you think they're not sick down there in the jungle too, if we are up here?"

"Dharamsala then—"

"Delhi was hit first; of course they have it in Dharam—"

"Lhasa!" he shouted, making a cutting-off gesture with the purse-hand. Like this was the end of the discussion, some kind of irrefutable truth.

The lightning was distant, she realized, as his eyes flashed with it. Her heart thudded loudly in her ears until the rumble of thunder finally came, several seconds later.

She couldn't believe it. Of all the things she'd seen in the last year, this was the most awful. It was a nightmare, it had to be. Not her Sonam.

But he just stared at her, looking wild and cold.

Finally, she forced herself to speak again. "Even if the roads hadn't been swallowed up by the landslides, do you think that Beijing wouldn't send the first sick Chinese right into the Tibetan quarter to finish the job for them?"

Sonam recoiled slightly, his shoulders slumped.

Pema knew damn well that this was playing dirty, reminding him about why they had to stick together — not just their family, but their people. But it wasn't half as dirty as his game.

He started forward, hands then knees on the foot of her bed. She pulled her legs up underneath her to make room for him. He sat, knees touching hers, and looked her in the eye.

He didn't look right, she thought. Didn't look like Sonam. Something was wrong...although that should be fairly obvious, by then. If something wasn't *wrong*, he wouldn't be acting like this.

"He's going to be dead in the morning," he said. He didn't look or gesture toward Tenzin. He didn't need to.

"And so will the rest of this city. But we're not sick. We need to go somewhere safe."

"We can't leave him. Sometimes people get better—"

"One in a billion."

This was an invented statistic and Pema knew it, but it was probably close enough that it didn't matter. So all she said was, "Nowhere is safe."

He closed his eyes, shook his head.

She reached out, pushing his hair out of his eyes, her fingers brushing his forehead. Her heart stopped. He was burning up. Even with that smallest touch, she could tell. "Oh my god," she said it in English, like they always did. "Sonam."

He opened his eyes. He didn't look like he understood.

"You're..." but she couldn't make herself say it. Her thoughts were frozen, this new revelation rattling around in her head uselessly.

But it didn't explain why he would want to leave Tenzin. And, she suspected, why he'd been about to leave her, too.

He shook his head and swatted at her hand, which hung in the air between them. One last look at her, and he was on his feet, swooping down for the purse and backpack.

"Don't leave us," she said, almost without thinking. It just came out, and her eyes started to burn for what felt like the twentieth time today.

He didn't turn back though.

"Sonam, don't leave me."

But even before he walked out the door, she knew there was no point. She thought about going after him, dragging him back, hitting him and kicking him until he *listened*...but she didn't.

Her eyes overflowed, and she buried her face in her hands.

Tenzin's frail figure convulsed again; this time, he coughed something like blood onto the sheets. Something *like* blood because it was blacker and thicker than blood should've been.

Pema wiped it up — first off his graying lips, then from his chin, and finally the bed. He winced slightly at her touch. There was no light behind his eyes when he opened them.

It wouldn't be long now.

The coughing died out after that, and Tenzin seemed to fall asleep, his shallow breaths growing further and further apart, his body relaxing under the sheets. Pema laid a new cold cloth on his head and peeked out the window.

The rain had stopped for the moment. Now was probably the last chance she'd get today — and there was nothing in the flat but biscuits. She'd better save those for when it got *really* bad — those things could survive a nuclear holocaust, let alone a plague.

Another glance at her little brother, to make sure he was asleep, and she grabbed a bottle of water and slipped out the door, down the pale lime green hallway, into the cramped stairwell, and out the door onto the stupa-circle.

Silence. Not even the thin, frantic gathering from yesterday. There were a few dead beggars against the stupa walls, but all the brown, blue, and green doors were sealed against them. Whether there was anyone inside to care, Pema didn't know.

She'd seen death before — it happened a lot near the stupa. The sick and poor came to beg, and once in a while they died there. Her mother had passed away in the flat upstairs, not long after Thinley had gotten his visa to go to the US. Bodies were paraded around the stupa in covered palanquins before being taken down to the ghats, in normal circumstances. Bodies in the street and on the sides of the road were almost common.

That was what she told herself, as she picked her silent way over gray cobblestones, the faded eyes of the stupa looking down on her blankly. But she couldn't fool herself into thinking this was *normal* death, no matter how hard she tried. Maybe, if Sonam was still there to smile and pretend with her, she could've done it. But Sonam had left them a long time before last night, really.

The only open door was the monastery's — the same one they'd stopped at yesterday. Pema approached on squelching-sneakered feet, eyeing the doorway suspiciously. Every corner could hold a new and horrific sight for her, and numb though she was today, she didn't think she could handle something ghastly. Not here. Not where her mother used to take her for puja in the mornings. She'd fall asleep against her, listening to the monks chant and ring bells, breathing the smell of butter tea...

But there was nothing ghastly, as it turned out. Two monks sat on the marble entryway now — an older man, in a fit of coughing, and a younger. The latter was the same monk from yesterday, who'd had his head symbolically crushed. He patted the old monk on the back and muttered something to him.

They both looked up when Pema approached. The old man blinked and smiled. The younger just stared, as if he were surprised to see her. He couldn't have been more than thirteen or fourteen — he still had baby fat in his cheeks.

"Lama-la," she bowed her head to them. "Tashi delek."

It felt odd to greet him like that, almost like a bad joke. Like nothing was wrong.

The older monk smiled, his eyes crinkling in the most charming way, and returned the greeting. "Are you hungry?"

She nodded, tried to return the smile, but failed. It made her eyes start to burn — but they were still red and raw from

43

last night. That was the last thing she needed, to cry more. "I was looking for something, but I didn't think any shops would be open."

It hadn't been a very good plan, now that she thought about it. Why had she thought she could get anything — without breaking into the stores, anyhow?

The old man gave the younger monk a slap on the leg, and the boy took off in a shot of red and yellow into the monastery. "Are you alone?" he asked.

"No. My brother...he's sick."

The monk nodded, looked like he was about to say something else, but started coughing into his robe instead. Pema saw that his eyes glowed bright with fever, and his high cheekbones made him look sunken. Too sunken for an old lama living in a rich monastery. She held out her water bottle to him and he accepted gratefully, chugging it. By the time his coughs had calmed, the boy had returned with round, flat bread for her.

Pema accepted it, and caught herself smiling when she met the boy's eyes. He was only a little younger than Tenzin, three years at most. They looked nothing alike, with the little monk's bald head and round face...

But Tenzin used to have pink in his cheeks like that.

"I'll come back tomorrow, to check on you," Pema promised, before she could start crying.

The old monk nodded, raising the water bottle as if to thank her for it. The little monk tried to smile back, but he couldn't seem to manage. He'd lost the composure of the boy who'd had his head symbolically cracked for vultures yesterday evening.

Pema decided to do some kora around the stupa. Just three rounds. Maybe she'd feel better then.

It took Tenzin one more day to die.

Pema held his hand for an hour, even after he took his last painful, rattling breath. Not because she wanted to pretend he wasn't gone — she was glad for him, she only wished it hadn't taken him so long to be free. But she held his hand because she didn't know what else to do, and that was what she'd been doing when he'd stopped breathing.

There was nothing left. Yesterday she'd wandered Boudha — winding alleys that used to be lined with booths selling cuts of meat, piles of garbage that needed to be burned, restaurants advertising everything from momos to apple pie, glass-windowed shops with turquoise jewelry and Newari-made bronzes of Chenrezig and Thankgas painted with Green Taras. But now prayer flags fluttered over empty carpet factories and monasteries, streets were clogged with abandoned autos and the bodies of people who didn't have anywhere better to die. Packs of dogs fought over the leftovers of the neighborhood. Flies were everywhere, encouraged by the lack of humans to whisk them away.

The smell was awful. She'd thought she'd get used to it, but no matter how much incense she burned in the flat, it was everywhere. In her hair, in her clothes, in her nose.

She wondered, letting her brother's hand go, why she hadn't gotten sick. She'd kissed Tenzin's forehead, she'd talked to the sick monk yesterday, when he'd looked like he was on his own deathbed. She hadn't tried to keep from it. She *wanted* it. Now that Tenzin was gone—

She covered her brother with a sheet, took a bottle of water and some of Sonam's drawings from the wall, and left. Wishing she could set the whole building on fire, knowing that she never could. It was home.

The monastery door was open, a few candles burning in the dark depths of the front chamber. She left her sandals at the entryway, noticing vaguely that they looked lonely there, all by themselves. When she went inside, the smell of butter lamps and juniper warded off the cloying death-smell that coated Boudha like a film.

She stopped, put her water down, and began her prostrations. Hands together — first at the head, then the throat, then her heart — and then down on her knees, head to the floor. Three times, offering herself body, speech, and mind, almost without thinking.

Only when she stood did she look at the massive statue at the far end of the hall: Shakyamuni Buddha in his robes, sitting as if under the bodhi tree at the moment of his enlightenment, shining and golden even in the dark. One hand reached over his thigh, to touch the ground. Calling the mother earth to bear witness for him; to show he wouldn't be swayed by Maya, the illusions of this world. He was serene, for someone being threatened by a demon. She'd never thought it was odd before, but now she did.

Had he really just laid down and died calmly? Did he come back, like these monks swore to do when they devoted themselves to the Dharma? Or had he simply disappeared, freed himself, and never had a thought for anyone else?

He'd died from bad pork, that much she knew.

The thought, inexplicably, made her laugh.

It wasn't that it was funny — in fact, it was awful. It didn't matter. She laughed so hard she couldn't stop herself, until she couldn't remember why she was laughing. Until her stomach hurt and she sank to her knees in front of the statue, rocking gently back and forth.

"Pema?"

She looked up, trying to get herself under control. She was hysterical, she realized, but it wouldn't stop.

"Pema Tsering." The young monk — his name was Tashi, of course his name was Tashi, everyone who wasn't named Tenzin or Pema was named Tashi — hit his knees beside her, giving her a shake.

She looked at him, his wide dark eyes and expression of fear — not for himself, for her. Poor little monk. What had he seen of life before this plague? The boys sent to the monasteries lived better than the families who sent them, generally. And here he was, lighting the lamps, doing the puja, burning incense, and sweeping the floors. All by himself.

"Where's...?" She gained control of herself and started to ask after the older monk, but the boy's expression told her everything. She sat up straighter, on her knees. "He's dead."

Tashi nodded.

"Why aren't we?" she asked.

He shook his head. "We'll all be dead, some day. But they went before us."

Her head cleared suddenly, looking at him. Remembering him whispering to the marble outside. He radiated calm. Acceptance. The boy from yesterday was gone.

She took a deep breath — astringent, beautiful juniper and warm, burning butter smells filled her lungs. It cleansed her senses for the first time in forever. There was silence for a moment, where she watched his eyes. Then, "I haven't seen anyone else in Boudha."

"No," he agreed. "No one comes anymore. I tried to use the booth, to call India..."

He didn't need to finish. She got to her feet, and he followed. When she looked around the hall this time, she didn't see anything much to laugh about. "I don't really want to die."

She hadn't realized it until that moment. But she didn't.

She missed her brothers. Sweet Tenzin and his dreams, who'd really disappeared the day he'd gotten sick. Sonam and his drawings, his temper, his affection, and his fears. Thinley and his funny emails from America.

Existence was impermanent; she'd always been okay with that. But she was here. Now.

"Is there anything we can do?" he asked, looking at the ground thoughtfully.

Thinley and his emails.

Pema looked up at the boy-monk. "No. But...maybe there's a place we can go. If...we can get to America; to Grants Pass."

It sounded insane to her when she said it out loud like that.

But Tashi smiled brightly. He reminded her of Tenzin again. "Will you teach me English?"

Pema smiled. "Of course."

BIOGRAPHY

K.V. TAYLOR

K.V. Taylor is an avid reader and writer of urban fantasy and dark speculative fiction, even though the only degree she holds in is in the history of art. (Or, possibly, because the only degree she holds is in the history of art.) Originally from the Appalachian foothills of West Virginia, she currently lives in the D.C. Metro Area with her husband and mutant cat. Her work can be found on the web at kvtaylor.com.

AFTERWORD

The mixing of cultures and religions in the Kathmandu Valley is dizzying and wonderful; when I lived in the predominantly Buddhist neighborhood around the stupa a few years back, it absorbed me as easily as the hundreds of other traditions with roots there, and became a true home away from home. (It's also home to the best apple pie in the world, I'm convinced.) And so, when it came to the end of the world as we know it, my mind went straight to the Himalayas, their sacred geography, and their way of looking at life and death.

'Boudha' is the name of the stupa at the heart of the neighborhood, the name of the neighborhood itself, and the Nepali word for Buddha.

HELL'S BELLS

CHERIE PRIEST

Along my windowsill I used to keep six small bells. They didn't match at all, because they came from different places. My mother called them tacky souvenirs, and she said they were cheap, and that she wished my grandmother had never bought them for me.

But I liked them.

I could sit on the radiator if it wasn't turned on, and I could hold the bells between my fingers while I looked out the window over the hospital parking lot. If I shook the bells gentle, they tinkled. If I banged them hard, they rang wild. I liked the loud sound best, when I threw the bells up and down, popping my wrist to make the noise bigger.

One of the nurses said I made her crazy with the bells. She was afraid that something was wrong when I played with them, and I was keeping the other patients awake, besides.

I told her that she was right and it was true, when you ring the bells something's usually wrong. The loudest bells mean danger, or sorrow, or warning. I heard them on the long red trucks with the white ladders, and on the bank building downtown — clanging crazy after the glass was broken. And I heard them loudest from the church down the road, every time someone died.

The nurse in her stiff uniform said that this was all the more reason for me to leave the bells alone. She scooped them up off of the windowsill and took them away.

I cried, but she wouldn't bring them back. I told her that my grandmother gave them to me, and that my grandmother was one of the early dead, and I thought it might make the nurse sad. I thought it might make her feel sorry for me.

But she had a headache and other patients had complained.

I begged her for my bells but she shook her head and left me in the white-walled room. No one felt sorry for me except for me.

My mother was one of the later dead; she followed Grandma, and then my brother followed her too. They shouted all the time, and they didn't like my bells either. So even if they'd been alive by the time I was in the hospital, they wouldn't have stopped the frowning nurse who took my bells away.

I bet.

I can't remember if the church bell rang for any of them, but I hope it did. I hope that the bell rang and rang, that you could hear it as far away as the next town over, and they couldn't stop it — they couldn't take it away — because they were dead.

When I was first left at the hospital, it was a very crowded place. I didn't even have my own room for the first week. The doctors left me in a hall with a bracelet on. The bracelet was plastic. It had a note on it that said NNOK.

In the hall, I met a little red-haired boy with a tired-looking mother holding his hand. He tugged on my bracelet and sounded out the letters he saw there. I told him it was my name, and he could call me "Nnok."

His mother shook her head and said no.

She said it meant "No next of kin."

I think she must have been right, because Grandma and my mom and my brother were dead by then, and there was nobody else who ever came to see me. I sat down on the floor and opened my backpack, where I kept the bells before I had a windowsill. I pulled them out one by one and held them tightly in my hand so they didn't ring, but only clattered.

After awhile, the hospital got less and less busy. I got my own room, and the doctor told me I could decorate it however I wanted, because it didn't matter anymore. I asked him what that meant, and he coughed when he answered.

"I don't think anyone else is ever going to stay in it anyway."

I took it to mean that this was my new home, and it wasn't so bad. I never saw the doctor again, though I heard him coughing up and down the halls. I only saw the nurses once in awhile, and sometimes they coughed too. They brought me a tray with food on it twice a day, once in the morning, and once in the late afternoon, just before sunset.

Mostly, everyone left me alone with my bells — until the one nurse took them away.

At first I was lonely; when the other, nicer nurses who were left began to cry in the corners rather than bring me coloring books and trays with runny white pudding.

And when I'm lonely I get bored.

I crawled out of bed one night, while the hospital was dark and empty feeling. I thought maybe the nurse had put my bells in the lounge with the big TV, because there was a desk there and some filing cabinets, and I knew sometimes the nurses put things inside them.

The TV was on when I tip-toed by, but it wasn't showing anything good. It had been left on a static channel, buzzing with black and white snow and throwing light out in funny patterns on the floors. If I were tall enough to reach it, up there in the corner by the ceiling, I would have turned it off.

But I'm too short, so I didn't. I didn't care if the TV played anyway. I wanted my bells.

On the back-side of the desk there were 5 drawers. I opened them all, starting at the bottom on the left and working my way around. I found lots of papers, folders and some envelopes too. There were pens and pencils, and metal clips for holding stacks of paper together.

I didn't find my bells, but I found something else and I took it with me. It was a tiny tape recorder, with a squeaky little tape and black buttons.

I pressed the button with the green triangle and the tape said, "For once, the man on the street corner was right. Every day for fifteen years he carried that damn sandwich board, the one that said 'The end is near.' And he stood on the corner in front of the coffee house and the bookstore, yelling at the intersection, converting the cars to his eschatology. Even a broken clock's right twice a day, I guess, because that son of a bitch—"

I pressed the button with two white triangles, pointing to the right. "And when we all are gone, who will bury the gravediggers?"

I pressed the button with the "X" on it and the voice stopped.

I thought that this might be fun to play with, but I would have rather found my bells.

Towards the end, before the whole hospital got silent and I didn't hear any more footsteps ever, the bell at the church down the street rang almost all the time. All day I sat at the window and listened with my ear pressed against the glass. I looked forward to it. I didn't mind that it meant danger or sorrow. The church bell sounded beautiful, and big.

I pressed a button on my tape recorder, the one with the two triangles pointing left. I let the tape rewind until it stopped. I guessed it was at the beginning, but I didn't play it. The man with the desperate-sounding voice didn't mean anything to me.

I stood on a chair and pried the window-clasp open with a clipboard. I then put my arm out the window with the tape recorder tightly in my hand, my middle finger holding down the button with a red circle.

At night, I pulled the tape recorder into bed with me, and I put it under my pillow. I did not press the green triangle button, though. I do not care who buries the gravediggers, but when there is no one left to ring the bell, I will push the button.

I had a bell again, but this bell was for the dead.

Three nurses — a blond, the brunette who stole my bells, and a redhead — were sitting around a radio in the TV lounge, their faces pulled down close to the round black speaker. Over their heads the TV was off, not even spraying static light into the room, which was okay because it was daylight and we didn't even need the overhead lights on to see.

A man on the radio was talking, asking if anyone was listening.

I laughed at him, because a radio is not a phone, and no one could answer him anyway.

"Shut up," hissed the nurses, all together.

The man's voice was shaky, and sounded like mine does if I haven't slept well.

"If anyone is listening, there's a place where I'm going to go, with what's left of my family and a couple of other people we've met along the way. We're going to a place called Grants Pass. It's in Oregon.

I know there are still people out there. I know someone must be. This is a hail Mary thing, really. I don't know if anyone'll be there. I don't know if anyone's going to go, but someone might."

"What do you think?" The blond nurse asked the other two.

"We can't stay here, not forever." The red-haired nurse agreed.

"It's better than nothing. A goal, anyway." She looked over at me and nodded. "We've got to find other people. We can't stay like this forever. And her — we'll load her up and bring her too."

I shook my head because I didn't want to go anyplace with them, but they ignored me.

The blond nodded. "Of course. We can't leave her here. Is there anyone else left? Anyone at all?"

"Not anymore. We're it."

"It's getting late," the blond nurse said. "We could pack up tonight. Leave in the morning. I don't know how far we'll get, but one of the ambulances has a full tank of gas. We could take it and run it 'till it stops, then see if we can't find another vehicle."

No, I shook my head. No. Not with you. No.

I got mad at the nurse again, the same one who took my bells. She cried all the time and made me feel bad. She came and went with my food, but only once a day, and I couldn't find anyone else to give me anything to eat.

She told me that I could go out and look for my own food for all she cared, if I was going to complain. I said that I didn't think I was supposed to leave the room, and she told me she didn't give a damn and that everything was different now.

"Look around!" She practically screamed it at me, and I don't like it when people scream at me. "Look!" She said it again, waving her arm around the room, and pointing it out at the hall.

I did, but I didn't see anything or anyone except for her.

And then it occurred to me that I hadn't seen anyone except her or the other two women for a long time.

She coughed and leaned against the door frame, putting her forehead to the back of her hand. When she walked out and left me, she tripped on her shoelace, caught herself before she fell. I wondered if she was getting sick.

That night while I lay in bed, listening to the sounds of nothing, I began to wonder if maybe I hadn't gotten it backwards.

Maybe the church bell rang and people died, not the other way around.

I didn't like the nurse. I thought maybe it would be okay if she died, as she didn't like me either. I could hear the bell — even if there was no one left in the church to ring it.

I reached under my pillow and ran my thumb over the button with the green triangle.

I pulled the recorder out, and I padded over to the window on my socked feet, sliding a little on the tile. I lifted the window and felt all the night air swirling cold, and I put the recorder outside — holding it with my hand and squeezing the green triangle button hard.

In the perfect stillness, the sound of the bells pealed out. I rolled the wheel on the side with my thumb and the chime went louder, louder. More. Higher. Bigger. The banging, clanging, ringing bells made my chest feel big and tight at the same time. They made me smile and forget to wish for anything else.

The next morning there were only two nurses left; the one I didn't like was gone. I asked the blond nurse where she was, but she didn't answer me.

"Did you shut the door?" the other asked over my head.

"Of course I did. What else could I do? She's dead, and there's no one to bury her."

"And now?"

The yellow-haired lady in the formerly white uniform looked over at her friend and then down at me.

My eyes were red and my face was probably puffy, because I hadn't slept well the night before. I'd sat with the tape recorder at the window, and I'd played the sound of the bell over and over again until I fell asleep, dreaming about the death bell at the church.

Maybe it looked like I'd been crying. Maybe they thought I was sad about the brown-haired nurse, but I wasn't. I was excited. I was happy. The bells worked both ways — you rang the bell when people died, and the bell rang when people died. Twice the bell ringing, the way I looked at it.

"I guess we're going to Oregon, unless you've got any better ideas."

In the ambulance, with the blond nurse driving, I rolled down the window and let my elbow lean on the top of the door. I pressed the green triangle and the bells trailed down the road behind us.

I told the nurses that the bell was for the dead.

It's for the people who are waiting at Grants Pass.

BIOGRAPHY

CHERIE PRIEST

Cherie Priest is the author of *Four and Twenty Blackbirds, Wings to the Kingdom, Not Flesh Nor Feathers,* and *Fathom* from Tor — as well as *Dreadful Skin* and *Those Who Went Remain There Still* from Subterranean Press. Her first novel won the first annual Blooker Award, and her third was nominated for an Endeavour Award. Two more books are forthcoming, one from Tor (*Boneshaker*) and one from Subterranean (*Clementine*). She lives in Seattle, Washington, with her husband and a fat black cat.

AFTERWORD

One of the first things I ever knew about Jennifer Brozek was that she was cooking up an anthology — an apocalyptic anthology, centered around an out-of-the-way town in Oregon called Grants Pass. As a fan of apocalyptic fiction in general, and Jennifer in particular, I was delighted when she asked me to contribute.

In my own reading experience, most stories of the apocalypse center around the adults — the powerful leaders, the craven scavengers, or the crafty survivors who make a go of post-civilization life on their own. I thought it might be more interesting to approach the situation through the eyes of a child, maybe even a child with some slight developmental issues, left alone and generally neglected, and unwanted. Hence, 'Hell's Bells' and its unnamed speaker. As someone who worked with children for years, I've never yet met another force in the human psyche's arsenal quite as pitiless and single-minded as the wrath of a child.

ASCENSION

MARTIN LIVINGS

From four hundred kilometers up, the Earth is still beautiful. Wisps of cloud drift in front of the small viewing window, obscuring the geology below. As I float serenely in the station's microgravity, I can see the faint lines of major motorways beneath us, the rectangular patterns of cities. From four hundred kilometers up, everything looks normal. I can almost forget what's happened.

Ignoring the bleeping fire alarm in the *Zvezda* control module is more difficult. It cuts through my concentration over and over again, sending a never-ending stream of piercing noises that makes my head pound. I try to tune it out, to look at the world below us, to pretend everything is normal.

"Come on, Pasha," my fellow Russian, Valentin, implores through the intercom from the adjoining module. "It shouldn't be like this. We're brothers."

I ignore him. We're not brothers; we're co-workers in the most isolated sweatshop on — or, in our case, above — the planet. The International Space Station is our home and work place, a string of tin cans flanked by solar panels that seems enormous until you have to spend twenty four hours a day inside it, week after week. It housed four of us for nearly six months.

Now there are only two. Valentin and myself.

"You know I'm right," he continues. But he's not right. He's utterly insane. Then again, who can blame him? And can I claim otherwise? "The Americans knew it. They accepted it."

"Accepted it?" I repeat, horrified. "How can you say that?"

"They knew the truth," Valentin replies. It's hard to understand him through the warning siren. "They made their choices. As have I." I wish I knew more about how this station works, how I could stop the alarm, or what would follow it. But I'm a biologist, along for the ride, my presence tolerated on some days, ridiculed on others. Valentin is the engineer. He should be in here, not I.

If he was, though, then we'd both be doomed.

"It's been six weeks," he continues. "Six weeks since the last transmission."

"A month and a half," I say without thinking. "That's not that long." I look out the window again. Just four hundred kilometers. I find that thought comforting. I know Valentin doesn't, though. He's a trained cosmonaut, went through years of training in the Yuri Gagarin centre outside of Moscow. He's always complained bitterly that he's never been any further from the Earth than the training centre was from Nizhny Novgorod. It's such a short distance, an easy day's drive. Valentin had wanted to be a cosmonaut his entire life, to explore the universe, penetrate the dark veil of space. He has always hated the fact that he is still so close to home, rails against it constantly.

I can't understand that, especially now. Four hundred kilometers is too near for him, but too far for me. Much too far.

As I watch, the world falls into shadow, as it does fifteen times a day up here. We orbit at around twenty five thousand kilometers an hour, or so Valentin has told me many times. My mind can't even begin to fathom how fast we're moving. It makes my head spin. I watch the planet go dark, and watch it closely, praying. A few months ago, the darkness would have been broken by a million pinpricks of light, cities and towns piercing the blue-black with their street lights and buildings. The Earth at night was once a mirror of the stars and galaxies above, a reflection in a deep, dark pool, shimmering with a breathtaking beauty.

Now there is nothing. Just cold, silent darkness.

"Ninety nine percent infection rate," Valentin says through the intercom, between bleeps of the siren. "That's what the woman in mission control said. And it was still rising."

"I know," I whisper, looking into the darkness, searching for any signs of life below.

"Ninety nine percent," he repeats. "With a survival rate of zero."

My wife and son are down there. I last spoke to Mischa two months ago, when the first reports of the outbreak were beginning. She assured me that she and Nikolai were fine; they were staying in our house outside Vladivostok, the house my family had lived in for three generations. The house where I was born. The house where I'd planned to die. Not here, four hundred kilometers above the surface of the planet.

They are down there. They have to be.

"Please, Pasha," Valentin says again. "Three minutes."

I close my eyes. "You won't do it," I say. "You can't."

"You're forcing me to," he replies, his voice cracking. It's the first sign of true emotion I've heard from him in days, weeks even. Since the second American killed himself. Dave Coulter had been a fine astronaut, an upstanding citizen, a patriotic family man. He was our electrical engineer and comms expert.

We found him in his bunk, his wrists sliced open. He'd tied plastic bags around his hands to stop the blood interfering with the life support systems. I think that might have been when Valentin lost his mind.

"How, Valya?" I ask him, my eyes still closed. "How am I forcing you?" I imagine myself sitting by the open fire in our house, the bitter cold kept at bay by the burning wood I collected during the day. Mischa sits by my side, her stockinged feet stretched across my lap. She is knitting a bonnet for Niki, using the rough wool from our own goats. I am happy.

If only that damned alarm would shut up.

"We can't stay here, *tovarisch*," Valentin says from somewhere very far away, a world away, four hundred kilometers and an apocalypse away. "Surely you know that. Nobody is coming for us. There is nobody left to come for us."

"No," I breathe.

"The Americans knew it," he continues. "Coulter knew it. Sutton knew it."

Commander Pete Sutton was the first to go. Not that long after the last formal transmission from Earth, I passed him in the access tube. He told me he was going to get some fresh air. I hadn't thought much of it, had other thoughts on my mind, selfish thoughts. We'd all said that exact phrase numerous times during our stay on the ISS; the Elektron oxygen generator and CO2 scrubbers kept us alive, but it could never quite free us from that stale smell of chemicals and exhalations. Ironically, the cleanest air in the station was in the EVA spacesuits, with their independent oxygen supplies, so sometimes we'd crawl into one, just for half an hour or so, to be free of the repeatedly recycled air for a while. Getting some fresh air.

That was the last time anyone saw Sutton. He went into the *Quest* airlock module, where the EVA suits were stored. All the suits were present and accounted for. The logs show that the internal airlock door opened and closed, and then the external door was opened. We closed it from the service module afterwards. I often think that I should have realized what he was going to do, should have tried to stop him. But I was caught in my own despair, thinking of Mischa and Niki down below us, and the ever-spreading plague.

"One minute, Pasha," Valentin's voice comes from the intercom. "What's it going to be?"

"I can't...I can't leave them."

"Pasha, they're dead. They're all dead. You know that."

"What about those short-wave transmissions we got?" I ask. I open my eyes again, certain that now, surely now, there will be a glimmer of light in the darkness beneath us. There is none. "The people talking about that place in America?"

"Grants Pass?" Valentin asks, derision clear in his voice. "It's a myth, Pasha. A desperate belief, based on a viral email. Don't be fooled into false hope."

"Any hope, even a false hope, is better than none."

"*Chush sobachya*," he spits, and the venom in his voice makes me flinch. The darkness of the world beneath the station suddenly seems to lunge at me, fills the control module, and I understand that my friend, my comrade, my self-proclaimed brother Valya's soul has also been engulfed in the shadow of a dead planet, a lost future. "There is nobody down there for us anymore, Pasha. Nobody to come and get us. Nobody to return to. The only way is up. Up and out and away."

"No."

"So be it."

The siren stops. For a moment my heart is filled with relief; he must have cancelled the false alarm, come to his senses.

Then, in the shocking silence, I hear a hiss.

A breeze plays with the sleeve of my jumpsuit, softly at first, then stronger. The hiss becomes a dull roar, and then a howl, as the emergency vents in the *Zvezda* service module open wider and wider. It takes me a moment to truly understand what's happening.

The module is open to space.

In an emergency fire situation, such as the one Valentin simulated, the system allows time for crew to evacuate the module before sealing the hatches to the rest of the station and opening the vents to space. The air is expelled, like one long foul breath, and the fire is instantly suffocated. As is anyone unfortunate enough left behind in the module. Of course, there are systems in place to prevent that happening. Systems that Valentin has overridden.

The air is growing thinner, the sound of the wind slowly fading. Each breath is a challenge now. I take a deep breath and hold it, reflexively, even though rationally I know it's the wrong thing to do. I know I can't survive this, but the body does what it must to at least try. Clinging to desperate hope, like stories of a town in Oregon, a haven from the end of the world. Too far, though, too far for Mischa and Niki. Too far for me, though only four hundred kilometers away, still too far.

Sparkles of light dance in the corners of my eyes. My lungs are burning. I don't have long. There is still air in the room, enough to flutter pieces of paper that pirouette past my eyes, but not much.

There is nobody down there for us anymore, Pasha.

No.

The only way is up. Up and out and away.

No. There's another way. One that doesn't involve dying here, trapped in an airless tin can, four hundred kilometers away from home.

I push myself away from the window, towards the hatch. I float to the wall beside the hatch, and press the release button, the one I'd locked earlier, to keep Valentin out, to keep him from carrying out his crazy plan.

The door doesn't open.

Of course it doesn't. I've unlocked it from my side now, but the fire alarm has sealed it. I'm going to die here after all.

I release my breath, the air oozing from my lungs like a sigh or surrender, a final exhalation, a death rattle. I can barely hear it. My hands and feet are swollen and numb. Something pops deep in my skull, behind my left eye, and pain fills my head. I try to scream, but have no breath for it.

Then the wind hits me in the face, and I'm hurled back into the *Zvezda's* comfortless environs. I hit the far wall hard and bounce away, tumbling in mid-air. My breaths in the cool, stale air are ragged but thankful. My eyesight slowly returns, at least in one eye, blurry and red as it might be.

The first thing I see is Valentin standing over me. No, not over me; over the controls I'm slumping against.

I hold my hands up to him, seeing the blooms of hemorrhages under the skin and down my arms, blood pooling beneath the thin layer in broad swirls and strokes, a red and blue finger-painting. "Wait..." I croak, though I don't expect him to.

He does. He looks at me.

"I can't leave, Valya," I tell him again. "But I know you have to. I understand now. I understand."

He nods. He asks me something, but I can't hear him; my head is filled with ringing, like I've been to a rock concert. But I can see his lips well enough; I know what he's saying. "What do we do?"

I tell him.

From four hundred kilometers up, the Earth is still beautiful. Wisps of cloud drift across the curved faceplate of my helmet, distorted by the thick polycarbonate fishbowl that's keeping the cold emptiness at bay. Or, at least, the cold emptiness that's outside my spacesuit.

"Pasha? How are you doing?" Valentin's voice is tinny but loud in my ears. It makes me jump a little.

"How do you think I'm doing?" I nudge my thruster controls and rotate to face the station. I'm surprised how far I've travelled already; the ISS is large in my view, but not as large as I expected. From here, maybe two hundred meters out, it looks like some kind of robotic insect, with its golden solar panel wings and spindly body. It's beautiful as well, much more beautiful from outside than from within.

Of course, my eyesight isn't what it once was. My right eye has almost returned to normal, its vision focused and clear enough. The left is still just a blur, though, from the damage it sustained. My hearing is still shot too, a maddening, relentless tinnitus filling my ears. Valentin told me my eardrums had nearly burst, that I'm lucky I'm not entirely deaf. At any rate, adjusting the volume on the radio in my suit did the trick.

"I'm going to activate the boosters in a minute," Valentin tells me. "Run them dry."

"Do you really think you can break orbit, Valya?" I ask. I'm no physicist, but his scheme doesn't really strike me as practical.

"Of course," he replies, but there's hesitation in his voice. I know him well enough to recognize when he's lying.

"Well, with only you on board, the food and water supplies should last much longer," I point out.

"Not that much longer," his voice crackles in my ears. "But long enough to finally become a true cosmonaut. My father would have been pleased at last."

"I'm sure he already was," I told him, thinking of my boy, my Niki. My chest hurts.

Valentin chuckles at that. "Well, I suppose I'll find out, when I see him in hell."

I smile. "You do know you're insane, don't you?"

"You can talk, *tovarisch*. I'm not the one attempting to walk home from outer space."

That makes me laugh out loud. "Hey, it's only four hundred kilometers. Piece of cake."

Valentin laughs as well, for a moment, but falls silent. For a long moment, the only sound is my breathing within the suit.

Then he speaks again. "*Do svidaniya*, Pasha," he says seriously. "It's been an honor working with you."

"And with you. God speed."

I imagine the face he would have made at the religious reference, but he says nothing, which I appreciate.

Bright light flares on the station's attitude and altitude control boosters. There is no sound, not here in airless space. Nothing seems to happen at first, but slowly the station begins to draw away from me, its orbiting speed increased bit by laborious bit. It grows smaller in my helmet's visor, becoming little more than an insect itself, then a bright star. Finally it vanishes altogether, hurtling around the curvature of the Earth. I know that, if I remain facing this way, it will come back into sight eventually, overtaking me as it speeds around the earth even faster than me, faster than twenty five thousand miles an hour. But I don't want to see it again. I've said my goodbyes to my friend.

It's time to go home.

I use my own thrusters to rotate back towards Earth. Once again, I watch the terminator drift across the planet beneath me, sending the world into darkness. I just stay there for a while, enjoying the peace.

But it won't last. I put my rear thrusters on full, and push myself towards Earth as fast as I can.

It takes only three minutes of solid thrust to empty my tanks, and it doesn't seem to make a difference, not yet. But once gravity gets a better hold of me, I'll start to notice it. It's like sky-diving. In fact, it *is* sky-diving, just from an impossible height.

And at an impossible speed.

I know I'll burn up like a meteor once I hit the atmosphere. Even if I'd used my thrusters to slow my orbital speed down, I'd never have managed to decelerate enough to survive this. But that's alright. I've accepted my fate, the same as Coulter and Sutton had. The same as Valentin has.

Something catches my eye, to my right. A glimmer of light on the ground, the first I've seen in weeks. My heart seems to stop for a moment. Could it be the town in America, Grants Pass, where survivors have fled to start a new life, a new world? Or perhaps it's a farm house near Vladivostok, miraculously spared the ravages of the worldwide pandemic that has killed so many others.

It makes no difference. Not now.

I watch the light track across my view as I fall from space, until it vanishes in the blur that is my damaged left eye. I couldn't leave them; I had to stay, to return home, as I promised my beautiful wife, my young son. Tears fill my eyes, beading in the weightlessness, floating inside my helmet like stars, like ghosts, like wishes.

A spark scintillates across the visor of my helmet. Then another. And another.

Don't be afraid, Mischa, Niki. Papa's coming.

BIOGRAPHY

MARTIN LIVINGS

Perth-based writer Martin Livings has had nearly fifty short stories in a variety of magazines and anthologies. His short works have been listed in the Recommended Reading list in *Year's Best Fantasy and Horror*, and had stories in both *The Year's Best Australian SF & Fantasy, Volume Two* and *Australian Dark Fantasy & Horror: 2006 edition.*

His first novel, *Carnies*, was published by Hachette Livre in 2006, and was nominated for both the Aurealis and Ditmar awards.

http://www.martinlivings.com.

AFTERWORD

When I first heard about the *Grants Pass* project, I was intrigued by the possibilities it offered. I wanted to write something about people trapped outside the pandemic, perfectly safe but perfectly doomed, and how they might react to this fate. And what better place than outer space? The International Space Station has always intrigued me, and I wondered what would happen to the people on board if there were suddenly no more supply ships, no more crew swaps, no chance of return. I wanted to know how they'd react.

I guess it's a dark story — hardly a surprise from me! — but in my mind it was actually about finding some kind of hope in hopelessness. When your options are all but gone, the choices you make are more important than ever.

ANIMAL HUSBANDRY

The city of Clayton was burning. I saw the smoke from over fifteen miles away, but I kept riding towards it, less from hope that the fire was a sign of civilization than from sheer, cussed stubbornness. My instructions said I needed to go this way. Since all the GPS systems failed around the time the networks and satellite uplinks died, I really didn't think that deviating was a good idea. Not if I was actively interested in living, anyway.

Fortunately for me, the wind was blowing out to sea, carrying the bulk of the doubtless carcinogenic smoke with it. I left the trailer about a mile down the road from the lookout point, choosing the minor risk that one of the other poor souls left in this god-forsaken world would stumble over it — you can't exactly Lo-Jack a draft horse — over the greater risks of smoke inhalation and panicked animals rocketing out of my control. My mare, the unimaginatively-named Midnight, would put up with just about anything I asked from her. She'd be able to stand the heat as long as I could.

Even with the wind in our favor, the air was so thick with ash that I could practically chew it by the time we got to the top of the lookout point. I shielded my eyes to block the flames, squinting through the smoke as I strained to see the city beyond. There wasn't much left to see. The fire had almost burned itself out, but it was still vigorous enough to make that particular route impassable.

There were two choices. We could try to find another route. Or we could back-track twenty miles to the superstore

I'd seen in San Ramon, resupply, and let the fire finish burning itself to death.

"We need a break, don't we, Midnight?" I asked, running a hand down the anxious mare's throat. She snorted, front legs dancing a half-panicked tattoo against the gravel. She was ready to bolt, holding herself in place solely because she assumed I wanted her to stay.

There was no need for that. We'd seen everything we'd come to see, and it was just more devastation. Tugging gently on the reins, I turned Midnight towards the caravan, and the road.

Before we rode out of the region completely, I stopped at the sign marking the city limits, pulled out my staple gun and another of my precious flyers, and set to work. Even if we didn't come back this way, even if the store managed to yield a better route, I would have done my self-imposed duty by the people who might still be living here. Wherever they were. When we finally turned towards San Ramon, white copy-paper ghosts glared from the city sign behind us, eye-poppingly clean in a landscape gone to ash.

It would never be enough, but it would have to do.

IMPORTANT - IMPORTANT - IMPORTANT
PLEASE READ
YOUR SURVIVAL COULD DEPEND ON IT

If you're alive and reading this, there are a few things you should be aware of. Firstly, those diseases everyone died of? The ones that barely had time to make the papers before it was over? They weren't natural, and that means there's no way to estimate their out-of-body survival rates. Be careful.

Keep contact with the dead to an absolute minimum. If you must handle human remains, wear gloves and be prepared to dispose of your outer garments immediately afterwards. Avoid closed-up spaces where people died, especially those which have remained moist. Diseases survive better in dark, warm, moist places.

Stick with bottled water whenever possible. Boil everything when you can't. All that plastic they said we needed to keep out of the landfills? Forget it. Bottled water could save you. (Not just from the manmade toxins. Cholera, dysentery, lots of other nasty things could be lurking in the water by now. Drink Crystal Springs or shit out your intestines. The choice is yours.) When selecting canned foods, check to be sure that the cans are whole and have not been dented. Exterior rust is fine. Interior rust is not.

On the bottom of this flyer you will find a list of basic nutritional supplements which are likely to be missing in your current diet. All items on the list can be found at any large grocery store or moderately-sized health food store. I recommend you begin taking them.

Watch out for dogs and other previously domesticated animals, as they may have turned feral in the absence of human custodianship. I have also included a list of standard poison baits and their doses. I do not recommend their use. They may still provide a measure of security while traveling.

I am on my way to Grants Pass, Oregon. I recommend you do the same as soon as you can. Time was short before the pandemics, and there's no telling how much we have left.

Hurry.

My name was at the bottom: Mercy Neely, Doctor of Veterinary Medicine. Possibly the last vet in the world. Possibly the last medical practitioner of any kind in California.

I really wish I'd paid more attention in class.

The San Ramon superstore showed signs of moderate looting, which was reassuring. I've come to see looting as a sort of hopeful omen, a little piece of proof that the human race will manage to recover from what it's done to itself. I was less pleased to see that my would-be looters had focused their attentions on the junk food aisles and cosmetics, almost completely ignoring the canned goods and well-stocked pharmacy. Maybe that was better for me, but it didn't bode well for the survival of the species.

After my brief solo reconnaissance was done, I cranked up the loading bay door enough to drive the wagon inside and parked it in what used to be the stock room. Midnight wandered off to investigate while I was unhitching the other horses and pouring their oats out on the concrete. I don't know what their names were originally; I call them Tweedledee and Tweedledum, and that seems to work well enough for everyone involved. The goats were hard at work trying to chew through their ropes again. I set them loose to wreak what havoc they could inside the closed superstore ecosystem. Goats can do a lot of damage, but even they can't chew through walls.

Finally, with everyone else roaming free, I opened the wagon's back door and released the hounds. Even indoors, it's difficult to overstate the value of a good guard dog in this brave new world we're all marooned in. They came bounding out with tails wagging madly, even Brewster, whose close-cropped stub of a tail could barely do more than vibrate rapidly back and forth.

The dogs inquired whether I might be interested in company while I explored the store, largely through the mechanism of trying to jump up and lick my face. I allowed that this might be acceptable. An agreement was reached. Who says animals don't communicate?

"All you be good, now," I cautioned the rest of the traveling zoo, and stepped through the swinging doors that separated the loading dock from the rest of the store, all three dogs at my heels. Time to go shopping. New-world style.

The world ended about fourteen months ago. Sadly, I missed this momentous occasion. I was home sick with the plague, and was thus not allowed to participate in the grand pandemic which wiped out the majority of the human race. Yeah. I get the irony. Still, I like to think I'm doing pretty well, all things considered. I've made it more than halfway to my eventual destination, despite some pretty major complications, and I've managed to do it without having a psychotic break. Talking to the animals doesn't count. That's what I went to school for.

As for how I missed the pandemic...bubonic plague has been endemic in California's small mammal population since the 1800s, when it was imported along with other luxury items such as silk, spices, and cheap immigrant labor. The state managed to hold on to all four imports until just recently. I doubt there's going to be much of a market for any of them these days, but hey, I also didn't think mankind was going to wipe itself out in a blaze of dick-waving glory, so what do I know?

California's ongoing plague problems are how I know for certain that the pandemic was manmade. Supposedly, Texas was hit by a form of bubonic plague that mowed down the population like a wheat thresher. It spread too fast for anything but a droplet-based transmission — person-to-person by way of sneezing or coughing — and it was resistant to all known antibiotics. Welcome to fourteenth-century Europe, where the Black Death was everybody's least-favorite neighbor. Only that's not possible, because that's not how bubonic plague works. Bubonic plague is carried by rat fleas, transmitted by rat fleas, and spreads slowly, since rat fleas are notoriously unreliable about when they bite you. Pneumonic plague is droplet-based, but that's not what killed Texas. Bubonic plague that wasn't bubonic plague killed Texas, and that means it wasn't bubonic plague at all. It was something somebody built in a lab, and I'm sure its creator won the Terrorist Science Fair before letting it out of the vial.

The Texas plague killed horses, cattle, goats, and most dogs, by the way. Texas may be the last place in this country where it's safe to sleep outside without fear of your neighbor's abandoned Rottweiler. Thanks, Texas plague. Thanks a lot.

As the only veterinarian in Pumpkin Junction, California, my practice covered basically anything that people wanted to bring me. Mercy Neely, Swiss Army veterinarian. If someone had a sick cat, dog, or other standard pet, I was their girl. If they had a horse that needed gelding, a cow that needed a checkup, or a flock of sheep that needed their shots, that was also me. I did parrots, reptiles, and anything else animal-like that happened to need medical attention. I examined an African praying mantis once; I extracted a mousetrap from the stomach of an escaped boa constrictor; I euthanized an emu with a broken leg. My practice was boring more often than it was interesting, but it was always vital. I was the only game in town.

I guess I technically still would be, if I'd stayed.

I'd been out at the O'Shea place the Sunday before the pandemic started, giving the goats their yearly exam. With thirty of the things in the flock, it was easier for me to go to them. The barn was hopping with fleas, and I must've been bitten a good thirty times before I finished for the day. Three days later, I got sick. You can't be a California vet and not know what's endemic to the population; I know bubonic plague when I see it. I diagnosed myself, gave myself an illegal prescription for tetracycline, doped myself to the gills, and went to bed. Not, sadly, before hanging a sign with a cute little hand-drawn rat on my door. 'Doc's got the PLAGUE!'

I even slept through the quake that leveled half the damn state. Remember, kids, vets get the *good* tranquilizers.

I like to think that there were other survivors in my home town. The pathogens that hit California seem to have caught and killed almost instantly, and I went to bed for six days starting two days before the pandemic came out to play. I like to think that some people made it through the sickness, saw the sign on my door, and decided that there was no point in checking. I wouldn't blame them if they did, but I would see them again when I got to Grants Pass.

Most of all, I like to think that I was exposed along with everybody else. I didn't miss infection because I was locked in my little room over the office; I missed infection because I had a natural immunity. In a healthy population, naturally immune parents tend to have naturally immune children. Maybe Dan didn't make it through, but if I was naturally immune, there's a chance that Linda was, too. There's a chance that she'll be waiting for me at the end of this road.

Wishful thinking, but hell. Everybody's allowed a little wishful thinking after they've survived the end of the world.

The dogs roved ahead of me as we walked through the dimly-lit store, never ranging more than about ten feet away. It wasn't just because they felt the need to protect me, although that was a part of it; the last six people we'd seen had been armed, and had taken shots at my little pack before I had time to tell them not to. When I left Pumpkin Junction, I had six dogs in my personal escort. They'd been picked off one by one, and the three I had left were the ones who'd figured out that hiding behind the human was the best way to survive.

Brewster was the most timid of the three, despite also being the largest. He looked back at me, buffing uncertainly. "It's okay, Brewster," I said, in a soothing tone. I was only half-paying attention to his unease. My eyes were too busy crawling over the shelves, noting the things we needed, the things we could use, and comparing them to the wagon's carrying capacity. If I hitched Midnight alongside the Tweedles and walked for a while, we could manage another few hundred pounds of kibble; that would probably get us all the way to Sacramento, where we could —

A gun hammer was cocked behind me. A very small sound, but one that had come to hold a great deal of importance in my life over the past year. It was the sound of someone who might decide that my surviving the pandemic was just a fluke that needed to be corrected.

I stopped in my tracks, raising my hands to shoulder-height. Brewster hunched his massive head down, a growl rumbling from the bottom of his throat. I could hear the other two dogs moving up ahead, still uncertain and unwilling to approach the stranger. "I'm sorry," I said, voice calm and level. Never be the first to show panic. Never let them think that you might be an easy target. "I didn't know this store was yours. If you'll just let me gather up my animals, I'll be on my way." *Please*, I prayed silently, *please let me gather up my animals.* I lost two goats to a man who saw them as fresh meat on the hoof; I lost my second riding horse to a man who fancied himself the Lone Ranger and decided that an old gray mare would do just fine as Silver. I'm sure one of her legs was broken before I'd even made it out of the valley that he took her from me in. The old gray mare, she ain't what she used to be.

"Turn around, miss. Real slow, no sudden movements."

Male; middle-aged, probably one of the white-collar workers who'd packed this sort of business park before the pandemic; artificially polite, which was a natural development under the circumstances. Even when you were the one holding the gun, it paid to be polite. Next time, the gun might belong to someone else. I turned as I'd been instructed, not dropping my hands or making any effort to avoid meeting his eyes. Confident without being challenging, that was the goal. Once you've stared down a bull that smells cows in estrus, you can handle anything humanity has left to throw at you.

The man behind me looked almost exactly like I would have expected, even down to the stained, slightly tattered white dress shirt. Even a year after the disaster, people still dressed like they expected the old world to be called back to order any second. The poor bastards. They'd been domesticated, and they didn't even know it.

"Those your dogs?" he demanded. The skin of his left cheek jumped and fluttered in a nervous tic, making it look like he might jitter apart at any moment.

"Yes," I said, not lowering my hands. "They're also my horses, my goats, and, if you've been inside the wagon already, my birds. They're well-fed and not a threat to you."

The pistol he had angled towards my chest wavered, almost perfectly in time with the tic on his cheek. "Are you some sort of farmer?"

"No. I'm a veterinarian."

Shock and relief chased each other across his face for a moment before he lowered his gun, saying, "Miss, I'm going to need you to come with me." He hesitated, finally adding, more quietly, "Please."

"Sir, I don't want to get your hopes up here. I'm not a people doctor. I'm—"

"It's my daughter. She's nine."

Linda will be nine this year. If the world can make it that long. I sighed.

"Come back to my wagon with me. I'll need some things from my bag."

His name was Nathan Anderson; he'd been a tech writer, churning out endless pages of instructions for machines he'd never use. Like almost every other survivor I've encountered, he never got sick at all. No pandemic for Nathan. No wife, friends, or job, either. Nothing but scrounging from the stores of San Ramon and taking care of Miranda. Until Miranda started getting sick; until he was lucky enough to catch a traveling veterinarian who'd been to some form of medical school, even if it wasn't the human kind.

He was quiet as we walked the three blocks back to the office building they called home, only the gun in his hand serving as a reminder of his status as my captor. Brewster, Mike, and Little Bobby trailed along behind me, an anxious canine escort. I wasn't willing to leave them behind. Too much of a chance that Nathan had friends who'd learned the hard way that dogs needed to be shot on sight.

Nathan paused at the office door. "She was awake when I went out scouting for supplies. She gets a little disoriented sometimes, but she's a good girl. She'll probably even like your dogs."

I could smell the sickness from here, that horrible combination of sweat and vomit and a dozen other bodily fluids that says 'something's dying nearby.' I kept my face as neutral as I could. "Let's see if she's up now."

Nathan looked relieved — like he'd been afraid right up until that moment that I was going to disarm him and run — and opened the door.

Miranda's room had been a corner office before the pandemic, probably much-prized for the floor-to-ceiling windows that comprised two of the four walls. Now it was a little girl's paradise. The once-white walls had been inexpertly painted pink, and flower-shaped plastic decals studded the window glass. Toys and books were heaped haphazardly around the floor. At the center of it all was a glorious fairy tale of a four-poster bed — God knows where they found that — and in the center of the bed was Miranda.

Any hopes this little jaunt would prove my theory about immunity being hereditary died when I saw her. Adopted daughter, maybe. Adopted after the pandemic, almost certainly. But biological daughter? No. Not unless he'd had a Korean wife whose genes had been able to beat his nine falls out of ten.

Miranda raised her head at the sound of the door, summoning a smile from somewhere deep inside herself. "Daddy." She paused, brow knotting. "We have company?"

SEANAN MCGUIRE

The question was uncertain, like she thought I might be a hallucination.

I swallowed the lump in my throat before it could turn to full-fledged tears. "I'm Mercy Neely, honey. I'm a veterinarian."

Sudden interest brightened her eyes. "Is that why you have dogs? I like dogs. I used to have a dog. Before—" She stopped, the brightness fading. "Before."

"A lot of people did." Nathan was standing frozen next to me. He'd ceased to be a factor as soon as I saw the little girl. Ignoring the possibility that he'd decide to shoot me, I started for the bed, setting my traveling medicine kit down on the mattress. "Now, your Dad says you don't feel so good."

"Uh-huh."

"You want to tell me about it?"

"My head hurts. I can't breathe sometimes. I keep choking when I try to sleep." She sounded ashamed of her own symptoms. Poor kid. "I—" A cough cut off her words, and she sat up to catch it in her hands, bending almost double in the process. It had a rich, wet sound, like it was being dredged up through quicksand.

"Just breathe," I said, and turned back towards Nathan. "It could be a lot of things. Without a lab, I can't really tell you which one. It's probably pneumonia, complicated by general malnutrition. I'm going to give you a list of medicines that I need you to go back to the store and find for me."

His eyes widened, then narrowed. "I'm not leaving you alone with her."

"My way out of here is back at that store. I'm unarmed. I'm not exactly going to take a sick little girl hostage, now, am I?" I shook my head, expression disgusted. "She

84

shouldn't be left alone. Either you trust me here, or you trust that I'll come back."

"I'll lock the office door behind me."

"You do that."

Still he hesitated, eyes flicking from me to Miranda and back again.

I sighed, and played the ultimate trump card: "I don't know how long she has."

His expression hardened.

"I'll be right back."

Things I don't need to explain: what it was like to step outside for the first time after I got better and the rest of the world didn't. I'm pretty sure everyone that's still alive has their own version of *that* story, and they don't need to be repeated. I woke up, I felt better, I went outside, I threw up six times, I went a little crazy, and I got over it. There wasn't time to have a nervous breakdown. Maybe if I'd been a doctor, but I wasn't a doctor; I never wanted to be a doctor. I'm a veterinarian, and my patients still needed me.

Four days isn't long enough for most animals to turn vicious; that made my job a lot easier. It took eighteen hours to canvass the town, letting cats out of houses, assessing dogs and livestock and making my decisions as impartially as I could. Domestic cattle aren't made to live without somebody to take care of them. They need milking, or their udders will split open and they'll die of infection. Sheep are worse. Goats are fine on their own; so are horses, most poultry, and pigs. Cats will go feral. Dogs will go mean. If it could be released, I either released it or fed it and promised to be back in a little while. If it couldn't be released...

Ending future suffering is one luxury veterinarians have that human doctors don't. I spent a lot of that first day crying, but I guarantee you that while the people of Pumpkin

Junction died just as badly as the rest of the world, our animals died better than they did anywhere else.

I held back some of the stock. A few milking goats, some horses I knew were gentle and well-mannered, several of the larger, healthier, friendlier dogs. I was already planning, you see. Figuring out what I'd need, and what *we'd* need when I finished the trip. Can't build a society without animals, and there's no point in re-domesticating when we have the potential to save the work we've already done. Some of it, anyway.

God, I hope she's there.

♥

Miranda turned wide, dark eyes on me after her adoptive father was gone, and asked, "Am I going to get better?"

"That's what medicine is for, isn't it?" I opened my bag, pulling out a needle and a small, unlabeled bottle. I never labeled that particular bottle. They taught us that in veterinary school. Even when they were the ones who'd decided that dear old Kitty was ready for that great scratching post in the sky, people didn't want to see the label.

They also taught us to be natural about it. To fill the syringe like it was any other vaccination. "Miranda's a pretty name," I said. "I like it."

"So do I," she said, watching me with gravity beyond her years. "Are you going to give me a shot?"

"Mm-hmm. Just a little one, to help you sleep." I glanced up, offering her a warm smile. "I have a daughter just about your age. Her name is Linda."

"You do?" Her expression turned carefully neutral, like she was about to walk into a minefield. "Is she...did she..."

"She's just fine. She's waiting for me in a place called Grants Pass. It's up in Oregon. I'm on my way there now." Linda would be there. Linda had to be there. She was the one who had told me to go there in the first place. Eight years old, smart as a whip, and gullible enough to believe everything she ever read. Gullible enough to believe the pandemic was coming, for one thing, and that it would probably come in our lifetime. "When they go crazy, Mom, you have to promise to come to Oregon," she said, with those big blue eyes just as wide and serious as they could go. Like my agreeing to come to Grants Pass was a matter of life or death. So I agreed. What else can you do? I only got her every other weekend, and if she wanted me to promise to take a post-apocalyptic road trip, I'd promise.

Linda had to be there. What I'd seen in Pumpkin Junction on the day I went a little crazy was just the shock talking. I didn't see it again. And if part of me insisted that I only didn't see it because I didn't go back there, who cares? There were no animals in that shitty little apartment. There was nothing there to save.

Miranda looked unsure. "How come she isn't traveling with you?"

"Well, see, Linda's daddy and I didn't think it was a good idea for us to live together anymore. So Linda was with her daddy when everybody got sick, and she had to start without me. I'll catch up to her sooner or later." I tapped the syringe, easing out the bubbles. "She promised to meet me there, and she takes her promises seriously."

Linda takes everything seriously, and has since she was born. So we sat down with the maps of the state, and we worked out four routes that we could take to get to Oregon. The Route Where They Closed the Roads. The Route Where Quarantine Kept the Roads Open. The Route Where There's Been An Earthquake and We Have To Go Around. The Route Where Too Many People Survived and We Need to Avoid Them. Even after the earthquake that took out most of the Los Angeles metro area, the bulk of California was mostly somewhere between routes one and two. Linda wouldn't have had any problems if she avoided the coast roads and skirted the area around Red Bluff.

"Can we come with you? Me and my daddy?"

"We'll talk about it when you wake up," I said soothingly.

She didn't even cry when the needle went in; she bore the brief pain like a trooper. Domesticated animals always do.

There are a lot of ways for people to die in the post-pandemic world; I've seen most of them. The human race was domesticated a long time ago, and like the cows that need someone to milk them, or the sheep too dumb to run away from a predator, the humans forgot how to stay alive without the trappings of their civilization. So they stagger along pretending they still have some quality of life while their teeth get loose from scurvy and their bowels get scarred by parasitic infections. Most of the people who lived through the sicknesses shouldn't have. They're just suffering now, without all the little luxuries they were so accustomed to.

Euthanasia is kinder. It's quicker. It takes the pain away. If we don't let our pets suffer, why should we let people do it?

Part of being a vet is knowing that the thing to do with suffering is end it, not prolong it just for the sake of being able to say that all your patients survive. I'm not a moralist. I see suffering, and I end it. It's that simple. Human doctors aren't allowed to have that luxury, but there's a reason I never wanted to work with people.

Miranda's eyes fluttered shut in a matter of seconds as the drugs took effect, her body effectively sliding into a comatose state that was deeper than any sleep.

I put the syringe away and took her hand, my index finger pressed against the pulse point of her wrist. Her heart sped up, fighting against the lidocaine. Her fingers tightened on mine with no more force than a kitten's jaws.

She gasped once, sighed, and was still.

"See?" I said, slipping my hand out of hers. "Nothing to be afraid of."

Nathan returned about ten minutes later, clutching a bag that bulged with medical supplies. I met him at the office door, motioning for him to be quiet. "She's sleeping," I whispered. He looked past me to where she was stretched out on her bed, expression peaceful, and believed me.

Outside, in the hall, I offered him a sympathetic smile, and said, "It's bad, but she should pull through. I've given her something to help her sleep, and I can show you which medicines to give her. But there's a fee for my help."

The hope in his eyes died like a switch had been flipped. "What's that?" he asked, warily.

I held up my bag. "After spending a year scrounging in all this rust? You need a tetanus shot. Let me give it to you, and I'll stay as long as it takes to get her better."

Nathan laughed, sounding utterly relieved. "I think I can stand a shot if it gets my baby girl better."

"Good." I smiled. "This won't hurt a bit."

BIOGRAPHY

SEANAN MCGUIRE

Born in California, Seanan McGuire has long been fascinated by the fact that bubonic plague is endemic in the local rodent population. This explains a lot about her, really. Seanan's interest in plagues and pandemics occupies much of her spare time; the rest of her time is spent taking inordinately long walks and working on her various writing projects. She is the author of the *Toby Daye* series from DAW Books. The first, *Rosemary and Rue,* will be published in 2009, with at least two more to follow.

Seanan has released three albums to date. The latest, *Red Roses and Dead Things*, includes a lengthy musical explanation of why the Black Death wasn't actually the bubonic plague. No, seriously.

Like many writers, Seanan is a cat person, and lives with several Classic Siamese. She watches too many horror movies, and reacts violently to people asking 'Is that you, Johnny?' (It's not Johnny.) You can catch up with her at www.seananmcguire.com, where she will happily geek pandemics with you.

AFTERWORD

As a fan of both pandemics and California history, I was fascinated to learn that bubonic plague has been locally endemic since at least 1900. Bearing that in mind, I wanted a protagonist who'd know the medical 'lay of the land' in my home state, and could really appreciate the devastation. Since a surviving doctor seemed a little too convenient, I went with a veterinarian.

A lot of our domesticated animals really can't survive on their own any more. That got me thinking about what would happen to most of my friends without their modern conveniences. How many would make it? How many would want to make it?

So there's Mercy. She's doing what she's trained to do: ending pain. The question is whether what she's doing is moral, and, if it isn't, why is it moral to do that to animals?

Plus, I like being able to write about plague.

MEN OF FAITH

IVAN EWERT

I'd never killed a man, not even after the world went to hell. But so help me God, Preacher would have been my first choice. In the dark of night, when everything was quiet and we were all huddled around the fire, I could hear the fluid rattling in his chest; hear that awful, sickly sound of a man struggling for breath. He said it was asthma, or apnea, or whatever the hell it was, and Sarge and Bo believed him.

Not me. I figured he was catching.

"You're dreaming," said Bo when I brought it up. "Flu's gone. Killed everyone it was like to more than two months back, and I don't think it's headed back up anytime soon. Burned itself out, the way I figure it. Besides, it moved quick, remember? Preacher's been snorting and snoring like that since the day we picked him up."

"Maybe it's a new strain?" I asked, but Bo just laughed. He knew I'd barely managed to stay awake in class back at Pat Henry High, and I should've given it up there. "I'm no doctor, but I know that stuff like that changes. Mutates, right? It changes and becomes something different."

"Hell, Dave. Look at him. Preacher ain't exactly the type to fight something serious off. If it was the flu, he'd be dead. End of story."

I looked back towards Preacher. There he was, nose in that Bible and barely watching where he walked. That pigeon-chest kept on swelling and collapsing like a blood blister, probably the only kind he'd ever raised. Never done a day's work in his life; never got a callous. Never even raised a sweat except trying to sleep at night.

"Still don't like it," I said. Hell, I couldn't help myself. "No reason to bring him along, and believe me, the folks up at Grants Pass aren't going to listen as nice as you do. I'll bet they throw us all out to the wolves the minute they hear him trying to breathe."

"No reason to bring him along?" Bo laid a thick finger along his nose and gave a solid farmer's hanky. "I think you're wrong. Just hold on, and put up with it a while. You'll see. I've got plans for Preacher."

Now, as much as I didn't like Preacher, I trusted Bo. He was the only good foreman we ever had; he listened to us when we were telling the truth about needing a day off but busted your balls when you called in with a hangover. You just couldn't lie to him and make it stick. He could tell just by the sound of your voice if you planned to spend the day fishing and watching hockey, or if you really needed the time to look in on your grandmother. After the first time I tried pulling something, and he gave me the business for it, we never had any trouble.

He could fight, too. Only time I ever saw Bo lose his temper was the day he found out his wife Jenny was sleeping around with one of the regulars at the Riverside. Bo knocked him cold inside of five minutes, and Jesus, even then we had to pull him off the guy. He was cool about it the next day, filed for divorce and never looked back, but I sure saw what he could do to someone in his way.

That's why I called him up, once my folks passed away from that flu. That was three months ago — back in July, when the world started falling apart faster than a politician's promise. I was low, just like everyone else who was still standing. It was like the world had ended, but you were left...and you were numb.

After a hell of a week spent trying to get them buried, I tracked down Bo. Figured if he was still alive, he'd have some kind of plan put together, and he'd need some guys watching his back to pull it off. Hiking halfway across the states through a Great Plains winter wasn't what I had him pegged for planning. But if that was the way it was, then that was the way it'd be. You pick your guys and stick with them.

So I kept my mouth shut and just watched the river as we walked along. The Musselshell wasn't much compared to the Yellowstone, but skirting Billings had probably been a good idea. The last few cities we tried getting through had been nothing but trouble. Even Miles City wasn't any kind of treat. Of course, that's where we picked up Preacher.

We'd generally holed up in churches along the way. They'd have been picked clean of everything worth a nickel long before we came in, but like Bo says, it was still the safest place to spend a night. It took a certain kind of coward to rob a church, and they weren't the kind to stick around once they'd finished. So Sarge and I, we took the sides with our shotguns like usual, since you can't be too careful, and Bo walked on in.

It was the strangest damn thing to see those candles going. First time I'd seen anyone praying in a church since the fall. I guess it might be different other places, where folks could hunt for their food or try and live off of canned goods from grocery stores and warehouses. But travelling through farm country, most of the living were out until dusk trying to get in as much of the seed as they could. There was plenty of ground going fallow, but with autumn half over, those people that were left were working like crazy to get the wheat and barley planted. Not a lot of time to light candles — and not a lot of time to waste on your knees.

There he was, though, casting a long shadow across the aisle, down before the altar. He was praying right out loud, praying forgiveness for the folks of Miles City, for Montana, and all of America for bringing down the wrath of God.

Sarge gave me a look, and I gave it to Bo, but Bo just stood there and listened until Preacher stopped. Then he gave a cough, and walked forward a piece.

"Excuse me, preacher. We didn't want to disturb your prayers, but I was wondering if we could rest here the night. Been walking all day and it'd be a favor to us all."

Preacher turned around, and that's when I first saw that swollen, puffed-out chest rising and falling. First saw those cracked glasses. I didn't like anything I saw, and I sure as hell didn't like the look he was giving Bo.

"There's nothing here worth having," he said, real nervous.

"Not looking to take anything but a piece of sleep."

"You're carrying guns."

Bo nodded. "Like I say, we've been walking. It's a bad time to be wandering without them if you're a stranger in a town. Boys, set the guns down. We're not in any trouble here, and I don't care to make any for the Preacher." He turned back to the Preacher then. "Let me tell you our story."

And he told him. Flat out, no hedging. Told him about our ganging up in Minneapolis, how he heard about Grants Pass and the girl's crazy dream. About bringing all these random folks together to this little valley town for the common good. About the importance of having someone around to be a leader.

"Now, I know we're not the types she was looking for when she spouted off on the Internet," he said. "But we're the types she's gonna need. Folks who used to spend their whole day behind a computer don't know how to set up a house, or straighten a roof. They don't know how to fix pipes or set up a water system. They might get a couple engineers, but you can't tell me there'll be a lot of guys who want to do the grunt work there. That's where we come in. We're just looking for honest work, and we're working hard to get there."

The Preacher had holstered his fish-eye now, and he was looking Bo up and down, real steady. Then he took another rattling breath and said, "Why walk, when there are plenty of cars to be taken?"

"You want me to tell you I wouldn't take them?" Bo shook his head. "I'd be a liar. We did manage to hotwire one back when we started, and I've thought on it plenty since, but the roads aren't real safe. Saw enough B-movies before the collapse to know that much. We've been sticking close to Route Twelve for a long piece now, but far enough away to hear anyone coming and get down in a ditch. We're not angels, Preacher, but we're not looking for trouble, either. We just want honest work."

That got him a nod. "All right...but why go so far? Oregon's a long way from Minnesota. I'm sure there are other towns that would be happy to take on a few strong backs. For that matter, some of the locals here could probably manage with a few more men."

"Are you a real preacher?" Bo asked bluntly. The question put Preacher off, but he nodded. "All right then. I figure you know a little something about waiting for a reward, and working toward it.

"I don't know if they'll let me in when we get to Grants Pass. I don't even know if anyone actually made it there. But if they do, they're going to have a lot of different folks from a lot of different places. I might not have gone to school much, but I can respect the folks who did. I figure they're like to have a doctor, or at least someone who studied some. They're like to have a couple business folks, who might be good to have around for trading in case anyone wanders through with goods to sell. They're like to have just about every kind of person you can find on the Internet, but like I said, there are two kinds that don't spend much time there: folks who are used to just working, and folks who know the word of God."

Preacher looked at Bo while I looked at Sarge. I didn't mind preachers as a rule. I went through Sunday school just fine and showed up at Ascension Lutheran for the holidays. We were barely making twelve miles a day as it was, though, what with staying off the roads and needing time to find food. Adding someone soft to the group was just going to cause more delay, and I could see what was going to happen if we got caught in a Montana winter. Figured by my count it was early October already, and that was just asking for trouble.

"Hey, Bo..." I didn't get to finish.

"Hold up, Dave. I want to hear what the Preacher thinks about working hard to get to an uncertain reward."

That was the only time I saw much life in Preacher. He could tell he was being sparked, and he gave this kind of wet and wheezy laugh. "You're not going to get a rise out of me that easily."

"Maybe not. But what kind of rise are you gonna get from the good folks here in Miles City when winter comes?"

"What do you mean?"

Bo shrugged. "Have you been helping them plant? Help them bring the crops in?"

"A little."

"A little. Then, Preacher, you're like to be entitled to a 'little' food. What are you living on now? Canned stuff, I bet, out of the local Super Value or whatever grocery chains you had up here. Now, come December, you might still be getting fed. It'll be the first Christmas since things collapsed, and folks are probably gonna want to stay in good with the Preacher. But you and I both know that it's not gonna be easy getting any fresh food before April.

"How well do you think you're going to fare in February, or in March? When the canned stuff's run out and your neighbors are running out of wheat? Are they gonna remember that you were praying for their souls all through the harvest? Or will they just remember that you stayed inside the whole time, letting them break their backs in the fields?"

Preacher looked a little doubtful, but Bo kept on. "Maybe I've got them wrong. Maybe they'll be persuaded by Easter coming up, or maybe they're just more religious here than I'm used to. Maybe they'll bring you fresh bread every morning until the day you meet Saint Peter. But it's nothing I'd bet money on. You might know God, but me? I know people."

That was it, I could tell. There'd be a little more back and forth, but Bo had put the fear of man into the raspy little loafer. There was more I wanted to say, a lot more, but Sarge motioned me to come outside before I had a chance to spill. We weren't like to be missed, so I followed him. Those crazy blond curls nearly spilled into his eyes now, and as skinny as we'd been getting on canned beans and fresh rabbit, he looked more like a washed-up rock star than ever before.

He stayed real quiet, just staring across the street, so I finally spoke up. "What do you think?"

"Bo knows guys," he said. "He knows how they think, and he knows how to talk to them."

"Yeah, but we hardly got enough food for the three of us. And winter's on its way. This preacher doesn't look like he could walk a mile without stopping to rest. He's gonna slow us down."

Sarge looked out across the darkening town. "Yeah, I bet he will. But Bo knows what he's doing. Always has before. I don't see him screwing up this time."

"I'm not saying he's screwing up," I said, a little frustrated. Sarge wasn't the sharpest knife in the drawer. "I'm saying he hasn't thought of everything, that's all. Adding another guy's a great idea if he's in good shape, but this guy?"

Sarge shrugged again. "Hell if I know, but Bo's got his reasons." And that was the best I could get out of him before Bo called us back in to introduce us to Preacher. We shared some hard bread and canned beans, bunked down in the pews, and that was the end of it. It was over three weeks ago, and I'd been right — we were moving slower since Bo talked Preacher into coming along.

"Hey, Bo," called Sarge from the roadside, "sign says we're only twelve miles from a campsite. Might be able to make it before night if we push it."

Bo just shook his head. "Might as well come on in, Sarge. We're not like to make that kind of pace. Map says we'll reach Ryegate first, let's plan on hitting that. Like to be another ghost town, we can pick up some real beds there."

"That's not the reason," I said to him, quiet, looking back at Preacher. "You know he can't make it that far, that's all. Won't be any beds left in this Ryegate place, any more than there ever are." Bo's look was mild compared to the one he could've given me, but I was getting sore. "Campsite ain't a whole lot better, but even a couple miles a day can make a big difference, Bo. You know I'm following you, but..."

"Then follow my lead," he said, flat as the autumn plains. "We keep spending our time arguing, there's going to be some kind of trouble, Davey. Now I don't want that, but I'm telling you there's a good reason to put up with Preacher. So stop acting like a spoiled kid in the back seat of the car and start walking. I want to get to Ryegate before nightfall."

I had a thick skin. I never minded getting cussed out or hollered down. But being called a kid...well, that did it.

That's when I figured what had to be done. It was going to be for his own good — for Sarge's, and mine too. Preacher was the kid here! Tagging along like some kind of half-wit brother who's got no more right to be there than a queer in a convent. Without him, we'd have been nearly to Idaho. We might've been able to get across the mountains before the snow came, and spend the winter in Grants Pass, where they'd have stoves set up and canned goods set by. Hell, I dreamed they might even have coffee and beer, and you couldn't get those no matter how hard you tried along the Musselshell River.

It was only Preacher standing in the way.

If there was anyone still living in Ryegate, we didn't see them. A few towns we'd come up to had guards posted along the roads, men — some women, too — who would turn strangers away. I figure Ryegate wasn't big enough to make any kind of colony. Even the church was a tiny, little place.

"Guess I was wrong," I said to Bo, putting a little grudge in my voice. "Ought to be plenty of beds around here."

He nodded. "All right, usual drill. Spread out and holler when you find one." It wasn't difficult in such a small town. Bigger houses had always already been looted, and folks would slash open mattresses looking for hidden cash. So you avoided those, even though they looked better. Smaller houses, that was the trick; finding a place that wouldn't attract so much attention. I didn't figure many folks would be wandering through Ryegate, but you never knew who else was on the roads.

The third house we tried was a ranch-style with the door shut but unlocked. There was a pullout sofa and two beds inside, one a queen-size; the other a single in what must have been a kid's room. Some stuff was missing — looked like the pictures had all been taken off the walls, probably someone looking for safes — but at least they hadn't messed up the beds, and that was all we cared about.

"All right," said Bo, "I'll take the floor, I had a bed last time we were under a roof. Preacher, you take the kid's room. Close the door so we don't have to listen to your snoring all night."

Sarge glanced at me. "Rock, paper, scissors for the big bed?" I took a rock and won the bed, and given what I'd planned, it took some doing to look happy about it. On top of that, there was an old-fashioned grill in the garage, and some coals left in a bag. I thought of all the nights I've spent wishing for hot food, and cursed a wish come true.

The sun had been down about an hour when we finished eating and turned in. The sheets were long since gone, but I could just feel that nice, big mattress under my shoulders before I even closed the door.

Now, I knew myself. If I lay down in a real bed after a hot meal I'd be gone to the world until someone shook me, so I put myself to walking in place. Once you get used to walking the way we'd done these past two months, you could pull it off without even thinking. I figured everyone else would need half an hour, tops, to get themselves off to deep dreaming. I could put off sleeping that long. I knew I could. I had to.

I did. Preacher's snoring was the first thing I heard, that sick rattling that made you think of an engine gone bad. It stoked the fire in me again, forced me to shake off sleep and march in place to the sound of that lousy drone. With every minute that passed, all I could think of was the past three weeks. The way he'd slowed us down, held us back. The disease I knew he was carrying around in his lungs. The way Bo was protecting him, shrugging off Sarge and me like so many afterthoughts, even when we'd walked so far across the country with him.

The porcelain lid to the toilet tank was good and solid, heavy in my hands. It came off with hardly a sound when I lifted it. The trick was going to be opening Preacher's door quietly enough to avoid waking Bo or Sarge. Then I could bring the damned thing down, and my problems would be over. I wouldn't have to share anything with that mouth-breathing son of a bitch a moment longer. Bo would be pissed, sure. Might even throw down with our fists for a bit. But he'd know I was right, afterward. He'd see I knew what was best.

I thought that until the minute I turned around and saw him in the moonlight, Sarge's shotgun held steady at his hips, aimed right at my crotch.

"Lay it down, Dave. Quietly," said Bo, and I did.

"Put your hands at chest level and step out here." He walked me to the back door of the house. "Open it."

I never scared easily. I'd never had a shotgun at my back before, either. I'd trusted Bo, sure, but he'd trusted me — and see what that nearly got him. I opened the door.

Once we were outside, away from the roof, the big night sky made me feel almost naked. We'd been away from roofs for so long that you'd think it would have comforted me, but I just stood there under a waning moon, waiting to hear a click and a roar from the man I'd betrayed.

"You ever killed a man, Dave?"

"No. Never have."

"It's not as easy as the movies make it look," he said, still behind me. "It's not something a normal man does. Might have been, once. Hasn't been for a long time." He got quiet for a minute. "Turn around."

I turned. He'd pointed the barrel at the ground.

"I want you to listen, now. I saw it in your eyes back when I passed on the campsite. I've seen it building in you ever since we picked up Preacher. You're getting worse every day, so I'm going to tell it to you straight. If you don't like it, well, that's something we'll have to deal with.

"You're right about Preacher, Davey. He's sick, and he's sick bad. But it isn't killing him and it isn't touching us. He's what they call a carrier."

My hands came down slow, but Bo didn't seem to mind. "Carrier?"

"He's got the flu but he isn't dying. At least, that's the way I figure it."

"So why aren't we sick yet? Why aren't we dead?"

"We're not sick because we're not getting sick." It sounded simple, the way he said it, with a quiet shrug of his shoulders. "You were around your folks when they caught it. I was the only one in my family that didn't die of it, same goes for Sarge. Figure we got a taste of it, near the beginning, and got lucky, like a kid that gets the measles and never sees them again."

It started dawning on me. "You're bringing a carrier...into Grants Pass. You want the flu to spread there."

"He doesn't even have to get in the town. Just get close enough to someone working the fields or guarding the road to breathe on them a little, and the job's done."

"Hell, Bo," I said. My throat was dry. "Why?"

"You ever stop to think how I heard about Grants Pass? I never had much use for computers. Jenny, though...you remember her. Jenny."

His voice got cold when he said her name. I swear it felt like the stars got darker and the sweat came easy to my skin despite the chill in the air. "Sure. I remember."

Bo took a deep breath. "She said she needed one, and you know me. I do for the folks who mean something to me. We got it, and she starts shopping online all the damn time, spending money we didn't have. Found some places where people chat online. Made some new friends." There was a tightness in Bo's voice now, like words had been building up and choked back for longer than they should've.

"Met that son of a bitch on the goddamned Internet while I was out working to help pay for all those damn stupid dolls she loved so much. And she's the one — before the bastard, you know — who told me all about this crazy girl in Oregon and her little pipe dream for after the fall.

"Made me promise we'd go. I told her she was nuts, the world wasn't going to end, but at the end of the day she was dead set on it. All right, I told her. The world goes down the toilet, I'll bring you safe to this Grants Pass place."

He took a deep breath, and shifted his hands on the shotgun. "I'm going to meet her there now, if she survived. And I'm bringing Hell with me."

"Bo," I said, real quiet. "Bo, listen. That's crazy. You're talking about damning a town full of people, just in case she's there?"

"That's the short of it, Davey."

"They're gonna be immune, too, Bo. You know that's a fact — if you and Sarge and I walked away safe, it's a safe bet the whole town did."

I let him chew on that a few seconds, hoping to God he'd lower the gun, agree with me, and leave Preacher in the dust come morning. I could leave him in turn, then, once we got closer to a town that might take me in — leave him and his obsession behind.

"No," he said, and he said it flat, with a coyote look in his eyes. "There'll be those untouched, and they won't last long. Worst come to worst and you're right — well, all that means is Preacher doesn't do his job. I'll still do mine." He ran his hand along the barrel of the shotgun. "I'd love to see the whole damn place fall apart, and let her know her whoring caused it. If it comes to just me and her and a minute alone, though...well, that's all I *need*."

"That's crazy," I said again.

"You've never had so much reason to hate."

I couldn't think of much else to say, so I stayed quiet and still, just watching him. He lifted the shotgun, casual, and said, "So now you know, and Sarge isn't asking. What's it going to be, Davey? You going to help me?"

"You pick your guys, and you stick with them," I said with a shrug. "You want to take Grants Pass, I'll be with you. You want to kill the bitch, I'll be with you."

Bo shook his head and raised the gun.

You just couldn't lie to him.

I ran, and as I ran, something tickled at the back of my neck. I jerked away from the sensation and heard both barrels go off, heard the window shatter on the house I'd been running toward a second before. I got to the street with Bo shouting for Sarge, to get my gun and come after me. I kept running through the dark, hopping between houses and buildings, moving to put any space I could between myself and the men I'd trusted.

I didn't sleep the next day. I walked on like a man half dead, making my way north, but the whole way thinking of how I'd survive on my own. Thinking of what a man could do with that much hate in him.

Thinking of what I'd have to do in order to stop him.

I'm writing this down in every town I come to, everywhere I find paper. I'm warning people at every guard post to keep watch for a blond beanpole, a sickly preacher, and a pale horseman who talks with a smile. Some folks say they've seen them ahead of me. Some folks tell me to keep walking on. Sometimes they'll give me a bit of food to keep me going. Most times they turn me away.

Tonight I'm alone, in a place they used to call Deer Lodge, and the snows are getting bad through the mountains. I picked up a gun and some bullets from a dead man in the woods a few weeks back, and once I've written the end of this I'll read some out of a bible they gave me in Missoula. Tomorrow morning I'll keep looking for them and sounding the warning.

What haunts me is the fact that Preacher saved my soul. If it hadn't been for him — if I hadn't got so close to killing him — I never would have known. I'd have walked right into Grants Pass at Bo's right hand, and if he ran into Jenny, well…I might have figured he had some right to do what he planned. I'd picked my guy. I'm afraid I might have stuck with him.

Then again…

We're no angels, Bo said, and he was right. But I'm no devil, either; and I don't mind saying that somewhere on the road I got fond of the idea of Grants Pass. Maybe it's just because there's nowhere else for me to go, but someone's got to beat them there. Someone's got to warn that girl, Kayley, and Jenny, and all the crazy dreamers who set themselves up for a world after the one we knew.

BIOGRAPHY

IVAN EWERT

Ivan Ewert's work has previously appeared online in *The Edge of Propinquity*. He lives in an old house in northern Illinois with a lovely wife and enough gardens to feed them for the first month after the fall. Once that's gone, he's ready to look for work on one of the neighboring farms, but walking to Oregon isn't out of the question.

AFTERWORD

The very concept of *Grants Pass* seems based on an unspoken faith in the idea that you *will* be one of the survivors, you *will* make it to this fabled promised land, and you *will* set up a new life there, regardless of what the current inhabitants want. It's a frontier mentality straight out of the American Westerns which I tried to echo here.

But that kind of faith, combined with the dark obsession that insists the world will end, gives rise to people like Bo — strong-willed bastards who can tear down the world for their own personal reasons.

There's also a school of faith that says a person can be tempted to the edge of madness, but can come back stronger for it. That's what I believe, and that's what changes Davey from a would-be killer to a post-apocalyptic Paul Revere.

If the future comes apart, then everyone's going to have to flirt with the darkness. Finding a reason to continue being human, being fundamentally decent, despite that temptation, is what makes a man — hell, what makes a hero — in my view.

I hope it never comes. But if it does, I hope my faith is proven right.

THE CHATEAU DE MONS

JENNIFER BROZEK

KimmyShan: You serious about Grants Pass?

Kayley98052: Serious as a heart attack.

Kayley98052: Actually, no. But it's a really good mental exercise. You know? I mean, what would YOU do if the world ended? Would you be prepared? How would you live? Where would you go?

KimmyShan: I can't go to Grants Pass. I'm in Belgium, remember?

Kayley98052: Oh. Right. Hard to get here. Guess you'll have to make your own Grants Pass. Need to have enclaves all over the world for survivors.

KimmyShan: The world isn't gonna end.

Kayley98052: Not the point. Point is to think about it. It's a mental exercise.

KimmyShan: It scares me.

Kayley98052: The end of the world is scary. But it's scarier to survive it. What then?

KimmyShan: I hope Dad's stationed back in the States if the end of the world comes. I'll just go to Grants Pass. Then, you'll tell me what to do then.

Kayley98052: What if I die, too? Nothing says I'm going to live through the end of the world. I've just written about it and suggested a plan. If I survive, I'm gonna go to Grants Pass. I hope my friends from all over will meet me there. Some have already said they would. But, if I die, my friends will meet each other and survive together. Grants Pass is a good place for that.

KimmyShan: You won't die.

Kayley98052: Everybody dies. That's the easy part. It's surviving that's hard.

Kim re-read that instant message log from over a year ago. She had taped it into her journal because she had wanted to remember it. It had changed her life. Kayley had not realized how young Kim was. Kim had just been an Internet friend after all. Since she had typed in mostly complete sentences, readers thought she'd been older than her fifteen, highly impressionable, years. This conversation, and others like it, had sunk deep into her psyche. In turn, she had peppered her parents about emergency preparedness and plans of action, just in case something 'bad' happened. At first, her parents had been amused, then concerned, at her obsession over the idea of the world ending.

Her parents had decided that Kim's obsession was a reflection of her nerves at being stationed in a foreign country for the first time. To fix this, her parents had gone through the motions of preparing for any eventuality. They stocked up on freeze dried foods, bottled water, power generators, propane tanks, emergency kits and contingency plans over and above what the military required of them. They even went so far as to run several disaster drills.

Reassured that her family would survive anything that came at it, Kim relaxed and thoughts of imminent death and destruction left the forefront of her mind.

No one had any idea that a year later the unthinkable would come to pass, and that this preparation would mean the difference between life and death. At first, the news of California's devastating earthquake had been interesting in a train wreck sort of way. Then, it became downright disturbing as the news of three, simultaneous plagues hit countries all over the world.

Kim closed her journal, trying to hold back the rush of tears that threatened to overwhelm her. It had been six weeks since her father had called from the military base to tell her and her mother that it was being locked down due to a lethal outbreak of the Super Flu virus. He ordered them to stay at home and not to leave or even open the front door for any reason until he called again or came for them.

They lost power four weeks ago, but due to the previous year's preparation, she and her mother had remained relatively comfortable. Last week, a woman and her young son had come begging for food. Her mother had answered the door against her father's orders and had given the hungry pair what was left of the fresh fruit and bread.

They had repaid the kindness with death.

Her mother had caught the flu by that evening. She had died this morning and Kim knew she needed to bury her mother's body as soon as possible, out of respect and safety.

She wrapped her mother up in the sheets she had been laying on when she died. Her mother was much lighter than she had expected. Always a small woman, her mother's body seemed as tiny and light as a child's, rather than the vibrant spitfire everyone was always saying she took after. Except, now, there was no one to say that to her anymore. She was alone and, perhaps, the only person still alive in Mons. Maybe, the only person still alive in Belgium.

Taking out her fury and fear at the realization of her abruptly singular status, Kim dug a large hole in the far left corner of the backyard, next to the stone wall that enclosed it. Once her mother's body was in the ground, she fashioned a wooden cross to mark the grave with her mother's name, date of birth and date of death. She spoke a prayer for her mother's soul out loud, her voice cracking with tired grief. Then, she walked to the base of the walnut tree and slumped against it, looking at the backyard and home her parents had fallen in love with at first sight.

"Jean Paul tells me that it is called the Chateau de Mons." Her father had said. *"It's over three hundred years old. In times of dangers, the villagers would come here and camp in the backyard within the safety of the stone wall. Can you imagine that?"*

Looking at the backyard that was bigger than a football field — with a vegetable garden larger than the backyard she had had on base back in the States — she could imagine it. Friends of her parents had jokingly started calling them the Von Taylors, to reflect their "landed gentry" status.

Kim had felt like a princess when they had first moved into the manor house. It had a full stone cellar that included both a root cellar and a wine room, the first floor with a library, the second floor with all of the bedrooms and her mother's art studio, a full attic big enough to be another bedroom if they had wanted it and even a working bell tower — though she had been forbidden to ever ring the bell that dwelled above the attic.

The exchange rate had been good enough to allow her family to afford a maid once a week. The house was large enough that a maid was needed. Marie Rose had come on her bicycle every week with a smile. In her broken English, she would tell Kim how much of a good girl she was. Not like the other "ugly Americans" she had previously worked for. Now, there was no more Marie Rose to spoil her. She was the only one who remained and the house's size dwarfed her; making her feel that much smaller and alone. She hurried back inside so she would not have to look at it any longer.

It only took two days of wandering through the empty house, futilely wishing and willing the electricity or phone to start working again, before she decided to venture outside. She armed herself with her mother's Sig-220 and her father's 9mm Smith and Wesson pistol. As a military brat, she had been brought up around weapons of all types and knew how to use most of them. The weight of the two pistols seemed to be her only security in this newly silent world.

She was surprised at how frightened she was of leaving the safe haven of her home. Part of her protested, insisting her father would come for her. The other part suspected that if he was not already dead, anyone still alive at the base would be under very tight restrictions — to ensure the continued safety of the Supreme Headquarters Allied Powers Europe. If SHAPE, as an entity, still existed. However, given the lack of any sort of air traffic in the last three weeks, Kim was almost positive that the base was as deserted as the streets of the city that she walked through.

After a few hours of wandering, she returned home, happy to be in familiar surroundings. She thought about the instant message conversation she had had with her friend Kayley, and all of the talks they had had about what to do if you survived the end of the world. Neither of them had ever honestly believed it would happen. But, here they were. The end of the world as everyone had known it had come. She wondered if Kayley had survived and thought about Grants Pass, wishing with all her heart that she was in the States, where she had at least a chance of making it to the meeting place.

"But, I'm not. I'm here in Belgium and I'm still alive." She dug out her journal again, to reread what she had written over a year ago.

"July 14th, Kayley asked me what I would do if I was still in Belgium and the end of the world came. I didn't have an answer for her but she really pushed me. She made me think about it. I really didn't want to think about it. I don't like the idea of the world ending. I don't like it ending with me in a country where I don't speak any of the languages.

"I answered her after I thought about it. I decided I would make my home like Grants Pass. At least, to begin with. We have everything we need: a large house, a working garden (oh, the tons of weeds I have pulled from that thing), a fresh water well on the property, weapons, wood burning fireplaces, a potbelly stove, a huge pile of wood, wild game in the fields and a fortified yard. I would call everyone still living to the house using the bell, just like they did in the old days. It would be kind of like Noblesse Oblige — the noble's obligation."

She closed the journal again, thinking about what she had written. *Noblesse Oblige.* The bell would reach farther than she could on foot. It would bring all the survivors to a central location that could house and feed them. The garden was ready to harvest. But, if she rang the bell, she might call bad people to her only place of safety. Or, she could call people like herself. Survivors who needed help and wanted to help others. She had the means to help and she did not want to remain alone. Fear of the unknown warred with her frightened loneliness.

She thought about Kayley and the idea of Grants Pass. Kayley had had no idea who would come to Grants Pass when she presented the idea to the online community. She just gave it as an open invitation: Come one, come all. If the Chateau de Mons was to be like Grants Pass, she would have to take the same chance.

She left the journal on her bed and walked into the large hallway. To the side there was the bell rope she had been forbidden to touch. It felt rough in her hand. There was a moment of shock and fear when her experimental tug met with a strong resistance. She had made up her mind to call everyone; the bell *had* to work. She did not know what she would do if it did not. Take a sledgehammer to it instead? However, her second adrenalin filled pull elicited the loud ringing she had been looking for.

The ringing was louder than she had expected, but she did not stop. If this first call did not bring people to her, she would try again at regular intervals over the coming weeks until she was certain no one was coming. Then, she would decide what to do. For now, she was willing to make the call and hope for the best.

AFTERWORD

I wrote this story about the 'Chateau de Mons' because I lived on an estate very much like it in Belgium, while my father was stationed at SHAPE, Belgium. Our home was referred to as "the Chateau de Mons" and was over 300 years old. It had a rich history of being a place of sanctuary in times of need. I was told, back when the Mons was a small village, if danger threatened, the estate bell would be rung and the villagers who could make it, would camp behind the protected stone walls on the chateau's grounds until the danger passed.

Being an American on foreign soil, the military required my family to be prepared for all dangers. We had our stores of extra food and water, as well as instructions on what to do in certain situations. As I thought about the *Grants Pass* anthology, I wondered what I would do if the End came while I was in another country, and unable to go to my chosen place of sanctuary. This story immediately sprang forth. My own memories of living abroad mixed well with the concept of a post apocalyptic world, and the chateau of my childhood would be an excellent place to gather people together and to start again.

THE FEW THAT ARE GOOD

SCOTT ALMES

Since when did you smoke?" I asked, watching my brother light up a cigar.

"It's a special occasion," Brett replied. He coughed a few times before he finally got the end to glow red. He was nineteen, a good seven years older than me. He was about six inches taller and was able to grow a beard. I always told him that I would be able to grow a bigger beard than him someday.

The two of us leaned on Brett's truck. We were supposed to retrieve supplies from one of our father's friends. Our father was part of a gang called the Ravens. This would be the first time Brett got to be involved without our father's supervision. In the last two months, the three of us have hardly left each others' sides. Ever since the world fell apart, our father told us it would forever be the three of us. Of course, when Brett came into my tent telling me that he was allowed to drive the truck by himself, I couldn't help but tag along. Besides, I'm sure Dad would be proud of us.

In the distance, one of the other Raven trucks started to roll over the hill. I could hear the engine whine as it climbed the steep road.

I glanced over at Brett. He was pale and sweating badly. I guess he was nervous. I would be too. This was a big opportunity. Still, it seemed a little unnerving that Father was not with us. But, I knew Brett wanted to be a man, and I supposed doing this alone was the next step.

"Don't be afraid, Ryan," Brett said softly.

"I'm not," I said. In truth, I wasn't scared. I felt perfectly safe with my brother around.

SCOTT ALMES

The Raven truck finally pulled up in front of us. The back was loaded with boxes that never looked more beautiful. Jimmy came out of the side door, smiling widely. He was always laughing about something, and was Dad's best friend.

"I'm surprised to see you here, Brett," Jimmy said. The smile seemed to change. There was something I didn't like about it.

"I came to bring the supplies back to camp," Brett replied, almost twitching.

"Really? After your dad's old job?" Jimmy's smile got even worse. "Why don't you just hit the road?"

"Our family is supposed to pick up the supplies."

"Look, kid," Jimmy said sternly, no longer smiling. "You don't need to get anything. Now, beat it. All right?" Jimmy then turned away and started to step back into his truck.

Brett reached deep into his pocket. It didn't take me long to figure out what he was pulling out.

"Brett, no!" I shouted.

It was too late. My brother had Father's pistol in his hand and fired off three rounds. The first one ruptured a cone of blood out of Jimmy's leg. The man tried to turn and draw his own weapon, but then the second bullet landed in his chest. The third bullet hit Jimmy right between his eyes, letting loose a small stream of crimson.

"What are you doing?" I shouted, feeling my breathing quicken. "What did you just do?"

"Just hold on a minute, Ryan," Brett responded calmly, holding a hand up in the air. He stuck our father's gun into his waist belt with his other hand.

"No! You just killed Jimmy! Do you know what you just did?"

"I know exactly what I did! Jimmy deserved it!"

"Not Jimmy! He was our friend. He was Dad's friend."

"No he wasn't! He killed our father, Ryan! Dad is dead. It's just us now! The Ravens betrayed him. It's just me and you left."

"What? That's not true!"

"Yes it is. You have to believe me. That's why Dad isn't with us right now. He was killed last night. He wanted to take his own supplies and take off. We were going to go someplace safer. People are fighting here, and he didn't want us to be in danger. He was trying to protect us."

"What are we going to do?" I gasped. I felt a rain of tears come out with every word.

"You are going to get into my truck and drive to the bridge. There are no more deliveries today, so there won't be anybody crossing it." He started to walk towards Jimmy's truck. "Though, to be safe, park under the overhang."

"But—"

"No, Ryan, you have to do this. My truck is an automatic, so you'll be able to drive it. It's just like when Dad used to let you drive the car up at camp. Okay?"

"Okay," I said meekly.

"I'll be back soon, so don't worry," he said. He lingered a moment, as if trying to make a big decision. Then, he simply nodded, and hopped into Jimmy's truck. I saw him drive off into the distance. I sat for a moment, fighting off an army of tears. I wasn't as strong as my brother. He was both older and braver. I could only hope to grow up to be as courageous as he was.

A few minutes later, I was driving myself to the bridge.

It took Brett two hours to get to the bridge. I was close to having an asthma attack waiting for him. At first I thought he could have been another Raven, since he was driving Jimmy's truck. But he was shouting my name as he drove up next to me, so I stopped worrying.

"Ryan, are you ok?" he asked when he finally pulled up along side me.

"Yeah," I replied.

I then gave my brother a quick look-over. He was splattered with patches of blood. I wasn't sure how much of it was his. He had a bandage over his left forearm that was soaked red. I found myself staring at it for a moment.

"It's okay," he said. "The bullet only grazed me. I was able to stop the bleeding."

"What did you do?" I asked, wide-eyed.

"Something for Dad," he said simply. "Now, quickly. We're going to siphon the gas out of that truck. I have a few extra cans in the back. It's more efficient to only take one vehicle."

I nodded my head and climbed out of my vehicle. As I dug the can out of the back of Jimmy's truck, I realized that we had a lot more supplies than before. Brett had almost quadrupled our stock.

The two of us canned the gasoline and threw it into the back. I crawled into the passenger's seat.

"You ready?"

"I suppose so," I said, almost a whisper. "Where are we going?"

"Away from here," he gave me a weak smile. "Don't worry. I'm going to take care of you." He reached into the glove compartment and took out another cigar. He put it into his mouth, lit it, and drove across the bridge and into the beyond.

Did you grab our stuff?" I asked after thirty minutes of driving.

"Yeah, I took everything that was in the tent," Brett replied.

"Including my books?"

"What were they in?"

"The brown chest, the one that Dad made for us to keep our toys in."

"That thing was full of books? No wonder it was so heavy. I thought it was more weapons."

"No, just my books. But I like my books, Brett."

"I don't understand that. I never liked to read. There were always a thousand better things to do."

"It was just good to get away sometimes."

"Away from what?"

"Everything."

"You believe a book can make the world disappear?" Brett asked, half-sarcastically. He noticed me frowning at the statement and instantly changed his tone. "I guess they could. Like I said, I was never much of a reader, so I wouldn't know. I'll tell you what: I'll make sure I trade for any books I see along to way."

"Ok, Brett," I smiled. "That sounds good to me."

We journeyed for a good two weeks before seeing another person. It was an old man, riding in a broken down jeep. The vehicle seemed to have lost all of its suspension, as it bounced like a jack-in-the-box with every bump. Brett had me lean out the side of the truck to wave the geezer down.

"Hello," the old man greeted us as the vehicles pulled side by side.

"Hi," Brett replied. "Are you willing to trade?"

"Certainly. That is, if you have something that suits my fancy. Can I see your stock?"

Brett nodded and got out of the truck. I noticed that he still had the pistol in his belt. The old man also got out of his vehicle, following Brett to the truck's bed. Brett waved to me to stay in the passenger's seat.

I couldn't understand what the two of them were talking about. They were discussing something intimately. Brett seemed really excited about it, but I couldn't tell what they were talking about. Unfortunately, the excited motions had stopped by the time I had the guts to roll down the window.

"You have a nice stock," the old man said. "Is it just the two of you?"

"Yeah, for now," Brett replied. "What are you interested in trading?"

"Well," the old man started, licking his lips. "I think I'll take the whole lot."

"What? What do you have? Gold?"

"I have this!" The old man was now holding a gun to my brother's cheek. "Your truck is a lot better equipped than mine. I think I'll just take it. Now, hand over the keys or I'll be forced to take them myself."

"Shut it, old man. You're not taking anything."

"Really now?" the man asked. There was a click as he pulled back the hammer.

My brother amazed me. He looked right into the eyes of the old man without flinching. He was a lot braver than I was. Then, with astonishing reflexes, he knocked the gun away from the old man's grip. In an instant my brother had our father's pistol in his hand and fired twice into the old man's chest.

I swear I could see a tear in my brother's eye as he walked back to the car.

We set up camp right by the two vehicles. Brett rummaged through the old man's supplies. It was mostly ammunition and alcohol. We had enough stuff to feed a group of ten for three months, and I didn't think Brett found a scrap of anything edible in the old man's truck.

I lit the fire and Brett cooked dinner. The two of us ate in silence. After dinner, we continued to sit quietly. There had been very few words spoken between us in the last two weeks. It had been as if Brett was in a different place. His eyes would look forward, but I knew his mind was elsewhere.

I tried reading to pass the time, but even the tales of dragons and elves weren't able to distract me. This world just seemed cold, and it seemed to be affecting Brett.

After looking into the fire for an hour, Brett dug for another cigar. He realized that he had left them in the truck, and decided he was too lazy to get up for them. Instead, he took a bottle of whiskey from the crate he was sitting on. He wordlessly began to drink straight from the container. It wasn't for another half hour, after Brett was a little woozy, that I had the courage to speak.

"What are we going to do, Brett?" I asked, hardly loud enough for him to hear me.

"I'm going to take care of you, little brother," he said, slightly slurring the words. I don't think he'd ever had much to drink before.

"I mean, where are we going to go?"

"Oh, I do know that one. We're going to Grants Pass."

"Where?"

"It's about a hundred miles north of here. The old man told me about it. Supposedly, there is a gathering there. It's supposed to be a safe haven."

"We're going to join with other people?"

"No, no, Ryan. We're not going to join the people in Grants Pass. We're going to get supplies from them."

"How? What are we going to trade them? I can drive the jeep if you need me to. We could surely trade it."

"No, that won't be necessary. We are just going to take the supplies we need."

"Take? Like from the old man?"

"Yes."

"But, what if they are willing to trade?"

"That doesn't happen anymore, Ryan. We're the only good people left in the world. It's just going to be me and you. But, we'll need to get more supplies if we're going to survive all of this. We just need to stay strong until things get better." He looked at the bottle in his hand. He had drunk nearly half of it. Satisfied, he corked it and set it down beside him. "Now we should get some sleep. We're going to leave early tomorrow morning."

We left before the sun rose the next day. Brett was already packing up the truck before I woke up. I was only awake for five minutes before I was back in the passenger's seat and we were driving away.

"What were you reading last night?" Brett asked, after driving an hour in silence.

"What?" I asked. I had been completely absorbed in the landscape around us.

"The book," he replied, "which one was it?"

"It's a fantasy story. It's called *The Griffin Rider*. The story is about a boy who finds the last griffin in the world."

"What does he do with it?"

"What do you mean?"

"Well, he found the last griffin in world. That means it's extremely rare. He could sell it for millions of dollars. They're big creatures, so he could even train it to defend him. He could do anything with it. So, I'm wondering, what did he do with it?"

"He befriended it."

"Oh," Brett said, and he drove on.

It wasn't before long that we saw a car in front of us. It was an actual car, a small sedan of some Japanese make. Once again, I was told to wave down the car.

The vehicles were soon stopped with our truck parked right behind the car. My brother pulled out my father's gun. He checked the magazine, making sure there was a full clip. He then put the gun back together and shoved it into his waist belt.

"Hello," called out the driver.

"Hello there," my brother called back, approaching the car. I was leaning out the window, watching what was going on.

"Are you interesting in trading?"

"That depends, are you going to Grants Pass?"

"Sure am. I'd be daft if I wasn't. It's supposed to be the only safe haven."

"Really now?" my brother asked. "That's too bad you won't get there."

Brett pulled out the pistol and fired into the window. I could see the flashes bounce off the inside of the car and the driver twitch as the bullets pierced him. My brother fired until there was blood splattered on the windshield, and finally shoved the gun back into his belt.

"Come on, Ryan," he shouted, starting to walk back to the car. "Let's see what he had in his trunk."

But, before I could even put my hand on the handle, the backdoor of the car swung open. It smashed right into Brett's legs, knocking him to the ground. I could see a man get out of the backseat. He must have been resting under a blanket, for a blue cloth fell off of him as he stood up. The man was wielding a shotgun.

It took the man the same amount of time to cock the gun as it did for Brett ready his weapon. I saw both go off. A splash of blood flew out of the man's back, right behind his heart. He started to fall. Brett, however, got a more gruesome wound. The man had been aiming for his face, and he had aimed true.

My eyes snapped shut at the sight of my brother. He was dead, instantly killed by the shot. There was no doubting that.

There was nobody left but me along the road. There was nobody else alive. There was nobody to protect me.

I could do nothing but curl up in the seat of the truck.

"Kid?" It was the first word I heard as I woke up.

"Wha—?" I started. I couldn't finish the sentence. Realistically, I couldn't even identify where I was.

"Kid, are you okay?" My eyes focused on the speaker. It was a woman. She seemed middle-aged, and it looked like she had been walking for hundreds of miles.

"Kid, are you okay?" she asked again.

I shook my head. I remembered what happened now. My father and my brother were dead. I was far from 'okay'.

"What happened here?" the lady continued. I noticed that there were a few other people behind her. They were investigating the bodies.

"They shot each other," I said quietly.

"Did you know any of them?"

"Yes, my brother."

"Oh, god," she stammered, stepping back a little. "I'm sorry. Do you have any other family?"

"No, my father is dead."

"What about your mother?"

"I never knew her." I could feel tears start to well up.

"Well, kid, do you have a name?"

"Yeah, Ryan."

"Well, Ryan, I think you'd better come with us."

"Where are you going?"

"To Grants Pass. It's one of the few safe havens in the States." Then, the lady's face switched to a frown. "Or at least what used to be the States."

I sat in silence for a few moments, pondering it all over. I made my decision in only a few seconds.

"All right," I replied. "Just let me say goodbye to my brother first."

As I walked over to my brother's corpse, the group of adults was already starting to take supplies from our truck. I leaned over Brett. I let a few of my tears fall into his body. I knew he had only wanted to protect me. He wanted to try and take my father's place, and now I had neither of them.

I noticed the pistol lying next to his hand. Without thinking I shoved it into my waist belt.

"Carrie," shouted one of the men rummaging around the truck. "Look what I found!" The man held my book, *The Griffin Rider*, in his hand.

"Literature will be worth a lot soon," Carrie nodded. "Put it in the safe."

"I found a few others, too."

"Put them all in."

"Those are mine," I stated, standing up.

"Sorry, kid," the lady said. She frowned as she spoke. "I've got a theory that things like books are going to be quite valuable soon, whether fiction or non-fiction. I don't want them to get destroyed."

"But, my father bought them for me."

"I'm sure he did, but there are better uses for the books. You will see what I mean later."

"I want my books back."

"Kid, that's not going to happen."

"I want my books!" I yelled. Before I knew it, my father's pistol was in my hand. I fired off the last of the bullets. I saw the lady and the other adults collapse to the ground. The man with my book was the last one to fall.

Silently, I shoved the pistol into my belt, just like Brett would have done.

Once again I was alone. Though, this time, I knew no one was going to protect me.

Hopefully I would be able to get one of the cars to start, but that was a concern for later. I made my way over to the man's body. He was staring into the air with open eyes, a small stream of blood flowing out of his chest. I ripped my book from his fingers, wiped the blood from the cover, and started to read the precious words. I would go to Grants Pass like Brett wanted me to, but for now, I needed to escape.

Brett was right: I was one of the few good people left in the world.

BIOGRAPHY

SCOTT ALMES

Scott Almes currently resides at the University of Pittsburgh underneath a stack of calculus and physics books, trying his hardest to get a degree in mechanical engineering. When he's not trying to learn the mysteries of gravity and flux, he enjoys movies and reading.

Generally, he prefers his books smart and to lead him to places that he's never been, but his movies simple enough to give his mind a break. He also thoroughly enjoys the suburban equivalents of adventuring, even if it means a backyard campfire, a simple trip to his friend's cabin, or an 80 mile journey to the nearest IHOP. He has been told that he has the ability to find humor in whatever life throws at him, and he agrees with that statement.

AFTERWORD

I wrote this piece to explore how younger people might react to an apocalypse. In this story, there are two boys. The main character is too young to be left alone, and his brother is just of an age where normally, he'd be looking to start his own life. This story is a thought experiment imagining how these two boys would react to the world changing at such a critical point in their lives.

RIGHTS OF PASSAGE

PETE KEMPSHALL

I missed it the first time, my eyes sliding across it like it wasn't there. I wondered about that later, why I didn't register the sight immediately. For a while I convinced myself it had been the salt wind making me squint, but to be honest, I probably wouldn't have noticed it even on a clear, still day. I think my brain had simply removed it from the list of possibilities — it was like walking into your back garden and bumping into a T-Rex.

Even when I did spot the white cloth billowing out past the Palace Pier, my mental gears continued to grind for a few seconds...then finally they meshed, and I was running.

"Woah, someone's had their spinach."

Diane's words were carried on a rush of warm air, redolent with the aroma of carrots, onions and pepper. In defiance of its nervous churning, my stomach rumbled.

She had her back to me, stirring the pot over the fireplace, and hadn't bothered to glance around when I'd come through the door like a charging elephant. After all, she didn't need to look to know it was me, just like I didn't need to see her face to know she was smiling.

When I didn't answer she turned from the fire. "Sorry. That was stupid of—" Her voice tailed off at the sight of me pale and panting: I could read the thoughts flashing across her face. The dread. "Oh God, you're—"

"No," I gasped quickly. "Not that. Boat. Out past the pier. I think it's going to the marina."

The flames from the grate caught in Diane's eyes, glinting. "Fucking hell."

When the little port where I lived started going from metaphorically dead to actually dead, I knew I would be the last man standing. Irony demanded it.

My problem meant that I'd been alone for years essentially, even amongst family and my few friends. So if anyone was going to be able to cope with the disappearance of every human on earth, I thought it would be me.

Truth was, I couldn't survive on my own. And I knew I couldn't stay at home, not with…not with them upstairs. So it was clear I had to leave. I had to find survivors.

West towards Brighton had seemed the best bet. The other way along the coast was Eastbourne — legendary seaside dumping ground for old folk — and I couldn't imagine anyone had survived there.

I'd never learned to drive. I was 17 at the time and had been legally entitled to start lessons for months, but it just hadn't seemed like a priority, not then. Now I had the freedom of the roads, I just wasn't confident enough to try. A little voice kept asking me what the point was in surviving the plague just to lose control of a car and veer off Telscombe Cliffs.

So I borrowed a bike. "Borrowed" — that was the actual word that popped into my head, like there was someone I could give it back to when I was finished. It belonged to the man next door — he'd been insanely proud of it, all lightweight this and gears that. I like to think he'd be happy someone was taking care of it.

Tiredness was still a big problem though. Fortunately there were towns all along South Coast Road, with convenience stores for food and clifftop pubs to rest in. After a while I even got blasé about the various occupants I risked disturbing every time I entered a building. Frighteningly, I was becoming desensitized.

But even with the frequent rest stops, fatigue pulled at me like quicksand. The more I struggled against it, the stronger it held. The *intervals between rests grew shorter and shorter, and what should have been a reasonably quick journey stretched on into days.*

By the time I reached Brighton Marina I was fit to drop. It would only have taken a short while to get to the town centre, but I knew I simply wouldn't make it, not before nightfall.

Besides, there were worse places to stop. The marina complex had shopping facilities and a cluster of homes — once fashionable and expensive — and that meant food and shelter. Plus, taking the slip road from the clifftop meant it was literally all downhill to get there.

Except that somewhere between the top of the road and the bottom, I passed out.

Looking back, I was lucky to wake up at all. If they'd found me first, I'd have been an easy meal for the wild dogs out scavenging for food every night. But I did wake up, tucked up in a bed so tightly that I immediately thought of hospitals. My side ached and my legs felt raw. I didn't need to open my eyes to know it was road rash, didn't want to look and confirm it.

Despite my closed eyes, I felt the shadow fall across me. I opened them — just for a second before passing out again — and when I did it was to brilliant light streaming through auburn hair, and a smile that gave the sunshine a run for its money.

"Morning, tiger. Sleep well?"

We took the bikes, hoping to make better time. Despite the wind off the sea doing its best to unsaddle us, we managed to coast down the marina road as the yacht slipped past the breakwater. While our eyes had been off it, someone had furled the sails, and now the sleek white vessel was chugging on its engines.

"They've got fuel," Diane remarked, her eyebrows raised. Another rarity.

Whoever was at the wheel was spoilt for choice for places to tie up. Almost all the seaworthy vessels berthed at the marina had vanished in the early days of the plague, sailed out to sea by panicked owners — or desperate thieves — in the belief that if they could just get offshore, they wouldn't get infected.

Except that by the time they sailed, they already were.

Many of the boats moored out to sea had since broken loose of their anchors and come back in on the tides. Shattered fragments had been washing up all down the coast from Rottingdean to Seaford for months. Against the odds, the anchors of two large yachts had continued to hold... They could still be seen off the coast at Saltdean, silent, floating tombs.

Diane and I dumped the bikes and padded silently down to the waterfront, keeping low as we went. Crouched behind a wall I could make out a figure steering from the back of the ship, gently nosing it into place before jumping onto the jetty with a mooring rope. It was hard to make out details at that distance — I guessed it was a man but the weatherproof clothing gave the figure a bulky androgyny that would only be decipherable closer up. One thing leapt out at me, though.

"Check out his belt."

"Yeah," Diane murmured. "What do you think?"

"Can't see anyone else on board."

"They could be below." She paused. "But if there was anyone else, wouldn't they be helping to tie up?"

She had a point. The sole sailor was clearly struggling with the ropes, and while some assistance wasn't essential it would certainly be desirable.

The breath hissed through my teeth. "Let's wait a bit longer. At least until we know for certain if there's anyone else on board."

And until we knew if they were carrying guns on their hips too.

♥

It took a couple of weeks for me to recover, during which time my savior breezily imparted her life story. Her name was Diane Platts, she informed me that first morning, popping another round of antibiotics into my mouth. Final year student of English Lit at the University of London, down from the city for a family party when the sickness hit. Her brother was getting married and the whole clan had gathered to celebrate the engagement. She'd really been looking forward to it.

As it turned out, she'd been forced to watch her entire family tree cut down in just a couple of days.

Eventually, she'd gone exploring and discovered a place near the seafront with a working fireplace for heat and cooking. Better yet, the owners appeared to have vacated so there was nothing to...clean up when she moved in.

For regular supply runs the marina shops were the closest to her new home, which is how she'd come to find me. She raised her eyebrows in mock exasperation as she told me of the trouble she'd had loading me into a shopping trolley and pushing me home. She had been hoping to fill up with tins.

When I could get a word in, I gave her the basics about me, keeping the more colorful details to myself. She didn't appear to notice I was withholding anything — she barely stopped talking for the first two days, flitting around me in a flurry of nervous energy.

So mostly I watched her. Outwardly, she was no different from the better-looking girls at school, but theirs had been a cold beauty. They knew they looked good and used that as a weapon. By contrast Diane's beauty had a warmth that came from complete unawareness — or disregard — of her attractiveness.

As I started to recover, I could also see there was pride in her eyes, stronger with each passing day. My return to health meant she'd done it; she'd actually saved a life. All those aunts, uncles, brothers, sisters, all those people she couldn't help...now at last she could chalk one up in the "win" column.

I let her believe that. After all, she did rescue me from a lunch date with roving packs of ravening hounds. But as far as my physical improvement was concerned...I didn't feel ready to tell her she had nothing at all to do with it.

The yacht was securely moored now, but still no-one had emerged from the cabins. On the contrary, its only apparent crewman had disappeared below, leaving us nothing to watch except the boat, bobbing gently in the water.

When he did reappear — and by this time we could tell it was a he — the yachtsman had swapped his thick rubbers and lifejacket for a chunky blue sweater, jeans and a ragged baseball cap. All that remained of his original outfit was the holster, heavy on his right hip.

He jumped nimbly onto the jetty and strode in the direction of the shopping complex, pausing only to rummage in his pockets for a cigarette. Sparking up, he walked on.

We slid from cover and followed.

If the yachtsman was at all worried that he was being watched, he didn't show it. He sauntered along the dockside in no particular hurry, smoking happily and stopping every now and again to glance in a window. We kept our distance, but were still close enough to see that he was tall — taller than either of us at any rate — and well built. The active type, it struck me. Outdoorsy.

Finally, he stopped outside a large chandlery, and gave the door a light push. It swung open unprotestingly, and he smiled. Shifting his weight to one side, he stuck a hand into the back pocket of his jeans and withdrew a crumpled piece of paper. To my side I could hear Diane stifle a snort.

"God," she murmured. "He's brought a shopping list."

"You have got to try this." Diane passed her glass across to me, the far rim slightly smeared from her lips. *"If that's not the best wine you've ever tasted I'm going to start giving you seawater to drink. You'll never know the difference."*

She smiled broadly. I could see her studying my reaction as I drank, eager for my enjoyment to parallel hers.

"It's good."

"'Good'." She rolled her eyes. *"'Good'? I despair sometimes, I really do."*

"What, should I spit some in a bucket?"

She stuck her hand out. *"Give it back. Now. Right now."*

I chuckled and passed the glass to her. She nestled into the huge leather beanbag that marked her favorite reading place, careful not to spill any of the wine, and opened a thick hardback. Then, poking her tongue out at me, she directed her attention to the pages.

And so it went. Once a week we'd loot the shops in the Churchill Square shopping precinct, her looking for books, me for music. MP3 players were useless now, but I'd unearthed a portable CD player and some speakers, and there were enough batteries in the shops to last me a lifetime. I'd let her pick the alcohol — largely because I didn't drink much of it myself — and we were set for the week.

Every night we'd sit by the fire, read and talk. At 22, Diane had a few years on me, had seen some of the world where I'd seen precisely none. She introduced me to writers, styles and concepts I'd never heard of, while I introduced her to...well, frankly very little. But unlike every other woman I'd ever known, despite the paucity of my own life experience she was still interested in everything that came out of my mouth.

And every night in a small house on the south coast, long after I'd come to believe I'd never hear it again, there was laughter.

❧

"Jesus fucking Christ!"

The yachtsman all but dropped the cardboard boxes he was heaving through the door. We'd watched him position a trolley outside the shop before making several trips inside, each time returning laden with goods to load into the cart. We simply waited until he came out, arms full of goods, and stepped into his line of sight. The idea was that if he had his hands full of supplies he couldn't pull his gun on us. Seeing him standing there, though, I suddenly wondered what we'd do if he just dropped the cartons.

"Mother of God, you scared the crap out of me," he blustered. His accent was American, and I put him in his forties, but fit with it. He carried himself with the self-confidence of a man who's in peak condition and knows it. That and the small cannon at his hip made me think he might be ex-military.

When he pulled off his hat to run his fingers through his hair — a gesture of disbelief at what he was seeing — I knew I was right. A buzz-cut, dark but graying.

"Where the hell did you come from?" he asked, repositioning his cap and pulling it on tight.

"I was just going to ask you that," Diane said. The grin she was rewarded with intensified her own.

"Germany, via France," he replied. "Been stationed with the Krauts for a couple of years." He shot out a hand, transferring the weight of the boxes to his leg. "Sergeant Aldo Quinn, at your service, Ma'am."

She returned the handclasp. "Diane."

"Will," I chipped in, taking his proffered hand. I winced slightly: he had one of those handshakes that grinds your knuckles together in a passive-aggressive show of strength. Diane hadn't reacted to it. Maybe Aldo had saved it especially for me.

"Just passing through?" Diane asked, like that was still a perfectly normal thing to be doing.

"Needed to pick up some things," he declared. "Didn't expect to see anyone, that's for damn sure!"

"You alone?" I asked.

"Sure am, boy."

"You've not seen any other survivors?" asked Diane.

"Not til you. Hoping to change that, though. Got a big trip planned." He fixed us with a look that was both amused and cagey. "What say you help me get this gear back to my boat and I'll tell you all about it?"

It was strange: you'd think that in the face of an eternity alone Diane and I would want to spend every waking moment together. I knew that being alone was what she feared most. She thrived on company. To have that taken away from her...I sometimes wondered if she ceased to exist when there was no one else in the room.

But enforced loneliness and voluntary time out are entirely different things, and from the offset we both seemed to understand that little breaks were not just necessary, but essential.

"We can't live in each other's pockets," she'd averred one morning as I asked nervously if she minded me going for a little walk. "That way madness lies."

The time alone took on a huge importance for me, if only because my "little walks" gave me the chance to see to my old problem. All the time I was bed-ridden I'd had to wait for Diane to go out for supplies before I could deal with it. Even then I had to be careful — I couldn't risk passing out and her coming home to find me flat out with a needle in my arm. Now I was finding that I could just slip away any time and see to my needs, no questions asked.

I hated doing it, tried hard to justify why I did. The whole reason I'd gone looking for survivors in the first place was that I couldn't manage the problem on my own, yet there I was, sneaking around, keeping it secret. I don't know why I didn't just tell her up front.

That's not true, I know exactly why. I'd been living with it for so long, living with the looks *people gave me when they found out...*

I didn't want to see the same thing in her *eyes.*

Below decks the boat was surprisingly welcoming. The hatch led straight into a living area and kitchenette, each making full, intelligent use of the available space. A short passage led off the cooking area to the front of the boat. There were three doors coming off it — one was a washroom the remaining two would be cabins, I guessed. While Diane was eyeing the rest of the interior appreciatively, I was wondering how I could get a look through the doors, just to be sure. Aldo may have been the model of the genial host, but we still only had his word for it that he was alone.

"Please sit," Aldo offered, gesturing to the seats in the dining nook. Diane slipped in behind the table, but I perched on the outside, just in case I needed to move quickly.

"Coffee?" The big American struck a match and lit the gas on the compact stove, before filling a kettle from a small tap and clanging it onto the hob. "I tell you, I can just about cope with the annihilation of the human race, but soon as I run out of joe..." He chortled throatily.

"You could always make do with something else," I muttered as he popped open a cupboard and reached for the coffee tin. The brief glimpse inside the storage space revealed it was also loaded with bottles — scotch, bourbon, vodka. The majority were down to half volume or less.

"You said something about a trip?" Diane prompted.

"So I did, so I did." He clinked a trio of tin mugs onto the work surface. "How's about your boy there reaches over into that cabinet."

Prickling, I remained seated. Aldo, busying himself with the drinks, seemed to interpret my lack of movement as confusion. Or idiocy. "That one there, boy, by the radio."

I stood and pulled open the wooden panel. Inside, the cupboard was stuffed with papers, from charts to handwritten notes. A second handgun, smaller than the one on Aldo's hip, sat atop the pile, alongside a tin with a red cross painted on it. Antithetic paperweights.

"That print-out on top there," Aldo coached. "If you'd be so kind as to bring that over to the table..." He spooned dark, aromatic powder into a pot, not even looking up at me. "That's the one. Now have yourself a seat and read what it says."

I scooted back into the dining nook and smoothed the paper out on the table. Diane shuffled in closer to me. Her leg pressed against mine as she scanned the words.

It was from a website, the top of the sheet dominated by a map and two words in a bold font.

"Grants Pass," Diane murmured.

Aldo set a tray of steaming mugs down in front of us and grinned. "Grants Pass."

It was maybe three months after she'd rescued me from the marina when it all came out.

We were sitting together in front of the fire, Diane working her way through a chardonnay that would have been way out of her price range before the plague, me just trying not to drop off. I suddenly noticed she was staring at me from her beanbag. Even with her glass to her lips I could see that smile of hers, tickling the edge of her mouth.

"Will?"

"Hmmm?"

"Why haven't you tried to sleep with me?" She took a sip of pale liquid, allowing me time to answer. After a few seconds of silence,

she took pity on me. "It's just funny, that's all. I always assumed that the last man on earth would try to jump me sooner rather than later." Her eyes twinkled. "You know, that whole 'It's up to us to repopulate the human race' thing."

"I—"

"You're gay, aren't you?" she posited. "God, how funny's that — we could be the last couple alive and you don't like girls!"

"No," I jumped in. "I'm not gay. I just…I can't."

"You can't?" Diane's smile was fading. This wasn't funny anymore.

"I can't."

"Why not?"

I sat, mouth guppying. At last, failed by words, I rolled up my sleeve.

For a moment Diane simply stared at the marks.

Then she hit me.

"You really think there's a community of survivors out there?"

Aldo shrugged. "It's a risk, sure, but hell, what do I got to lose? Course, it'd be less of a risk with a couple of extra pairs of hands aboard."

Diane gripped my leg under the table. "You want us to come with you? Just like that?"

"Way I see it, I can sail this tub on my own, but it's a long haul to be doing it solo." He stared at us, intense. "And neither of you two can steer a ship to save yourselves or you'd have found something seaworthy and been off looking for survivors already. You're stuck here, I could sure use the help…it's win-win."

"Why not just use the engines?" I asked. "Got to be easier."

"Hell, boy," Aldo smirked, "I got just enough juice to get me in and out of harbor. I could maybe manage sailing in a dead straight line for a couple of hours, all assuming the weather's good, then the tanks'd be dry." He looked steadily at Diane — obviously he'd decided she was the one who called the shots — and cranked up his grin another 100 watts. "So what do you say? Are you in?"

"Are you insane?" She looked at me with wild, disbelieving eyes. "Everything we've survived, all those people who died and you're pissing your life away with drugs?"

"I'm not—"

She hit me again, raging, tears running down her face as she landed blow after blow on my head and chest. I was too run-down, too weak to stop her. All I could do was wait for her to run out of steam.

When at last she subsided, sobbing, I flopped back to the sofa. "I'm not doing drugs. I'm sick."

She raised her wet face, the anger melting into shock. Shame.

"There's too much iron in my blood. It's rare for someone as young as me to get it, but it's not like we haven't seen any weird illnesses lately, right?" I smiled weakly, hoping it'd catch, like a yawn. It didn't.

"It makes me tired. Weak." I snorted bitterly. "No sex drive, amongst other things. When you found me, I'd let it get on top of me, let it build up…"

The silence made the air in the room seem heavier. Diane sat, perfectly still, digesting the information.

"And you inject drugs to treat it?"

"No, I have to draw blood. Drain it off."

"How much? I mean, how often—?"

"More often when there's more build-up. About the same as you'd take for a blood donation, except I can't handle drawing that much by myself. I can only do a couple of syringes at a time."

"That's it? That's the treatment?"

"Like I said, it's a rare type. The doctors were looking into other options, but — you know. Drawing blood will slow it down, but not stop it."

"What happens if you don't stop it?"

"Eventually? Organ failure. Liver. Heart."

She looked at me with eyes that barely masked her emotion. "Why didn't you tell me?"

I sighed. "Before the plague, everyone treated me like I needed wrapping in cotton wool, or like I was a freak. As long as you didn't know, I was…normal. A person, not a patient. I didn't want to swap your friendship for your sympathy."

She slapped me. Hard.

"You fucking child! What did you think I was going to do when it got serious? When you died? Didn't you think I deserved to know about that? Asshole!"

"I'm sorry. I didn't—"

"Next time you draw blood, you tell me. I can help you take the extra if you need me to. But you fucking tell me."

And she took me in her arms and held me tightly. "I can't lose you, you dickhead. You're all I've got."

"God, Will, there's hope. If we get to this place and there are doctors — you could *live*."

Aldo had gone up on deck for a smoke, to give us a chance to talk things through. I already knew Diane's answer. The chance of a few years more life for me was important to her. More so than the idea of a community full of new people? I pushed the thought away, disgusted with myself. "It's not a guarantee, you know."

"But it's better than sitting here trying to keep you alive one syringe at a time." She squeezed my hand. "We're going, right?"

"Right."

"God, I can't believe it. We're going to America." She slumped back in the seat, as if just thinking about it had exhausted her.

"So you're with me then?"

I turned quickly. Aldo was propping up the wall at the rear of the cabin. We'd been so wrapped up in our discussion I hadn't heard him come down from the deck. That or he moved like a ninja.

"Yes," Diane responded. "We're with you."

"Great!" He clapped his hands together with a sound like a cannon shot. "If we load up now we can be off at dawn."

"We need to pack," I said.

"Well, I could use some help with these boxes…"

Diane looked at me. I knew she'd want to pack her own clothes and keepsakes. I also knew she'd have no trouble with mine…

"I'll stay," I said. "But I'm not that great with heavy lifting."

Aldo stepped forward and punched me on the arm, good old boys together. "Damn it, son! A couple of weeks on board with me you won't need your mama around so much! I'll soon get you into shape!"

"Oh, he's not—" Diane piped up. I shot her a glance and she fell silent.

"I'll be fine," I reassured her. "You go. Pack for both of us."

"If you're sure?"

"I'm sure."

We stood on the jetty and she hugged me warmly. "Don't overdo it."

"No problem. I'll be as quick as I can, and see you back at the house."

"It's a date. I'll open some wine."

"That'd be different."

"Git." She trotted off down the walkway, stopped and turned back. "Think you can change his mind; get him to come back to the house with you when you're all done?"

I shook my head. Aldo had decided that if we weren't sailing until dawn, he'd remain with the boat while Diane and I gathered our belongings. "No, he's pretty sure he wants to stay here tonight. Keep an eye on the boat."

"From who?"

I laughed. "I'll be back by dark. Get packing."

"Thanks, boy." Aldo dumped another box on the deck. The trolley was almost empty now, and we'd restocked the ship with everything from fresh water to antibiotics. "You ain't as runty as you look."

I ignored him and lugged a pallet of tinned sausages and beans down through the hatch to the kitchen area. From the moment Diane had left, he'd started sniping at me and I was losing patience. As it was, we'd been hefting boxes for hours and I was starting to wane. I'd need to rest soon. Sleep.

"Getting dark," I called up the steps. "I'll have to get back to Diane."

Aldo clumped down into the cabin. "Got to say, you surprised me there, sonny."

"I'm sorry?"

"Woman like that with a boy like you…Guess the plague wasn't a disaster for everyone now, was it?" He flashed a mouthful of perfect white teeth at me, luminescent against in his tanned skin. "You *are* hitting that, aren't you?"

"It's not like that. We're — you know."

He furrowed his brow at me. "You some kind of faggot?"

I gritted my teeth and tore open a cardboard carton of first aid supplies.

"Been a long time since I seen a woman, never mind one as good-looking as her." He licked his lips. "I'd be all over her in a second."

I popped open the chart cabinet, and reached for the first aid kit. Keeping my back to him so he couldn't see my anger, I started replenishing the tin's bandages.

"You want to get your shit together there, boy. Where we're going there'll be plenty who'll get on her if you don't." I could see him behind me, reflected in the cabin window. He was brushing at his sleeve with one hand, dusting himself off. Preening. "Hell, it's going to be a long trip, I might just get some myself. A girl's got to pay her way!"

I replaced the tin and started to close the cabinet door...hesitated. Aldo had wandered into the kitchenette and was stacking tins under the work surface. His head ducked out of sight, and the decision made itself. I shut the cabinet loudly. Aldo looked up from his work and winked at me broadly. "You done, boy?" I nodded. "You best get back to her then. Spend some time together before we go. Cast off time's six in the ay-em."

"See you then," I muttered, and plodded up the steps.

I couldn't see him, but as I trudged off into the twilight, I could feel Aldo's eyes, burning into me. Zipping my jacket against the cold, I told myself I hadn't made my mind up about anything, not yet.

The new heaviness in my pocket called me liar.

Diane pulled the stops out for our last night in the house. We gorged on what perishables we had left in the pantry, while she put most of a bottle of wine away. As ever, I had to limit my alcohol, so only needed one drink to get a buzz on.

"Can't let it go to waste!" she proclaimed, glugging herself another glassful. She ended the night dancing to her favorite CD, an 80s compilation I'd found for her in the bargain bin of an abandoned music store. She bounced around in a blur of hair and limbs, laughing and spinning until the room started to spin for her too, at which point she collapsed heavily onto the couch.

I was still too drained from heaving boxes around to help her to bed. Instead, I fetched a duvet and covered her. As I tucked her in, she reached up a hand, slowly, like she was moving through water, and touched my cheek.

"Thanks, Will." She smiled crookedly.

And she was asleep.

It wasn't so easy for me. Despite my fatigue, my mind was still whirring a couple of hours later. I sat in the window, watching the stars and listening to Diane snoring lightly from her feather cocoon. She always slept heavily after a drink. Most people do.

I pulled on my jacket, padded across to the front door and quietly snicked open the latch. I paused, just for a second, to listen to Diane's rasping breath. Then, my fingers drifting to the cool metal in my pocket, I slipped out.

"Wake up." I shook Diane's shoulder gently. She moaned, squinting at the brightness pouring through the window.

"Sleeping. G'way," she grunted, her stale breath catching me square in the face.

"Di. Wake up. It's Aldo. He's gone."

In an instant she was upright, red-rimmed eyes boring into mine. "He's what?"

"Bastard!"

Diane screamed out to sea as we stood on the promenade and watched the yacht grow smaller. "Prick! Bastard!" She jumped down onto the beach, seized a pebble and flung it as far as she could into the waves, so angry that the futility of it didn't even occur to her.

"How could he?" she asked me, tears running down her cheeks. "How could he just steal our supplies and dump us?"

"I don't know. Maybe he thought extra supplies were more valuable than extra hands."

She came to me, threw her arms around me. "We'll find a way," she said. "We'll get you help somehow. I won't let you—"

Suddenly she couldn't look at me. Disengaging from the hug she worked her hand into mine, lacing our fingers together. "I won't leave you like that," she promised, staring out to sea. "However long you've got, I won't ever leave you."

"I know," I said, squeezing her hand and watching the boat chug over the horizon in a dead straight line.

"I know."

BIOGRAPHY

PETE KEMPSHALL

Pete Kempshall lives in Perth, Western Australia, a city that often seems so far away from anywhere else he'd be surprised if a humanity-destroying disease could even find it. 'Rights of Passage' is his second story for Morrígan Books after 'Just Us' in the anthology *Voices*. He has also written a novella and several short stories for Big Finish's *Bernice Summerfield* and *Doctor Who* ranges.

Like most writers, he has a blog. Feel free to pop along and double the readership:

www.tyrannyoftheblankpage.blogspot.com.

AFTERWORD

I'm one of those people who can't just sit down and write. I need the security of having plotted each scene from beginning to end before I'll even type word one. It's like a map, and without one I'm not confident enough to start. But now and again, in spite of my carefully planned itinerary, I find a character seizes the wheel and veers off in new and darker directions. And of course, that's where the fun starts.

When I was plotting 'Rights of Passage', the central question was simple: would Will sacrifice the chance to cure his illness if finding that cure meant Diane would suffer? As I wrote the story, however, the focus began to shift. I always knew the decision Will would make. The question now became *why* was he making it?

In my mind, there's no doubt Diane loves Will. There's a spark there that says if Will were only up to the job, Diane would happily take things further. In Will's mind, however…well, given his past experiences with women, you can forgive him some insecurity. And as the story took shape, that insecurity suggested to me that his final decision might not be entirely altruistic.

Does Will kill Aldo to stop him raping Diane? Absolutely. Does he also kill Aldo to stop Diane getting to Grants Pass? That'd be telling…

One other quick note: as far Will's illness is concerned, I needed to find something that, without proper treatment, would slowly and inevitably kill him. It couldn't be something you could treat simply by popping pills because there'd be no shortage of empty pharmacies where he could find medicine. Nothing quite worked, until a couple of doctor friends suggested a blood disorder. It wasn't perfect, but it was close enough for me to be able to 'tweak' something to fit. Any factual errors, therefore, are for dramatic purposes. They're my own doing and are quite intentional.

A PERFECT NIGHT TO
WATCH DETROIT BURN

ED GREENWOOD

The sky was clear, only the gentlest of breezes blowing, and the night was warm enough to ward off the shivers.

It was a perfect night to watch Detroit burn.

Motor City had been on fire — the downtown, that is, all those newer towers that soared into the sky around the old Penobscot Building — for three days and nights, now. Ever since the lightning storm.

A good, solid pounding of a storm, cloudburst after roaring sheets of rain after bolt after bolt of lightning stabbing down blinding-bright, from sunset until darned near sunrise. A fist of a storm, the sort that came a dozen times a year or so. Loud and hard, but nothing apocalyptic.

With no firemen, though, and nothing much roaming the streets but hungry dogs, a few slinking coyotes, and a patient pack of wolves that had been howling up Grosse Pointe way for a week or so, it only took one bolt in the wrong spot to breach some rusty tanker in the dark and silent maze of downtown factories, to start flames whooshing into the sky, and — from weeds to timbers to blowing newspapers and all the usual trash — a fire was underway.

It would have been the sort of fire the talking heads on nightly television and the Net would have called "stubborn," if there'd been any news networks nattering about anything, anymore, and any sweating firemen left to stare into a camera and grimly tell the watching world what a "tough one" this fire was — but all the firemen, it seemed, were dead, and there wasn't much left hereabouts of a watching world, either.

There were just a few scattered and wary handfuls of men and women who had come down out of the great silent expanse of Ontario farms and along the St. Clair shore, seeking gasoline, tools and the canned food that they could scrounge out of the reeking, rat-scurrying labyrinths most supermarkets had become in Windsor. Which should hold tools and fuel in plenty. Even with most of the car plants shut down these last few decades, Windsor had boasted, if that was the word, an airport and rail tunnels and the bridge, too.

The bridge they had to block if they wanted to stop the raiding.

Stop the Americans pouring into Canada, most of them so loaded down with guns and grenades and night-goggles and rolls of barbed wire that they might as well have been army platoons in some bad Hollywood movie.

Clint Heston had wondered how bad it must be in the old U S of A for them all to come flooding up into the Great White North, a place most of them "knew" just as a land of snowy mountains, growling bears, Mounties, and scantily-clad babes in beer commercials.

Or *was* it all those beer commercials?

Were hundreds of good ol' boys — if there were still hundreds of good ol' boys, that is — sitting in the ruins of America thinking Canada was a charmed never-never land of laughing, beckoning women who'd escaped the plagues and kept the beer cold and kitchen ovens hot, where supermarkets were still full of food, football games and sex-mad hospital workers and forensic hero-cops were still on TV every night, deer wander obligingly up to every porch on sunny mornings to be shot dead for dinner, and life was all still good?

The guy they'd found dying in the cab of his rig on the bridge had thought so.

Gut-shot and covered with flies, staring out through the shattered windshield at the bloody aftermath of a gun battle that had raged and literally died out before any of the farmers had got there, he'd more or less gasped out all of those things, before struggling to ask them for a beer and if "It was still safe, this side." And then dying before hearing the scavenging farmers try to stumble through answering him.

But then, why be cruel enough to let him hear and understand the word "No" before he slid into everlasting darkness?

It was, after all, the truth.

No, it wasn't "safe" in Canada. It wasn't safe anywhere.

The plagues had rolled through the provinces just like the border States to the south of them, and the wild weather, too. Leaving almost everyone dead, dogs and coyotes and wolves fat and bold and roaming everywhere, and...and frontier days come again, for the fortunate — fortunate? — few who'd survived.

Were all Americans stupid enough to think wind and rain and swarming flies respected borders? With "the greatest country in the world" shining brightly on one side of a line drawn on a map and the endless gloom of God-forsaken terrorist tribesmen, or in a few places unspoiled wilderness, on the other?

McTavish had asked that, but the trucker had been too dead to answer — and Heston, who'd asked that question himself a time or two, had just shrugged back at Derek McTavish, still having no good answer to give.

Then they'd started up two or three of the bullet-riddled pickups and rigs that would still start, slammed them into each other, and let them all burn. The battle that the dead trucker had been caught in had managed one good thing: the bridge was blocked now, with great holes fire-melted in its pavement. Some of the burnt-out vehicles had sunk into those pits and glued themselves there. Nothing that would stop men with guns from clambering over them and crossing the bridge, but they'd have to walk. Only a tank could bull its way through the wreckage — and a tank, or anything comparably heavy, would fall through the bridge decking. In a dozen years, with no one repainting the steel or repairing welds and rivets, the whole thing would start to sag.

The tunnels had all flooded months ago, with no power to work the pumps and no one left to fix them. Gunfire from both sides of the Detroit River greeted any motorboat piloted by someone stupid enough to try a crossing in daylight, these days. Motors still purred by night, but they weren't exactly quiet, and though nights were now very dark times when the clouds and moon didn't oblige otherwise, there wasn't much noise aside from the peepers to hide motor sounds now; landings were often deadly.

There were still plenty of people alive enough to fire guns, of course.

The plagues hadn't been *that* good.

Everyone who was left probably wouldn't die of plague until some new sickness arose, and those same survivors were much too busy trying to find food and water and safe shelter by night — shelter they wouldn't freeze in, come winter, which was why so many Americans were seeking the endless trees they thought all Canada was thickly cloaked in, for firewood — to worry about plagues, or the fact that darned near every doctor seemed to have either died or become precious gods to, or captives of, bands of people who guarded them night and day.

Heston had shot down men who'd said they'd come across the river to find and seize doctors and nurses, and take them back.

It had been late last year when he'd admitted it to himself: the world was going wild again, with the humans who were left too few to stop it and too busy killing each other, in endless skirmishes between those who roamed taking things at gunpoint versus those who hid and cowered and crept around foraging, to care much.

Right now, all the flames across the river were giving Heston and McTavish and Breskbro — *their* treasure, a Cree woman who was a doctor and a better shot than either of them, with bow as well as gun, and whose dirty, sweaty curves were more beautiful than half a dozen pale, underfed cheating wives on television — light enough to see by, to loot one of the rare convenience stores on Riverside.

The flames lit up the always restless water amber bright, displaying the dark shapes of two small motorboats heading towards Canada, but the idiots in them were already shooting at each other, and slinking shadows that were either coyotes or wolves were gathering on the near bank to await the survivors' landfall. If there were any survivors.

That was another thing that had changed. It sure hadn't taken long for most wildlife to stop fearing humans.

"Shit," Mary Breskbro snapped, jolting Clint out of his remembrances. She crouched down and hurled a can loudly through the glass of one of the few windows that had been intact, making sure she got the attention of both her men. "*Trouble.*"

Clint stopped scooping cans into one of the hundreds of blue recycling boxes they'd found in garages all over Windsor, and snatched up his rifle. McTavish was already running along the next aisle in a crouch, like some movie Marine, the submachine gun he'd liberated from a dead American raider a week back up and ready.

There were people outside, people wearing hardhats with headlamps on them, headlamps that were dark. Small wonder, that, with no electricity for most of a year and precious few batteries lasting through the freezes and thaws of a winter. Three people, two of them waving — God damn! — *white flags*.

The third was trailing her flag — a shirt nailed to a rake, it looked to be — behind her, and wandering aimlessly about as if she was drunk, mumbling something soft, off-key, and endless, that might have been singing.

The other two — a man and a woman, the woman clutching a motorcycle helmet as if unsure whether to swing it as a weapon, or use it as a shield — had their arms raised in "stop!" gestures, and didn't look to have any guns. Just homemade white flags.

"Peace!" the man called through the broken front store window, sounding a little scared, a lot earnest, and American. Indiana, maybe southwestern Michigan.

"We don't have guns," the woman added quickly. "We don't want to be any trouble." By her voice, she was from the same place as the man standing beside her.

"You already are," Mary told them flatly, not a hint of friendliness in her voice. "Whatta you want, and who else is with you?"

"N-no one."

"No one else, creeping up on us while you talk?" McTavish snapped at them, waving his gun.

"No! There're just the three of us!" The man cleared his throat nervously. "I'm Jim — Jim Adams — and this is my wife, Ida."

McTavish asked a silent question by pointing his gun at the mumbling woman.

"Oh. That's Jess. She's...harmless."

"Uh-huh," McTavish told them, clear disbelief in his voice. "What's wrong with her?"

"She..." Jim Adams ran out of words and looked to his wife.

"She has Jesus where her brains ought to be," Ida said flatly. "Lost her family a few months back to someone — we don't know who — shooting from far off. She follows us everywhere, now. Nice enough. Good cook."

"I'm sure she can fry squirrel just fine," Mary told them in a voice like ice, "but I asked you what you wanted, and I haven't heard an answer."

She hefted a can back beside her ear, ready to throw, and added, "We don't plan to spend the night standing here talking, when we could've been back out of here by now and heading somewhere safer."

"Safer?" Ida Adams asked her, just a touch of a quaver in her voice. "In all this?"

"Up on a roof," McTavish told her, "of someplace that won't burn easily, with no buildings or trees near, when there's enough of us to stand watch through the night. Now *what do you want?*"

"Help," Jim Adams replied quickly.

"To do what?"

"Get..." Adams cleared his throat again, sounding almost ashamed. "To get to Grants Pass."

His words fell into a little silence.

After it started to get longer than "a little," he grounded his white flag — it trembled, all the way down, so his hands must be shaking a lot — and stammered, "Y'see, just before all the — everything went bad, Ida read this message from someone on the Internet, about meeting in—"

"We know." Mary's voice was still flat, but not quite as cold as before. "Grants Pass, Oregon. Someone named Kayley, wanting to meet her friend Monte there. A sort of peaceful-people rendezvous, if the end of the world happened. She was scared of tough guys with guns setting themselves up as warlords. We printed it out, back before the power went."

Clint knew that Mary's precious handful of printouts were far fewer than she wanted them to be. She'd made them in spare moments snatched at her job, back when computers worked and people everywhere were living lives so fast that they never had time to look up and think — so the plagues had hit them like a brick in the face, one two three, making most of them fall over dead without even having time to blink, or say more than, "Shit, now, what—?"

Not that Mary was going to tell these strangers any of that. She stood up. "But why're you *here*? Oregon's *that* way, a lo-o-ong way behind you, not this direction!"

Ida suddenly burst into tears. "You *know!*" she sobbed, "you know about it!"

"Uh," Jim said awkwardly, putting an arm around his wife, "ah, we...I once saw a stack of maps in your railroad station here. The map was big; covered all the northern US as well as Canada. I hoped I could find some of those maps. I thought we could follow the rail lines to Grants Pass; I don't know any other way to get there. Our library — we're from out past Lake Orion — didn't have a good atlas, it just used the Internet. I hoped..." His voice ran down again.

"Are you..." Ida Adams fought down tears enough to speak, her voice soaring in hope. "Are you going to go there, too?"

"Nope," McTavish and Mary both replied, more or less together.

Ida wilted, slumping back into her husband's arm. "But...but you printed it out, you said..."

"Lady," Clint almost growled, "Oregon means the Rocky *Mountains*. Getting *through* them, that is. And it's a *long* way, across land we don't know, most of it not the forests — the firewood — we *do* know. And this Kayley was just a kid, a teen; we don't even know if she made it there, or Monte or *anyone* did. You're chasing not much more than hope."

"Hope that might be nothing at all," McTavish told them sourly.

"And just what's wrong with that?" Jim Adams blazed up into sudden anger, waving his arms as if no one had guns and he wasn't silhouetted against a burning city, with boats of armed men getting nearer behind him. "Just what the Sam *fuck* is wrong with chasing hope?"

"Nothing," Clint replied. "But moving across this land, this continent, chasing it — hoping things'll be better somewhere else, instead of trying to make the best of it right where you are — that's the mistake we always make. The mistake we've gone on making for more than *three centuries*."

He started to pace along the aisle, long-broken glass crunching under his boots, as if he was back in some classroom teaching to bored teenagers. "The settlers came across the Atlantic, hoping for land and food enough for a better life, then moved west. Always seeking something better, somewhere else, until they ran out of land and found themselves staring at the Pacific. Later, with banks making millions, oilmen making more, and everyone being told a lot of crap about the American Dream, we hopped on planes or packed up and moved from state to state — or province to province, up here — chasing better jobs. Or any work at all. Always 'moving on' to somewhere better. Instead of making 'better' right here." He sighed. "That's always been our mistake, all of us."

"Not *all* of us," Mary said sharply. "We — we natives, we Indians — we lived 'here' first, until the rest of you came and walked all over us. Looking everywhere for riches, and taking everything, and messing up everything you couldn't take. Back then, we — *my* people — knew all about living our lives right here."

"All *right*," McTavish told her. "Not you Indians. Point granted. Now can we get back to grabbing cans and getting the *hell* out of here?"

As if his words had been a proverbial cue, a boat engine roared and then died out on the river, someone down by the bank cursed, there was a gunshot, more cursing, another shot, then a shriek of pain from what sounded like a wolf but might have been a man.

The crazy woman giggled suddenly, loud and high, and turned to wave her white flag at all the noise — or perhaps at burning Detroit.

Which promptly erupted in a ground-shaking explosion, as something went up over on Slug Island as the flames reached it.

Clint ignored all the tumult.

"We know all about hope," he told the Adamses. "That's why we printed out this Kayley person's post, and kept it. But we're staying here. Back where we can farm, I mean, not down here in what's left of Windsor, where it's men with guns roaming around day and night. We're not, repeat not, going off on any wild goose chase to Grants Pass."

"Y'see," McTavish told the Adamses, "for us, nothing much has changed, really."

Jim Adams gaped at him.

"Nothing much has *changed?*"

Adams was so incredulous he thrust his head forward through the big open space where the shop window had been, to try to get a better look at McTavish's face.

Then he glanced at giggling, mumbling Jess for a moment before looking back at McTavish, making his opinion of McTavish's sanity more than clear.

Surprisingly, McTavish chuckled. "Yeah, all right, everything's changed, but look at it this way: for me, life is still a lot the same. I need to be with people I can trust, and to get enough to eat. To do that, and get through the days, means the usual sweating, never-ending shitload of hard work. All that's changed is that there's no one left to come looking for taxes — and numbers on a bank's computer monitor mean nothing anymore. No bank, no monitor coming on, and no one left to look at it, either. Now *things* have value again, not...not dirty scraps of paper with dead presidents on them."

He ran out of words, and looked at Heston. "*You* tell them, Clint."

Who shrugged and said, "Oh, I think you put it pretty well. There're a whole lot less people around, but we meet nasty, desperate ones. And wild animals who'll kill you just as dead."

"We're *not* nasty," Ida Adams insisted, sobbing, "but we *are* desperate. We hoped you'd help us!"

"We will," Clint told them firmly. "Come back here tomorrow. Not early, but before sunset. We won't be here." He slammed his hand down on a freezer. "But I know where those maps that you're looking for are — and some better ones. I'll leave them in here."

"I—" Jim Adams seemed to be having trouble finding words again. It sounded like he was fighting to keep from crying. "I...thank you."

"You're welcome," Mary told him. "Now get the hell out of here before we *all* get killed!"

Not quite sobbing again, Ida stepped out of her husband's arms to tug at the mumbling woman's sleeve. Looking at no one, Jess turned and came with her, singing to herself of the love of Jesus for her and everyone.

"Thank you," Ida said into the darkened shop. "Thank you *so* much. I thought you wouldn't help us, after what you said, and — and—"

Jess stopped singing, turned her head to look Clint Heston right in the eye, and asked, as courteously and yet as sharply as if she'd been a Supreme Court judge, "Why are you helping us?"

Everyone was so startled that they stared at her in silence long enough for someone else to noisily and profanely shoot a wolf down on the riverbank.

Then Clint replied quietly, "Because you're right; we all need hope. And you can be ours. If you get to Grants Pass, by damn and all you still hold dear, you find a way to get word to us and tell us who's there and how you're getting on, you hear?"

Jess nodded approvingly — and started singing again, turning to look at the flames of Detroit.

"We'll do that," Jim Adams promised. "We *will* get to Grants Pass, and we'll find a way to let you know. Somehow."

"We'd better go," Ida said, towing Jess.

"Get away from the river," McTavish advised them. "Find a roof you can get to, not a high one if you don't have a rope. Stay quiet and don't make any light." He waved at the flames of Detroit. "And stay out of that firelight as much as you can; you can be seen a long way off. By people who'll shoot you just to cut down on the competition for stuff — or to take what you might be carrying."

"But we're not carrying anyth—"

"They don't know that," Mary told them flatly. "Good luck."

"You, too," Jim Adams replied, with a strange sort of dignity, and turned away from the window. Ida and Jess turned with him as smoothly as trained dancers or skaters — and they were gone.

McTavish crouched down again, and darted forward to where he could watch them go. "Cans, remember?" he reminded Clint and Mary, over his shoulder.

Mary let one crash noisily down into her blue box by way of reply.

A few busy, hard-breathing moments later, Clint came up to McTavish's elbow and said, "We're all done. Here's your box, full. They're gone, right? Not watching from somewhere, so they can follow us?"

"They're gone. Down past the casino parking lots; too far to see where we go, unless they've got nightscopes and still-working batteries for 'em."

"Let's go," Mary said softly. "There are *more* boats out now; see? I swear Detroit is still effing *full* of men with guns!"

They went, seeing no lurking Americans in hardhats or anyone else that moved, except something that was probably a raccoon, and something else, farther off, that might have been a coyote.

They made it to their chosen roof without incident and drew up the last bit of ladder, marooning themselves for the night where no one could get at them. The housing of a long-silent air conditioner sheltered them on three sides, leaving them only a view of Detroit's flames.

In silence they put down their boxes and got out the blankets they'd left there earlier, and in silence they lay down together — still fully clothed and booted, with Mary in the middle, as usual — and looked at the stars.

Clouds like dirty smoke were racing across the sky tonight, not letting them gaze at any stellar twinklings for long. Clouds that were an angry, flickering orange on their undersides, courtesy of Detroit.

"Grants Pass," Mary murmured, head pillowed on the extra blanket. "I wonder..."

McTavish groaned disgustedly. "Aww, for Chrissakes! They'll be dead, those three, before they even get out of Detroit."

"You shut up," Mary told him, cupping his crotch with firm fingers to back up her command. "I know you're right, but have the effing decency to let me go on pretending you're wrong. Hope, remember? That's what Kayley, whoever she is — and those Adams idiots, just now — gave us. Don't you pee on that, or it'll be no more bed-and-tickle for you, hey?"

"You play dirty," Derek McTavish told her, his voice sounding even more disgusted.

"Shut up and watch the city," Clint told him. "It's not like there's anything else on any of the other channels."

"*Haw* haw," came the reply, but it sounded amused.

"Besides," Mary added, from between them. "It's not raining for once, or hurling down lightning. Nice and clear. In fact, it's a perfect night to watch Detroit burn."

BIOGRAPHY

ED GREENWOOD

Ed Greenwood is an award-winning Canadian writer and game designer, best known for creating The Forgotten Realms® fantasy world (featured in board, role-playing, computer and card games, comic books, and a bestselling novel line). Once hailed as "the Canadian author of the great American novel" (bestselling fantasy author J. Robert King)) and "a true genius" (bestselling sf and fantasy author Elaine Cunningham), Ed has published over 170 books that have sold millions of copies worldwide in over a dozen languages. He has written three fantasy novels already this year, and by the time they are all published, this fall, he will have written at least the first drafts of three more.

Ed was inducted into The Academy of Adventure Gaming Arts & Design's Origins Awards Hall of Fame in 2003, has been a Guest of Honor at more than four dozen conventions worldwide, and has judged both the World Fantasy Awards and the Sunburst (Canada's sf awards).

In real life, Ed Greenwood is a large, bearded, well-padded man who is all too often mistaken for Santa Claus. He has worked in public libraries for over thirty years, and lives in an old farmhouse with more than 80,000 books. Ed has been an editor of DRAGON® Magazine and a columnist for more than a dozen periodicals.

AFTERWORD

Three things have always fascinated me about post-Big Doom stories set in North America. One of them is something I've had ever since I was a child: the imagined fun of foraging in deserted stores and homes and factories, being able to take and have, for free, just *anything* to carry off to have and use (the same fun I get when re-reading the chapters of *Robinson Crusoe* while the title character scavenges useful rope after useful board after vitally-important tool off the wrecked ship).

The second thing is the juxtaposition of gleaming modern society with enforced back-to-the-land self-reliance (or at least fumbling attempts at same) of survivors, clawing amid the wreckage and abandoned belongings and homes of vanished people.

The last and most important thing is hope. The hope that, whatever happens, we (the characters in the stories that a reader can identify with, no matter how different from us they may be) can survive and struggle on to some sort of success, even if it's just managing to stay alive amid the ruins. Hope is what drives us all on, and hope is what a *Grants Pass* story must be all about, in the end.

And I find I very much like creating hope.

FINAL EDITION

JEFF PARISH

Dusk settled on Paris, Texas. The sun, hidden all day behind dark clouds, took advantage of its last few moments to create a nearly perfect sunset, painting the cloudbank in glowing blues, reds, oranges and yellows.

It was, as Matt Godwin's father liked to say, enough to knock your eyeballs out. It was also a wasted effort, as Matt's own eyeballs remained firmly fixed on the ground spinning slowly beneath him. The sun slipped below the horizon, stealing its momentary beauty along the way. Sullen, leaden clouds hastened night's approach.

Matt stopped turning the merry-go-round. He lay there for a moment. His chin hung over the edge, his hand tracing random glyphs in the pine bark mulch some city official or other thought would make the playground safer for children. Scooting back, he rolled over and rested his head on the metal surface. His five-foot-six frame barely dangled off the other end. His girth just fit between hoops meant to hold children despite his weight loss in the last few months.

He lifted his left hand and turned his wrist this way and that in an effort to determine the time. The hour and minute hands showed 4:27, and the minute hand hung motionless. Matt cursed the watch for a few moments, but stopped with a wry chuckle. What was the point? Time meant little anymore. It was morning, noon, dusk or night; what else did you need to know these days? He unfastened the band and slipped the watch off his wrist. He hefted it for a moment, and then tossed the offending timepiece into the night.

"Hey, squirrels! Do you know what time it is?" he called, laughing once more.

As usual, no one answered except a passing breeze laden with the scent of more rain. The wind ruffled his close-cropped black hair as it played across seesaws stuck somewhere between teeter and totter and pushed swings that might never again hear kids demanding to go higher, Daddy, higher.

A soft crunching noise cut his laughter short. He raised his head, casting about for the source. Surely Bill wouldn't have followed him here...

The noise came again. Head swiveling like a radar array, Matt's attention centered on a corner of the fence surrounding the playground. He sighed with relief, and his entire body sagged with departing tension as a bois d'arc dropped a third green, wrinkly apple on the ground.

Thunder boomed across the yard, warning anyone outside to get indoors.

Matt stood, wincing as tight muscles protested a new position. Had he been on that merry-go-round all day? His stomach rumbled, a small echo of the thunder overhead. He supposed he had been. Matt stumbled around the carousel, disoriented after hours of slow turning.

"Where did I leave my backpack?" he muttered.

His feet found it first, stumbling over the black fabric. Hoisting the bag onto one shoulder, Matt headed out the gate. He needed to catch a City Council meeting.

Mayor Gary Hamilton pounded his gavel on the table.

"That is enough out of you, councilman! I will not tolerate such rudeness at my meetings! Do you understand me?" He glared at an alderman, who sat stiffly in his seat, hands poised a few inches off the tabletop.

The mayor swept his glower around the horseshoe, pointing at each seated figure with the gavel. Flickering light from several oil lamps gave him the look of a stern medieval judge. Satisfied an outburst was not forthcoming, he turned to the audience.

"I'm sorry you had to witness that, ladies and gentlemen. Sometimes the democratic process gets a little heated." Gary ventured a small laugh. "I hope this won't make top of the fold in tomorrow's edition, Mr. Godwin."

Matt smiled, shook his head and kept writing in his reporter's notebook. The last edition of *The Paris News* lay weeks in the past. But so long as anything happened here, it was his duty to record it. He was the city reporter, after all. Of all the changes seen here since the Crash — as people around here called it — three months ago, Gary offered one of the strangest.

Voters elected this slender, balding black man to represent one of the city's two minority districts last May. Timid and soft-spoken, he always made Matt think of a mouse. That changed once the councilman realized he was the only surviving member of Paris city government. As Gary saw it, that made him mayor — and that put him in charge. Power transformed this small, mousy man into a thunderous orator who held the reins of power tight. That the reins controlled nothing meant little to Gary. He just forged ahead, calling nightly City Council sessions to deal with what he saw as pressing problems.

"Now on to our last order of business," he said, reading from an agenda he painstakingly copied by hand each morning for the council and the dozens who attended the sessions. "Ducks in Lake Crook were staring at me again yesterday. This sort of impertinence simply cannot be allowed. I propose we form a subcommittee to enter into discussions with them. Perhaps we can find a mutually agreeable solution. If not, I'm afraid the police will simply have to arrest all of them."

The mayor adjourned the meeting with a quick rap of his gavel. He stood and walked over to the council member who had so recently been the target of his wrath.

"No hard feelings, I hope, Frank. You raise some good points; I just wish you would learn to curb your enthusiasm a little. It's unbecoming in a man of your position." He leaned over to shake Frank's hand, which came off in his grip.

"Well now, that's embarrassing," Gary said with a chuckle as he pushed the mannequin's hand back into place.

Matt stood and walked out of the council chambers, leaving the only empty seat in the house. He still couldn't believe Gary found enough mannequins in Paris to fill six City Council seats and dozens of chairs in the audience. He must have raided every department store in the city. It would explain why they all wore different clothes every time he came here.

He turned back for a moment. Gary wandered among the rows of chairs, grinning and patting shoulders as he schmoozed with his 'constituents'. Matt shuddered and walked down the stairs and out into the night, eager to be gone despite the rain. The sight of all those dummies no longer disturbed him as much as it once had, but it still creeped him out. And he could only take so much of the unhinged, small-town politician. At least Gary's obsession gave him the illusion of productivity, even if it did centre on ducks and dress-store dummies.

Bill was a different matter altogether.

Matt supposed he should have seen it coming. "Big Bill" Vance of Clarksville was the most persistent letter writer *The Paris News* had seen in years. Even with the newspaper's policy that nobody had a letter printed more than once a month, Bill's name showed up more than any other on the opinion page. The policy didn't stop him from sending his missives every week, either. The subject changed from rant to rant, but each contained the same two themes: The government did it, and the media couldn't be trusted. Had the various local, state and federal agencies paid Matt all the money Bill claimed, he could have retired two years ago, before he even reached thirty.

It probably shouldn't have come as any surprise that Bill would focus all that mistrust on Matt. After all, he was likely the last member of the media left in Northeast Texas. But who would have thought he would turn violent?

Looking back now, Matt could see the first warning signs. He could even pinpoint the time — 5:30 p.m. on June 24 — since he set the meeting. That was the benefit of hindsight. At the time, everyone worried too much about survival to think of anything else. Sure Big Bill had been edgy, but so was everyone gathered there. And why wouldn't they be?

Even now, three months later, Matt saw the small crowd with crystal clarity. It was a pitiful group of shell-shocked survivors from three counties. These three dozen or so men, women and children were all who responded to Matt's message in the last edition of the paper. It was a single sheet, front and back, detailing what he knew about the happenings of the last few weeks. He closed with a request: Everyone still up and about should meet at newspaper office on Loop 286 to discuss what they should do.

The meeting started with a rehash of what people knew, which wasn't much.

America was more or less gone, both in government and people. The dreaded Big One had finally hit California, followed by smaller ones that shook the entire West Coast. Hundreds of millions were dead or dying of some particularly nasty germs.

Elsewhere, the world fared much the same. No matter where you looked, everything trembled on the point of unraveling. The same diseases had run rampant in every nation, decimating populations before medics had time to blink.

That led to personal stories. Everyone knew several people — mostly loved ones — who were dead. Matt listened with as much patience as he could muster, but it was hard. They weren't here to tell war stories. But he knew if he interrupted too soon, they would turn on him. As if he hadn't suffered! A souped-up version of the Black Death that appeared to have originated in Austin took his fiancée. Matt had held her hand as she wheezed and rattled her last few breaths. His sister had died of the Super Flu, for crying out loud! A cousin succumbed to some bizarre strain of Ebola or something like it. And what about his parents? Dead in one of a pair of twisters that hit Paris in the last month — the first the town had seen in two decades. Did Matt whine about it? Of course not; he went to work so this bunch of babies would know what was going on.

Eventually, his patience came to an end.

"All right, people. That's enough," Matt said, standing on a desk. His voice rose over the inevitable protest. "Enough! We can talk about this later, but right now, we've got more important stuff to think about, like what do we do now? Where do we go?"

The small crowd erupted. Where could they go? Why would they go anywhere? The cities were desolate wastelands, home to only the rotting dead. At least they knew the land here. So what if a couple of tornadoes had taken out a few buildings? Most of them still stood; even if the Love Civic Centre and Paris' landmark Eiffel Tower had been obliterated, at least its giant red cowboy hat had survived to adorn a Cadillac in the parking lot. Others pointed out that this town was just as empty as any of the bigger metro areas. Were forty people going to keep a town alive that once had about twenty-six thousand? Besides, most of those here lived outside Paris. Did they plan to leave their homes and move here?

Where — that was the question everyone shouted eventually. Matt wanted that question; he needed it to make this meeting work. He had an answer. He raised his hands and yelled, "Hey!" until the clamor quieted.

"Actually, I have a suggestion," he said. "I agree we can't stay here. There just aren't enough of us. I also understand your reluctance to leave this area. I share it. This has been my family's home for generations. But if we are to survive, we're going to have to find other people. I think I know where some are headed."

"And how would you know that?" Heads turned to identify the speaker. Matt could have told them who it was. He heard that voice at least once a week over the phone. Bill stood near the back, leaning against a door with arms folded across his barrel chest. He was an imposing figure, a foot taller than Matt and big enough to fill the doorway. Gray hair and beard did nothing to soften his look. "Big Bill" was tough, and he knew it.

"It's my job to know," Matt shot back. He instantly regretted the quip. This had to be handled delicately, but the man grated on him. He forced himself to soften his tone. "Look, I shouldn't have said it like that, but you know it's true. I was researching an article about how people felt about the end of the world — it seemed to be coming up on us real quick — after I saw a preacher on TV talking about a blog post from a girl named Kayley. He spent a lot of time talking about it; it even made some of the national news casts."

"What'd they say?" a woman asked from the back.

Matt paused. He hadn't counted on questions. He was surprised they didn't know already, even if most of them had been too wrapped up in their own affairs to pay much attention to the world outside Lamar County. He figured they'd have heard the televangelist, at any rate. But if they didn't know, he wasn't about to tell them that he'd seen the preacher holding up a crumpled sheet of paper and quivering with such righteous indignation that even his immaculately styled grey hair trembled in rage while he denounced those "attempting to flee God's righteous judgment". *What was that passage he quoted? "Then they will say to the mountains, 'Cover us!' and to the hills, 'Fall on us!'"* Matt had laughed and started searching immediately for the posting. He printed out his own copy to reference, which proved fortuitous. Traffic to the blog grew so heavy in the following days he'd found it nearly impossible to access it.

His mind racing, Matt shook his head. "That's not important right now. What is important is that she was planning for this. She knew the importance of gathering people together in one place. She wanted them to join her so that maybe something could survive."

Not that he planned to tell them what the preacher had thought of her plans.

"You knew this and didn't tell anyone? Why didn't you put it in that rag of yours instead of calling us all here?" Bill demanded. "I knew we couldn't trust you reporters. You're in cahoots with those government people, the ones who started these super germs in the first place. I bet you're still hiding stuff from us!"

Matt indeed hid more information than he offered. The region's Congressman had confessed a great deal over the phone shortly before his death. Terrorists had finally mounted a major offensive, but not with airplanes or nuclear bombs, as everyone had feared. They'd managed to get their hands on some of those "super germs" from the well-guarded stores of several world powers. The old politician had been delirious with fever, but Matt thought he had told the truth. His raving quietened toward the end of the interview, winding down until he gasped, "You're not recording this, are you?" Then he had hung up. Matt had been trying to confirm some of the details for a major story when everything fell apart. Not that he planned to tell these yokels that. It'd only play into Bill's hands at this point. And he certainly wouldn't tell them Kayley said her online note was as much a mental exercise as a practical solution.

Instead, he said: "I didn't put it in the *News* because people don't need to go off willy nilly. We need to band together. Do you want old Mr. Ferguson there trying to make the trip by himself? Or what about Sally here, with her three kids? People out there are scared, and fear turns men into animals. I've seen it time and time again."

"Well, you just got an answer for everything don't you? So where is this magical place?"

"You're not going to like this part," Matt warned. "It's a town called Grants Pass in Oregon." The protest rose once more, louder than before. Leave Paris to become a Yankee? It took several minutes to die down enough for him to continue. "Look, people. I told you that you wouldn't like it. But just hear me out. It's a nice place, and not all that different from Paris."

He told them what little he found out before the Web imploded. Grants Pass nestled in the mountains of southern Oregon about an hour north of the California border at the intersection of I-5 and U.S. Highway 199. The town sat on the Rogue River; Paris lay between the Sulphur and Red rivers. They both had about the same population. He told them about the giant redwoods and the so-called House of Mystery at The Oregon Vortex, where people supposedly changed height.

"No one said we had to stay there. It might not be more than a staging area. But we can't stay here, and we can't roam aimlessly around the United States just hoping to come across some other people," Matt said.

"We need a target, and this is as good as any. Better, really. Before it went down, people were searching the Internet for anything they could find about the end of the world or the apocalypse. This page was near the top of every search.

"*'When the end of the world comes, meet me in Grants Pass, Oregon,'* Kayley wrote. If this isn't the end of the world, what is?"

Bill walked out first, glaring murder at Matt as he shoved his way past the reporter. Seven or eight more looked at each other, shrugged and filed out at erratic intervals. The rest exchanged glances, but remained and planned. They would leave in a month.

Matt laughed. *A month!* Another month proved pestilence still walked the land. By the end of July, he was sure everyone else was dead until he wandered downtown and saw flickering lamplight — electricity had died weeks before — in a second-floor window of City Hall and witnessed his first meeting of the new City Council.

A week after that, he wished everyone else had died after Bill tried to blow his head off with a shotgun. Matt lost count of the number of close calls in the last two months as Bill tried to shoot him and run him over. The last incident, about two weeks ago, was certainly more memorable. Bill decided to take a more biblical approach and stone him to death. Fortunately, few rocks hit their target. Even in this new world where Matt could say with some confidence he was the best journalist alive, no one would pick Bill to pitch for the Texas Rangers. Since then, Matt hadn't seen hide nor hair of his would-be assassin. He hoped Bill had given up and gone back to Clarksville for good. If not, maybe he should head to Oregon by himself.

The rain slackened as Matt walked up the street to the newspaper offices, before dying altogether as he turned the key in its lock. The long walk from City Hall to the paper gave him much needed exercise, plus the building offered plenty of room and hiding places should Bill ever try to force his way in. More importantly, the lights still worked.

It had taken him several days to find the generator. He knew the paper had one to keep computers running in case of an outage, but he never thought to ask where. Once located, a length of hose, gas can and a wagon pilfered from the local Wal-Mart let him keep the generator running with fuel siphoned from cars in town. Matt figured there was probably a way to get it out of the ground storage tanks at nearby gas stations, but he could not puzzle out how.

The generator couldn't power the building's air conditioning system but proved sufficient to run a few lights and his Macintosh.

Exhaustion threatened to pull him under, but Matt had a job to do. He needed to get the day's story filed before he went to sleep. He did not want to get stuck in a backlog where he had to spend all day writing just to catch up.

An hour and a half later by the clock on the wall, Matt saved his story with the hundred or so others he had accumulated in the last three months. He turned out the light and made his way to a pallet on the floor of the editor's office. Sleep claimed its due, pulling him under almost before his head hit the pillow. The night passed peacefully.

The morning brought a gun to his face.

Matt blinked once and scrambled back, hitting his head on the editor's desk. The shotgun barrel followed, tracking every movement of his head in perfect synchronization.

"Time to wake up, news boy," Bill said.

Matt looked about wildly. The side doors locked automatically and he chained the double doors in front every morning.

"How?" he said.

"You shouldn't put chains on the outside if you really want to keep somebody out," Bill said with a chuckle. "A hacksaw doesn't make much noise, you know."

He straddled Matt and dropped the shotgun slightly as he leaned over. "This is all your fault. If it weren't for you and the government, my Betty would still be alive. Our kids would still be alive. Do you have any idea what it's like to bury your wife and children in the back yard, news boy?"

Matt didn't bother trying to answer. His foot shot upward, straight into Bill's crotch.

Big Bill fell hard with a strangled croak. The shotgun clattered to the floor as he clutched himself. Matt scrambled to his feet, grabbed the gun and smashed the butt into Bill's head, who fell limp as a boned fish.

Matt dashed out the front door. One foot kicked the cut chain and sent it slithering into the grass. The city's new fire truck sat in the parking lot, a red behemoth blocking his path. Matt barely paused as he skidded into a turn and ran around. The shotgun fell from hands and clattered to the ground. He let it go, not daring to stop or even slow to retrieve it. Panic held him in its grip and refused to let go. He barreled down Lamar Avenue and headed west.

His flight carried him nearly to downtown before his body decided to call a halt. Matt sank to his hands and knees, gulping air in great gasps. His heart galloped in his chest, and black spots danced in and out of his vision. Matt thought he might either have a heart attack or vomit. After a few moments, he decided on the latter. He remained staring at the remains of last night's dinner until loud growls and wild howls reached his ears.

Turning, Matt saw the fire truck racing up the street, careening off parked cars and utility poles. Its engine growled in protest at the pace Bill forced it to while its sirens howled with murderous intent. Too bad he didn't have a camera; this would make a spectacular photograph.

"What is your deal, dude?" Matt yelled.

He climbed to his feet and started an unsteady trot west. Maybe he could lose Bill among the buildings that remained downtown — if he could reach downtown. He crossed the road and dashed through yards and onto a side street. Lamar Avenue was a major thoroughfare, but many of the residential lanes were much smaller. Given Bill's difficulty just keeping the fire truck on the road, these smaller streets with cars lining the curbs might well prove impassable.

Following a path of turns, dead ends and backtracks, Matt soon lost sight of his pursuer. Bill never fell out of earshot, however. The engine and sirens rose and fell. Metal screeched in protest a few blocks over, followed shortly by a loud boom as he ran into something he could not simply push out of the way. Once or twice, Matt even caught a whiff of the fire truck's diesel engine.

His shambling flight eventually brought him to First Street. Turning north, he started toward City Hall, taking advantage of buildings, piles of rubble, trees and any other hiding place he could find. He stopped in a doorway across the street. The storms had carved erratic paths through downtown, flattening some buildings while leaving structures like Culbertson Fountain on the Plaza and the Peristyle in Bywaters Park intact. City Hall stood alone, exposed.

Matt paused, uncertain, until Bill made his mind up for him.

The fire truck raced past in a red blur. Matt jumped, and ran from his hiding place. Tires screeched behind him as he wrenched open a door and ran up the stairs.

Matt crouched, half-crawling his way to a corner office. Reaching the window, he pulled himself up to peer over the ledge. He saw no sign of Bill or his fire truck, but he could hear the siren warbling somewhere behind City Hall.

The noise grew louder. Matt stood and leaned out the window, straining for some sight of his attacker. The fire truck barreled through an intersection and leapt up the square, smashing into the marble fountain. Matt stared for several minutes at the mangled rescue vehicle. Surely no one could have survived the impact.

The driver's door opened, indicating Bill indeed lived, if not in perfect health. He limped across the street with blood streaming down his face. He paused at the corner, looking around. Matt pulled back. The motion caught Bill's attention. He grinned and pointed up at the reporter before resuming his limping march. The swish of the front doors announced his entrance into City Hall.

Matt's head swung side to side. What was he going to do? He could hear Bill's stuttering gait coming up the stairs. He took off his shoes and ran silently across the hall into the City Council chambers.

As expected, he found the council in session. Apparently not everyone agreed with the mayor's approach to the duck problem. Matt ran to the horseshoe-shaped bench and crouched behind it. Gary squawked in surprise.

"Mr. Godwin, what do you think you are doing? You know better than to just barge in here!" Matt tried to shush the mayor, to no effect. "Get out of there! If you don't get up right now, I'll..."

Bill kicked open the doors. "You in here, news boy?" he shouted. "I hear clucking, so this must be where all the chickens are!"

Gary stood as he turned from Matt to the new intruder. His eyes bulged and a vein started throbbing in his forehead at sight of the shotgun cradled in Bill's arm.

"Firearms are *not* allowed in here! Signs are clearly posted at the entrance!"

"Shut up," Bill replied.

He swung the shotgun around and pulled the trigger. A mannequin's head disintegrated. The second blast caught Gary in the gut, knocking him back against the wall and out of sight.

Matt took advantage of the commotion to scramble from behind the table and rush along a wall toward the door. The shotgun roared to life and punched a hole through a dummy's chest. The next shot blew the arm off another, which caught between Matt's legs. As he struggled for balance, Bill caught up and swung the shotgun in a wide arc. The impact buckled Matt's knee and dropped him to the floor. He managed to push himself onto his elbows before Bill planted a boot on his groin. The big man slowly rocked forward, grinding all his weight down on the ball of his foot. Pain exploded through his abdomen.

When Matt could focus on anything again, he found himself staring down the barrel of a gun for the second time that day. Bill's finger tightened on the trigger. Damp warmth spread across Matt's jeans.

Click!

"Aww, crap!" Bill yelled. "You reporters are just like cockroaches, aren't you? You just won't die!" He grinned savagely. "Well, my mamma always said the best way to kill a roach is to crush it."

Bill turned the shotgun in his hands and held it like a club over his head.

"It's all your fault," he growled.

Matt closed his eyes.

"OUT OF ORDER!"

The voice sounded familiar, but surely Bill's massive chest never issued such a high-pitched sound. Matt's eyes popped open.

The mayor stood behind Bill, one arm clutched around his stomach. The other rose over his head, gavel clutched in his fist. The hammer fell with a muffled crack. Bill's eyes rolled back in his head and he fell to one side, knocking over several chairs. Gary went down with him, still swinging. He kept hammering, grunting with every wet *smack*, until the head snapped off the gavel. Gary pitched forward over Bill's motionless body. He lay there, breathing shallowly.

"Firearms not allowed," he muttered. "Killed Frank...ruined my gavel...not on the agenda..." He trailed off into incoherence.

Matt sat still, staring at the pair until the mayor stopped breathing. As the sunlight started to wane, he finally grabbed a chair and pulled himself upright, standing still for several moments before limping out.

A double murder at City Hall, and he witnessed the whole thing! This was going to make a great story. He just needed to get one of the paper's digital cameras and come back. Maybe if he shut off everything else, the generator could power the press. He'd get another if necessary. Matt paused. Newspaper policy forbade photos of dead bodies on the front page. He turned back, surveyed the scene once more and nodded to himself. Screw the policy.

"I'm editor now," he said, rubbing his hands together. He planned to make the final edition of *The Paris News* the best this town had ever seen!

After that, who knew? Maybe Grants Pass needed an editor.

BIOGRAPHY

JEFF PARISH

Jeff Parish, author of 'Final Edition', is a 30-something native Texan. He and his wife, Melinda, have a girl and two boys. He has been writing since middle school, where he concentrated mostly on (bad) fantasy tales and (even worse) poetry. His writing skills developed over time, much to his delight and the relief of everyone he forced to read his work, and he gravitated to prose over poetry. He even decided to make a living as a writer, starting work at a small newspaper in Greenville, Texas, nearly a decade ago.

Since then, he's worked at several papers of varying sizes, including the *Dallas Morning News, Galveston County Daily News* and, yes, three years at *The Paris News*. His last newspaper job was as managing editor of two weeklies in Rockwall County. His newspaper career was suffocated in its sleep in February 2006 after he realized journalism might be a noble profession, but slowly starving his family to death was not.

He is now an English teacher at a high school in Paris. He's had stories appear in *Andromeda Spaceways Inflight Magazine, Bits of the Dead, Triangulation: End of Time, Courting Morpheus, Abominations, Flashing Swords, Speculative Realm* and *The Edge of Propinquity*, among others.

AFTERWORD

Write what you know — that's what they tell writers. When I found the guidelines for *Grants Pass*, my mind immediately turned to Paris, Texas. It's easy to focus on the big cities in a post-apocalyptic setting, and it's quite dramatic with all kinds of opportunities for a good story. But I wanted to explore a smaller town.

Small-town folks are among the best on earth, but they're also a bit rabid about local politics and local happenings. You can't dig them out of the town with a backhoe. Shock tends to push people to the extremes of their natural inclinations, right to the edge of madness or even beyond. I thought about some of the people I'd worked with in my career — the obsessive journalist, the local politician, the guy whose family has lived in the same house for generations — and 'Final Edition' was born.

THE DISCOMFORT OF WORDS

CAROLE JOHNSTONE

Another storm was brewing.

Louise sat upon a stool close to the vast picture window that looked down into New Town, watching the clouds chase the fleeing sun over the thin strip of blue that was the Atlantic; watching their obtrusive return cast the resort into grey twilight shadow, whipping up sand devils and bending low the spines of palm trees.

There were no signs of life. This should have been the beginning of the *Fiesta de Carmen*. The promenades and cobbled streets should have been swollen to capacity and filled with lambent light and dance and song. The bars and restaurants of the *Avenida de las Playas* should have spilled their illumination onto road and pavement; their neon welcomes stretching from new town to old in wavering lines of pink and green and gold. Fishing boats strung with fairy lights, their bows painted gold and silver, should have shone in stark relief against the darkening ocean as they called for good summer catches.

Instead there was nothing.

She considered that such dearth of life might have lost some of its capacity to shock, to frighten. But she could remember those who had crept into new nights of drum fires, barricades and shouted noise – rendering it only more insidious. And the encroaching dark more absolute.

In the beginning, she had locked herself away in her own little two-bed villa on the *Calle Lapa*, doing her best to ignore the sirens and the wailing screams. But she had been too close to the main resort. And when everything started to get worse – a *lot* worse – that cool whisper at her back had started up again; the same intangible fear that had found her leaving London for her holiday home on the island months earlier than usual. *Run away.*

But her options had dwindled somewhat. Lanzarote was an island less than 900 kilometers in area. Much of the north was lost to old volcano fields and a barren lunar landscape too inhospitable to afford safe refuge, and the capital to the east had been on fire too many weeks.

A stagnant air — now bereft of the north-east trade winds that had cooled the equatorial heat from the south — had hung great clouds of smoke and debris over Arrecife and the island's only airport, choking any lingering idea of escape. In the end, she had been forced to take to the hills high above *Puerto Del Carmen.*

Louise turned away from the dark beyond the picture window. The heat was an oppressive cerement that made her feel claustrophobic, clinging to her back and chest, and chasing away her fear. She no longer opened the windows at night. The arid island had previously suffered only mosquitoes and the occasional cockroach. Now insects, often the size of her fist, invaded the resort every sundown — even this high in the hills — battering their grotesque bodies and thrumming wings against the opaque walls of her lit prison.

That was all she now allowed herself. Light in the dark.

Her new sanctuary was far more luxurious a villa than her own had been: an abandoned *mansión* complete with generator, wrought-iron gates and a walled enclosure. All she needed to do was sit this out — whatever *this* was — and when it was safe again, she could go back down and find help.

There was still plenty of food in the freezer, but this comforted as much as the false solace that there would *ever* again be help to be found. The generator was still working, humming away in the sloped subterranean garage under her feet, but even with the air-conditioning turned off, there was no denying that it was fast running out of juice.

And there was an even more immediate concern. There was less than half a water bottle left. Despite always adhering to such prohibition before, she was more than prepared to drink water from the taps, but what was still in the cisterns likely wouldn't last very long. There were no rivers on Lanzarote, no natural supply of water anywhere on this *Land of a Thousand Volcanoes*. Severe drought had been the norm even before the world had fallen apart.

But she would not go down. Not while her courage still failed her. Not while fires still raged; while madmen doubtless still prowled the streets with knives and clubs — and grins so terrorized that they were beyond reason *or* fear; while barricades distorted the familiar, creating a patchwork of hasty and oft-disputed territory that stretched as far west as the harbor and as far east as the still-burning capital. Nor while bloated bodies stacked up alongside the promenades and restaurant bars like rank, slack-mouthed sentinels.

Louise returned to the window and sipped her tepid water, and tried not to think. She eyed the blank television with something between resentment and longing. It hadn't worked for weeks. The last storm had torn down the roof aerial, although the screen had been showing only static by then. The phones had gone out long before that. In a way she had been glad. The Internet had been screaming and unrestrained, and yet she had come back to it again and again, picking over its dire portents and accounts of mayhem and disease like a scab.

She reached into her shorts pocket and felt the reassuring square of paper there. *Kayley.* A sudden spike of lightning danced across the sky, exposing the desolate landscape in horrible silver relief. She swallowed a scream, bringing out the folded paper and pressing it hard against her mouth.

The following thunder was too loud, too close. It trembled the tiles under her feet and put out the lights. She sank onto the couch with a sob, feeling around the coffee table with desperate fingers. The dark was a monster — a plague all of its own — and one that threatened her more than any other had done before it.

In the days before all stations had been lost to the same static as the TV, the radio had shrieked *muerte* and *peste* and then *Apocalipsis*. On the last day, a frightened Spanish voice had muttered over and over the numbers already dead: a *mortanada* so huge it was hardly comprehensible. The only one that she now remembered was two million. That had been Madrid.

Finally she found the lighter, sparking it close — but not too close — to the now opened sheet of paper. She had found it tacked to the bedroom wall of whoever had fled the villa: a teenager's bedroom papered over by white-toothed boys with floppy hair and tattoos. The journal entry had evidently been printed off an Internet site. Of the many posts (there had been dozens more tacked behind it), Louise had only noticed this one, had only read it, because its third sentence had been highlighted in an untidy neon slash.

When the end of the world comes, meet me in Grants Pass, Oregon.

It mattered little that the post was more than two years old; nor either that it was likely only adolescent fantasy. Pretense. Kayley's voice (and Louise had instantly imagined her a fresh-faced all-American cheerleader) was childish — even mawkish, while managing to still sound blasé. An exercise born out of boredom, perhaps even a school project. Most probably little else.

But still. There was the neon slash. And even if *that* meant nothing either, Kayley spoke to Louise when no-one else had done for weeks. Even from another time and another world; across reaches of terror and despair — and ever stoic denial — Kayley had whispered in Louise's ear. Had whispered kindness, possibility. Hope.

Now, in the dark and the storm that bellowed but taunted with no rain, and the monstrous insects that yet banged against the windows in angry, mindless thumps, Louise read Kayley's message again. She knew it almost by heart anyway, but to see it, to touch it — to breathe it — was the greater comfort. Before the Internet had hung up for good, she had Googled Grants Pass. Just to look.

As far as the Pacific Northwest was from those Spanish islands less than 150 miles off the coast of Africa, Louise had still been able to seek solace in Grants Pass' parks and green spaces, its evergreens and pines, its summer night concerts and Boatnik Parade, its historic downtown lined with animal statues and Christmas murals, its antique shops, carnivals and firework displays. It reminded her of lazy Saturday afternoon films on Channel 5. It comforted where nothing else could.

Louise carefully folded up the paper and let go of the lighter's lever. Her thumb grazed its hot spark wheel. She curled up on the couch, the heat an oppressive blanket above her; the storm moving off towards the mountainous north in dry and angry flashes.

Tomorrow. She would go back down to the resort tomorrow, and no longer dwell upon the reasons why she shouldn't. As she drifted towards sleep, she thought only of green and trees and rivers and cool. And Kayley. Blond-haired, freckle-faced Kayley. Who waited for her there.

The next day it was hotter still. Grabbing hold of brittle flora, clambering past clusters of date palms, dragon trees and cacti, the sun beat down upon her through an ugly haze of sand and hot breath. It took even longer to get down from the hills than it had done to climb them — which was disheartening enough before she reached what was left of *Puerto Del Carmen*.

As she stepped out of the barren wilderness of the north and onto the incongruent paving stones of *Calle Lapa*, she longed for the return of boisterous noise: the chinking of glasses, the fractious screams of too-hot children, the better humored squeals of women — a job-lot of paperbacks, cocktails and psychedelic knock-off kaftans — thrown into kidney-shaped pools courtesy of boyfriends and husbands who were drunk by lunchtime, and who bellowed at each other from tiny balconies less than twenty feet apart.

Instead there was only silence. Horrible, empty, windless silence. And a smell so dreadful that not even the briny taste of the Atlantic could disguise it.

The white-walled apartments on the other side of the street were still deserted. She remembered finding her first dead body there in the days before she had fled. In the days before she had believed in the plague or in the end of the world, or in the terrible things that people could do in the face of either. It had been lying on a sun-lounger. A grey-skinned figure painted patchy red by the sun.

She had approached that body despite the whispered *Run away* at her back. She had approached it despite the incredible stench that came from it; despite knowing what she would likely find. Her fear had been a dazed anger that clutched hard at her chest. But still she had looked.

He had already begun to rot. Whether that was down to the heat or his terrible affliction hardly mattered. Huge dark lumps inside his armpits had splayed out his arms; more of the same protruded from the leg holes of his bloodied trunks. His face was the bloated dark purple of thunderclouds. Black viscous fluid had pooled and congealed beneath his eyes, while his mouth — a bloody and crusty mess — let escape a grey and flaccid tongue, leaving space for whistling breath.

It had taken that for her to believe. Not the sirens, the screams, the pall of smoke over the capital. Not *Breaking News!* alerts and grainy satellite pictures, or an endless dial tone whenever she tried the British Consulate or the *Cabildo Insular*. Her denial had demanded better proof than any of that — and a rotting, still-alive body had been it.

The day after that *she* had gotten sick. She had locked her doors and stayed in bed along with everyone else. When she had ventured out again: a gnawing hunger sending her back down towards the *supermercado*, she had not even glanced once towards the neighboring apartments or their pool.

Now heading again for that same *supermercado*, she looked only straight ahead, a memory of that bewildered anger tormenting her again. She ignored it. As she walked down the street towards the beach and promenade, her legs jarring against the unfamiliar paving stones, a sudden sound came to her. In the otherwise silence, it was an approaching wall of noise — though no more recognizable for that.

When the biting-hot wind suddenly found her, the hackles rose higher on the nape of her neck and she gripped a lamppost in trembling fingers. The sound moaned ever closer. Now she cursed the return of all that was familiar. Only once before had she felt that peculiar searing wind; heard that singing approach. A Christmas Eve more than ten years ago, when she and Patrick had first bought their island villa; when they had still sought each other's companionship. Each other's welcome company.

Eyes now filled with gritty sand, Louise backed up a little, determined to continue down to the beach despite what she now suspected was coming up from it.

"It's the wrong time of year," she whispered to the empty street and its frantically waving palm trees, to the cracks between paving stones. A Gallotia lizard scuttled past her on squat, frantic legs, and the moan that escaped her was too brittle.

The *Sirocco* wind roared around the corner of *Calle Lapa*, bringing with it the floating, blinding dust that the islanders called *Calima*. The sandstorm had originated in the Sahara; had travelled over one hundred kilometers of ocean to block out the island's sun in a violent haze. But that was not the worst of it. The *Sirocco* carried with it a cargo so dreadful that the warning of its approach was akin to that of the worst kind of hurricane: prompting boarded windows, nailed shutters and breathless empty streets.

There was no such warning afforded to Louise now. All she could do was follow the lead of the disappeared lizard. Turning on her heel, she sped for her old villa, fishing the keys from her pocket as she ran. The folded square of journal suddenly flew from the same pocket. Buffeted by the rising hot air, it danced out of her reach.

Sanctuary forgotten, a reedy scream escaped her lips, and she careered towards the apartments and their awful stench, the sobs stinging her throat as hot sand rushed in.

"Don't leave me! Kayley, no! Come back!"

She tripped over a body — this one spread-eagled upon the tiled surround of the apartment pool: stained khaki shorts below a pitted grey-white back half trailing in stagnant water — and picked herself up with another scream. She lunged for the fluttering paper even as the locusts found her in their swarming, clacking hundreds, dropping her to the ground. Her fingers closed around the sharp edges of the paper, and she drew it tight to her chest in reflex.

She crawled back to the villa — now unable to breathe much less scream or sob. It took too long. By the time she made it back to the gate, the locusts had swarmed over her back and legs, and had tangled in her hair. Their beating hind wings were the amplified thrum of Mediterranean cicadas and crickets; their sharp legs scratched and pulled at her in mindless, endless hunger.

There was no time to make it inside the villa. Sprinting around the pool, Louise stumbled down the steps of the pump room, batting insects from her face and hair in frenzied shrieks.

The dark was cool and quiet and empty. She crouched within it, rocking herself too quickly; now paying little attention to the frantic insects that still tangled in her hair and beat against her clammy flesh. She thought of green and trees and river and cool. As the *Sirocco* roared overhead, its cargo thrumming hard against the roof, the tiles, and the plastic covering over the swimming pool in horrible mimicry of torrential rain, Louise thought of green and trees and river and cool. And Kayley.

❦

By the time she awoke, all was silent again. Louise stood on too shaky legs, brushing dead and dying insects from her body with revived and disgusted slaps. She mounted the steps back into the world above quickly, terrified that night might have already taken hold — she had intended to be back in the hills far above the resort well before nightfall — but she had evidently not been asleep as long as her aching body suggested. The relentless sun probed long fingers inside the upper reaches of the passageway, so much so that Louise had to shield her eyes before she had even made it as far as the top steps.

The pool area was covered in a twitching pale carpet. Swallowing bile, Louise picked her way through the *Sirocco's* debris: the sound of dry, cracking limbs and wings swiftly assuming the same connotation as that of twigs snapping deep in a creeping forest. As she drew closer to the stone arch that led back into the road, she winced at every too loud footstep, the pads of her fingers stabbing at the hard edges of the rescued square of paper in her pocket over and over. Long after they grew numb.

But the street was still deserted. By the time she made it out of her cul-de-sac and onto the main road that climbed down into the resort proper, Louise had almost gotten used to the prickly carpet under her feet; the hideous crunching noise that every footstep precipitated; the otherwise utterly breathless silence. And the emptiness: the total absence of any life at all, except the flies and bluebottles collected in ugly restless patterns inside passing apartment windows and screen doors.

Somewhere during her hundred yard descent into the *Terrazza* complex ahead of the promenade and beach, the cool urge to flee returned to whisper at her neck. And this time within it there was something — some horrible little niggle inside her brain — whose warning she couldn't quite yet catch. That niggle was like waking up from a bad dream unable to remember, yet still suffering the hangover of its dread.

The long faceless rear of the *supermercado* heralded the beginning of the complex. Louise crunched her way past grey brick and thick chained emergency exits. The goods entrance, where the Spanish kids — most often the children of the *supermercado's* employees — had always played tag or musical statues before growing bored and terrorizing sunburnt drunken tourists, was empty except for scattered litter and discarded cardboard boxes.

When Louise turned the corner into a car park still full of cars, she saw that the front of the shop was in a far worse state than before. Its entire Plexiglas face had been knocked out, the displays inside overturned and ripped apart, bright cut-price banners hanging limply in the stagnant air. Louise only fleetingly thought about venturing inside. Its cavernous shadows were far from inviting, and she was too readily discouraged by the reminder of her last visit.

Then, the *Terrazza* had been far from empty *or* quiet. The *Avenida de las Playas* had been alive with angry horns and whining mopeds: the daily grind of holiday rentals and beleaguered white taxis replaced by a panicked mass exodus east, towards Arrecife and its closed airport.

The fighting had already begun, although at that stage it had been confined to squabbles over rights of way and the spoils of looting. The violence had been at its worst inside the *supermercado*. Louise had made only as far as the first checkout before losing her nerve and turning back.

She had not returned. Locking every steel gate and shutter in her villa, Louise had stayed indoors, enduring day after day of noise and rattle and fury, until those days had grown quiet and empty. Until the snatched view from her balcony had become only merciless sun and fiery savage nights; the stench of the dead carried inland. Until she had, quite literally, run for the hills.

As she ventured further westwards through the *Terrazza* complex, she tried to forget by remembering happier days spent there with Patrick. Close to Paddy's Karaoke Bar within the main courtyard, she glimpsed the old tapas bar that had played live Jota and Mariachi every night in high season. Under the shade thrown by the metal stairways leading up to a now battered and graffiti-scored Moonlight Lounge, various narrow shops stood shuttered and silent.

Their wooden stands — before weighed heavy with inflated lilos, fringed T-shirts, sarongs, imitation watches, belts and handbags — now stood empty. Where they still stood at all.

Perhaps that accounted for the still enduring niggle. And the dread crawling inside her belly. It was too quiet. Too empty. The lack of wind she had gotten used to. Even the desertion of the gulls and gannets that had plagued seafront restaurants and bars no longer struck her as unusual. Or frightening.

It was something else. Something that was somehow far worse.

Suck it up, the Kayley in her pocket stoically advised — and not without some measure of irritation. *You're here to find water, supplies. So find them.*

Louise doubted that there would be anything close to an REI anywhere in the resort. For perhaps the first time since leaving her sanctuary in the hills, she wondered exactly what she thought she was doing. Yes, she needed the water, that was a given. But it didn't explain the vice around her chest; it didn't explain the Kayley in her pocket — *in her head* — or the frenzied sense of urgency that suddenly saw her leave the *Terrazza* complex at too fast a run, in spite of the heat, in spite of the danger. In spite of the dropping sun, and the memory of those screaming, whooping, fiery nights.

The smell was somewhat diluted on the *Avenida*. Louise stopped running only because her own body betrayed her. The heat was incredible: it seemed to scorch even her lungs, forcing her to a wheezing, breathless standstill close to a deserted crazy-golf enclosure on the old beach road.

There were very few bodies here — although Louise was not fooled for an instant. People were, by and large, creatures of habit. Those unable or unwilling to flee the resort would have sought familiar refuge. The barricaded villas and apartments were evidence enough of that, even ignoring the mottled, moving curtains of insects inside them. In the oppressive heat, Louise shivered to her feet and back again.

Still she kept going. *Playa Grande* gave way to *Playa Fariones*. Its empty deckchairs and sun-loungers had fallen foul of the rising Atlantic. Many swept relentlessly back and forth in the high tide; many more were stuck low in the shallows, thrusting stranded arms and legs upward in silent and unanswered cries for help.

Louise drew close to the main crossroads to the Old Town. Climbing over a crude barricade of overturned barrels and traffic bollards interspersed with charred oil drums; she wondered again what she thought she was doing. The sweat ran in sticky rivulets down her back and thighs, though the sun had all but disappeared behind the high cliffs in the west.

She still needed water — that much was now truer than ever. And there was the rest of Kayley's checklist. Fuel, food — maybe even weapons. But Louise had already passed a great many shops and restaurants — barred or no — and not once had she stopped. That queer crawling started up in her belly again, almost nullifying whatever urge still kept her going; kept her moving further from *Calle Lapa*. Or her better sanctuary in the hills.

She suddenly thought of the friends that Kayley had arranged to meet in Grants Pass. She fingered the hard corners of paper again. Louise had had no-one for a very long time. Only now that the world had turned on its head — only now that she found herself shuffling alone through what should have been the busiest thoroughfare in the whole of Lanzarote — did she suffer such isolation so acutely.

It was perhaps fitting that she should then come across the round white lanterns and dark-stained balconies of *Casa Siam*. Here she had spent many an evening in the long months before the divorce: its obsequious Thai owner sequestering her in the darkest, quietest corner, commiserating with superb prawn curries and free shots of Maekhong whisky.

But it was not the eerie, empty desolation of *Casa Siam* that made Louise stop. It was the sheer number of bodies inside its entrance. There were dozens littering the space between bar and tables: a tangle of grey limbs and pulpy flesh spread liberally over a dark red floor that once had been black and white checkered tiles. The door to the kitchen had been ripped almost off its hinges, and there were bloodied handprints smeared across both it and the nailed wooden beams that now hung uselessly from its frame.

These men and women — and God help them, children — had fallen prey to perhaps the worst plague of them all. Louise backed up, her fingers splayed across lips that tasted of her own blood. The battered remains of Kam Pramoj sprawled close to the neighboring Perspex-fronted amusement arcade — the left side of his head horribly concave and writhing white above a deflated, bloody eye socket.

Her sob echoed too long in the hot, deserted vacuum — and when she started to run again, she hardly cared that the sun had sunk so far beyond the cliffs in the west that its reflection had turned much of the breakwater blood red.

It is better to travel in groups, I think, Kayley reminded from the damp corner of Louise's shorts pocket. Louise gave that pocket an angry, frightened squeeze before looking away from the road and back out towards the choppy Atlantic.

Where were they? Where were the riotous mobs; the perpetrators of such mindless horror? The shouting, jeering engineers of every barricade and fire these past endless weeks? *Where were they?*

Keep going, Kayley admonished. *Having a plan can make the difference between life and death.*

"Shut up. Shut the fucking hell up." Louise snatched her hand out of her pocket. She was beginning to dislike that earnest, pitiless whisper in her ear. She was beginning to loathe it. Daydreams of Evergreens and pines, summer's night concerts and Christmas carnivals — *of green and trees and river and cool* — were all very well when there was no whisper in your ear. No righteous purpose. No diaphanous promise of a plan.

Yet still she did not turn back. As she headed further west, past the tropical-fringed colonnades and tax-free designer shops of the new *Biosfera* Plaza, she waited for that whispered *Run away*. It didn't come. Instead she made do with a long and forlorn glance towards those empty, white-tiled buildings and the darkening way back home beyond them, before she stepped down into the Old Town proper. The cobbled, shadowed walkways of *La Tiñosa*.

Here, that crawling dread — that relentless *niggle* — found her too fast. And this time without any warning at all. It stripped her of the very last of her denial; it prized its fingers from the rock face before dropping her into the empty abyss beneath. She careered into a white stuccoed archway — and then backward into the cobbled road. She clutched at herself in panicked misery. A cockroach crawled over her exposed legs. Her voice was a reedy whisper.

"Hello?"

Louise managed to stand again with sobbed effort, clutching at a lamppost. She saw that her palms were studded with grit, smearing blood against the hot metal — and she snatched them back to her chest with another moan.

She looked back up the steps. Back towards the static summits of the palm trees on the *Avenida*; towards its promenades and squares, and then the wilted flags of the *bureaux de change* and basement nightclubs beyond. The sun was an angry red ball sucked slowly beneath the horizon.

Was it so inconceivable to imagine that out of an island population of almost 130,000 she might be the only one now left alive within its largest resort? Perhaps it was. But the desertion of that whisper at her back suggested otherwise. As did the silent dusk that she shared with the dead.

She reared up from the warm cobbles with another plaintive cry, half-running, half-crawling her way back up the steps. The main road stretched east and west into empty shadow; upon her right, beyond the palms and their squat wide bodies, the Atlantic had swallowed *Playa Fariones* completely, the ocean's back and forth wash now an ugly, malignant sound. The only sound.

Louise stepped into the road, walked right to the central median, and drew in a shaky breath. This time the question came out as a half-strangled scream that shot through her like electricity.

"*Hello?*"

It echoed unanswered in the darkening silence, and the panic that rushed stinging bile into her throat was dampened only when her fingers found that sharp-edged square of paper in her pocket.

"What do I do, Kayley? Oh God, what the fuck am I supposed to do?"

Kayley didn't answer. A long swollen finger of gold sunset followed Louise's resumed and limped progress towards the old harbor; her thirst suddenly choking shut her throat. Close to the vast banners wrapped around lampposts that advertised boat and catamaran cruises, Louise collapsed again. Her scream was raw and savagely afraid.

"Kayley, I'm sorry! I didn't mean what I said before. Please come back! What do I do? *Please!*"

The approaching night mocked both her screamed plea and futile efforts to stand again. She truly *was* alone. That knowledge terrified her. Not even pressing the damp and battered square of paper to her mouth helped dilute its horror anymore.

Likely all that saved her from herself was the sudden recognition of a sound she had missed beyond that of the roaring, closing Atlantic. She looked up at the dim outline of the vast balcony that stretched above the length of promenade — from the shadows of New Town to Old. A generator. A light.

You're going to go back down to La Tiñosa, Louise. You're going to go down to the harbor, and you're going to find a boat. You're going to sail to America. You're going to find Grants Pass.

Even in her hysteria, Louise struggled to disguise an incredulous snort. But she couldn't risk antagonizing Kayley again. It was enough that she had come back. A boat was maybe the best idea after all. She glanced back up at the invitingly bright oasis above her head. But she needed to rest first. She needed to *drink* first. Perhaps she could sail to Africa instead. Perhaps—

I'm only a voice in your head, Louise. That *voice* had taken on a hard, brittle edge that was somewhere between fury and petulance. *I'm not here. I'm far away, and I'm getting tired of waiting. I'm getting tired of waiting for you.*

Despite the warning; despite the snide threat of desertion, Louise sped towards the spiraling stairs that led up from the promenade. Toward the light. Hope — even hopelessness — was too easily defeated by something else. Something that was more than just thirst or the need to rest. Or the need to placate her only remaining friend. The bar was everything that Louise had lost. Everything that she had been in danger of forgetting.

At the top of the metal steps, she veered right, running into an easel depicting a chalked outline of a grasshopper above a scrawled promise of Big Screen Football and Fishbowl Cocktails for €12.

The bar was in darkness apart from a long tube of UV that ran the length of the bar and the neon cycle of its jukebox. Louise ran for the jukebox first, her fingers stabbing at the scroll buttons too furiously. The track lists snapped over and over in the silence. She forced the last of her change into its plastic slot. To hear a voice — one outside her head. Just a voice.

In the end, she chose more carefully. Her hands had stopped shaking when she lifted the hatch of the bar; when she liberated a cool Corona from a fridge beneath a poster advertising Ladies *Nite* at Caesar's. *Free entry before 11pm* had been scrawled underneath in Sharpie ink.

She perched on a stool overlooking the darkening street as she sipped her beer in steadier-still hands; as Billie Joe Armstrong sang about a Boulevard of Broken Dreams; as thoughts of plague and death and apocalypse left her momentarily behind.

A faint, almost imperceptible breeze came off the salty Atlantic, and she breathed it deep — for a moment pretending that this was just another balmy Canarian night in high season. The crawling dread in her belly almost abated. Almost quietened.

Until she thought of the stubbornly silent and folded square of paper inside her pocket. That last frightened voice on the radio. Kayley's too easy faith in her friends and in her sanctuary. In survival.

The last of the sun's rays sunk deep inside the slick black surface of high tide, and the promenade and its palm trees vanished into darkness. Louise trailed her arms over the balcony and closed her eyes. The heat clung to her like a shroud. In the distance, she could hear the whined return of insects doubtless still the size of her fist.

Louise remembered the eerie cornfields ahead of Mother Abigail's rocking chair; she remembered that ugly pink neon slash. She remembered Patrick. Her fingers suddenly twitched for her pocket again.

Obviously, not everyone who reads this would survive an apocalypse. Maybe I would not survive it. My want for immortality says I would but that's just me.

That breeze suddenly whistled through invisible palm trees, snatching the hair from her face and tickling the flesh on her stretched-out arms. The paper fell away over the balcony, its careful folds opening like wings as it caught the bar's illumination in the last breath of updraft. As it winked away into absolute darkness, Louise stared in horror at her open palms, their steady spread-out fingers.

The jukebox settled back into hummed expectancy. Louise's moan was a low, sobbing, childlike plea. "Kayley?"

There was only silence. Silence and dark empty windless space. No more than that.

BIOGRAPHY

CAROLE JOHNSTONE

Carole was born in a small town east of Glasgow. She now lives with her fiancé, Iain, in the southeast of England, working as a radiographer and medical dosimetrist.

A relative newcomer to the world of published fiction, she was first featured in *Black Static Magazine* in early 2008, and is to appear in the anthologies: *In Bad Dreams Vol.2*, *Scenes from the Second Storey*, *Voices*, *Dead Souls*, and *In the Footsteps of Gilgamesh*.

Her website can be found at www.carolejohnstone.com.

AFTERWORD

There are few things more effective or powerful than the beginning of a certain type of post-apocalyptic story. Into a scene of utter devastation — or more often desolation — a character wanders invariably alone. Confused and afraid. And — we're pretty certain — in a whole world of trouble. Whatever the setting: a slum, a hospital, an overgrown metropolis, an isolated mountain retreat, the intention is always to shock. To frighten with the altered familiar. To make us think of ourselves and wonder, What If?

I chose Lanzarote as a setting only partly because it is an island in a comparatively isolated archipelago. Lanzarote is an island of volcanic origin. In contrast to its few coastal resorts, its interior is made up of vast mountain ranges, desert landscapes and volcanic tunnels. To stand upon the *Montañas del Fuego* and look down upon alien fields of rock and solidified lava streams is to imagine another world. Or the ending of our own.

I wanted to write a story that begins with monsters and ends with worse. A story where the protagonist is *left* alone, confused and afraid. Maybe *I'm* alone in feeling a little disappointed when the crazies do finally come out; or when that lone survivor meets others like him and sets about rebuilding their version of civilization. For me, no monster — human or otherwise — can ever match that initial skewed perspective; that wonder that is part adolescent fantasy and part innate terror.

I believe that. Maybe you don't. But one thing we probably can agree on is that we all need hope. Even if it's lying. And we all need someone. Even if it's just a voice in our head. No more than that.

NEWFOUND GAP

LEE CLARK ZUMPE

JOURNAL ENTRY, MONDAY, SEPT. 4, 0001 AE:

Five weeks since last airplane spotted flying overhead — pretty sure that it was military, heading southeast, probably to Charleston Air Force Base. It's been two weeks since the last sign of traffic along US 441, heading north out of Cherokee towards Gatlinburg. I'm running low on packaged food but there's plenty of game to make up for that. It rains daily: The storms move north out of the Gulf of Mexico. Tropical activity should peak in the next few weeks. Last night, the skies to the east glowed red. This morning I saw smoke lingering low on the horizon. I think Asheville may be burning.

JOURNAL ENTRY, SATURDAY, OCT. 14, 0001 AE:

Winter will come early. Temperatures have been falling steadily at night and I expect to see snow next week. Tomorrow I hike over to the road, just in case. It's been too long. I don't expect to see anyone, really; but making the trip every week gives me something to look forward to.

Everyone Ethan knew was dead.

Friends, family, co-workers — all dead. Distant relatives living all over the country, all over the world; acquaintances he had made online, in chat rooms; sons and daughters and wives and husbands of former school friends — all dead to the best of his knowledge.

"Told you the place was deserted." Lamar walked down the middle of the road, eyeing the vacated tourist shops and art galleries. His boots shuffled across the pavement, his long black coat billowed in the breeze. Normally, Gatlinburg would be teaming with vacationers drawn by the changing seasons and the colorful autumn leaves. "It's been a ghost town for months, just like Pigeon Forge, just like Sevierville and every other town I've been through."

"There must be someone..." Ethan glanced at a newspaper resting in the gutter. The headline simply read PLAGUE.

He missed Hannah the most, of course. Though their intimacy had never evolved into a more permanent romantic attachment, he considered her the closest thing he had to a partner. They shared secrets, complained about the world in general as if kindred spirits. He confided in her, confessed both his fears and his weaknesses.

He missed his brother, too, and his bowling partners and the elderly lady who lived down the hall and the guy at the gas station on the corner. He missed hearing music on the radio in the car. He missed the group of kids that played football in the vacant lot by the grocery store.

"I've been getting supplies here," Lamar said, pointing his walking stick at a nearby market. "Door was wide open when I showed up. There was a rotted corpse in back. I hauled it out and left it next to the dumpster." In his fifties, Lamar had managed to survive in the midst of metropolitan Atlanta. He had lived in the house his father had built half a century earlier, during the height of the Cold War. Lamar spent months underground in an old fallout shelter, rationing his food and monitoring the demise of civilization on shortwave radio. "There's still plenty of bottled water and canned food in here. We should stock up before we head north."

Following a late season hurricane that devastated much of the Carolina shoreline, Ethan had relocated to the mountains of western North Carolina, leaving behind his beloved ancestral home in downtown Southport. Nothing really remained of the coastal town — a thirty-foot storm surge had obliterated most buildings, scattering debris through the tangled lowlands of the Green Swamp or washing them back to sea as the wall of water receded.

He shared a FEMA trailer with several other single men for a few weeks. Once he had managed to liquidate his assets, he paid cash and rented a vacation chateau outside Maggie Valley. In those last days, watching the news became an obsession for some; bleak images played out while monotone news anchors read what would become an epitaph for a nation. Every day seemed to bring another upheaval and new tales of tragedy.

When word of the plagues came, Ethan reluctantly abandoned the comforts of civilization and headed into the wilderness. A trilogy of epidemics arrived to trounce humanity, causing excruciating deaths in city after city across the globe. And it was all done by terrorists.

He settled in an abandoned cabin built by the Civilian Conservation Corps deep in the heart of the Smoky Mountains. Situated along a spur connecting to the Appalachian Trail, the place had long been frequented by hikers and was by no means a secret. Ethan expected others to join him, woke up daily expecting to see another survivor staggering up the mountainside eyeing the ribbon of smoke spilling from the chimney.

None came.

Beginning in July, he hiked to Newfound Gap weekly. He had once told Hannah to look for him there should anything happen to separate them — in reality, it was more a joke than a plan: He teased her that if bill collectors became too demanding or litigious, he would have to stage his own death.

Like everyone else born in the second half of the 20th century, when confrontational superpowers waged an unending war of words bolstered by enough nuclear warheads to reduce the planet to a smoldering cinder, Ethan had dreamed of a global holocaust. Though he had imagined end-of-the-world scenarios, he never really expected any of his wild, apocalyptic nightmares to unfold. Unlike his recent acquaintance Lamar, he was no survivalist. He simply knew how to effectively remove himself from society — and he had good enough sense to know when it was time to leave.

"Ethan," Lamar called to him from the market. "Hey, Ethan — what do you want for lunch?"

"Not hungry." Ethan shambled along the sidewalk, peering through store windows. Some windows had been shattered, merchandise strewn across the floor inside the shop. Looters had carried off goods after law enforcement failed, too short-sighted to realize they would have little time to enjoy the acquisitions. "I'd like to go ahead and find a couple vehicles."

He had found Lamar at Newfound Gap. Actually, Lamar found him. Ethan had left notes posted on the wall of the Rockefeller Memorial in hopes of reuniting with Hannah. The notes read:

Hannah: I'm alive. Wait for me here. Build a fire if you can — I'll see the smoke. I'll be back in less than seven days. I miss you. Ethan.

Lamar found the note and waited four days for Ethan to return.

"We'll find something at that dealership I told you about in Sevierville." Lamar emerged from the market with pockets packed. He carried a bottle of water in one hand and several packs of beef jerky in the other. "We've got a long haul ahead of us. You should grab some grub, boy."

Although Ethan was a good 25 years younger than Lamar, he still winced at being called 'boy'.

"I'll get something later. No sense leaving 'til morning," Ethan said, watching as the sun drifted low over the ridge embracing the city. "I'd like to clean up, get a good night's sleep in a comfortable bed."

"Sure, sure. There are plenty of vacant hotel rooms. But the service at the restaurants is lousy." Lamar caught up with Ethan and handed him a bottle of water. "Drink something at least. We'll hunker down for the night and head out in the morning, just in case your girlfriend shows up. We'd see the smoke from here, I reckon."

"Yeah," he nodded. He looked over his shoulder to the southeast, back toward Mount LeConte and Newfound Gap. "I know it's crazy to think she's still out there. It's just hard for me to convince myself I won't see her again."

"You never know. We might find her out west."

Lamar had convinced Ethan to join him in a cross-country trek. Someone else had been up on Newfound Gap recently; and, like Ethan, they had left a message. The mystery survivors provided no indication of their identity, no note to specify their point of origin or the number travelling in their party. They left a road map, highlighting their destination — like a beacon for stragglers, a welcome objective for the vestiges of humanity.

The map pointed them toward Grants Pass, Oregon.

JOURNAL ENTRY, TUESDAY, OCT. 17, 0001 AE:

Goodbye, Gatlinburg. Goodbye, Newfound Gap. Goodbye, Hannah.

JOURNAL ENTRY, THURSDAY, OCT. 19, 0001 AE:

Spent today exploring Nashville. We arrived just before dawn and Lamar thought he saw lights in one of the buildings downtown. We searched for hours but found no one. The smell is awful — sewage, bodies, rotten food. One thing Nashville is not, though, is dead. There are packs of wild dogs, feral cats and rodents everywhere. Lamar had to kill a dog that came after him in a store. If he hadn't been fast enough, he'd probably be dead. We'll be more careful.

Ethan, driving a late model SUV filled with supplies, watched Lamar in his rear-view mirror. Trailing him on the Interstate, his companion had appropriated an ambulance in St. Louis. Filled with pharmaceuticals and life-saving equipment, Lamar had picked it up outside a hospital emergency room, keys in the ignition and gas tank filled. He even found sodas floating in stagnant water in a portable cooler.

A mile separated them as they raced toward the setting sun.

"How are you doing, Theresa?"

"I want to go home," the young woman said, her gaze focused on the passing pavement. "I want to go home and see David."

"David isn't there anymore, Theresa." They had found her wandering around a shopping mall in St. Louis, dehydrated, emaciated and gibbering incoherently. The 29-year-old woman tried to elude them initially, panicking at the sight of strangers and screaming as she fled down the mall's central corridor. They caught up with her in a darkened department store, convinced her they meant her no harm. "You remember, we went to the house to get him, but he was dead. We buried him in the backyard."

"David is my friend," she said, choking back tears. Whether her delicate mental state existed prior to or resulted from the end of the world did not really matter. They could not leave her to die. So they adopted her. "When will we stop?"

"Pretty soon," Ethan said. He preferred to stay off the road at night. He did not want to chance falling asleep at the wheel, particularly with a passenger. "Are you getting tired?"

"Little bit. Where did everyone go?" Theresa noticed a number of cars parked along the road; shadowy figures slumped over steering wheels or huddled in bony heaps in the weedy scrub. Ethan had already grown used to seeing carcasses, so much so that even the most grisly display of human mortality scarcely fazed him. "Why did they go away?"

"Well," Ethan looked at her, trying to find the right words to make the situation clear, trying to summon up a suitable explanation that would not simply serve to inflate her confusion. "Did anyone tell you about the plague when it first happened — about people getting very sick? Lots of people?"

"David said it was a virus. He said it was like a cold, only worse."

"That's right — it was a virus. Actually, several different ones, all at once." Ethan remembered the last few days he had lingered in Maggie Valley, watching as the horror spread like wildfire, burning through the population. Governments vowed to contain it, scientists frantically tried to calm the masses. Cities were quarantined. Bulldozers pushed the dead into vast landfills where flames consumed their diseased bodies. Fires burned incessantly, smoke blackened the skies. Seeing no reason to share such unpleasant memories, Ethan tried to change the subject. "Did you have a family? Parents?"

"Everyone has parents," she snapped. "Mine couldn't take care of me and let me go when I was little. I don't remember them." Theresa turned toward Ethan, a look of sudden puzzlement in her eyes. "Are they dead now, too?"

"Probably," Ethan nodded. "There are very few people left, Theresa. Very few."

Ethan momentarily turned his attention to a fast-approaching road sign. In another thirty minutes, they would be in Kansas City. Ethan flashed the interior lights a few times to catch Lamar's attention. "Ever been to Kansas City?"

"No."

"Well, looks like we'll be staying there tonight."

"Okay."

Twilight finally caught up with them. As they continued, the land on either side of Interstate 70 blossomed with housing developments, apartment buildings, shopping plazas and tall offices. They slowed to a crawl when they neared the city limits, finding the roadway littered with abandoned vehicles of every make and model. Weaving through the maze of cars, vans, buses and trucks, Ethan paused and waited for Lamar to catch up.

"How long were you by yourself?"

"I wasn't alone. I had David. He took care of me."

"But," Ethan started, unable to settle on the least upsetting way to phrase his question. "When did David stop taking care of you?"

"When we played the drinking game."

"What's that?"

"One morning when I woke up he said he might have the virus. He said that he might not be able to take care of me anymore, and that made him sad." She hesitated, stared at her lap and rubbed her forehead with her right hand as she recalled the event. "He said he had a special drink — he said it was magic, like a potion. He said if we both drank it, he could still take care of me." Theresa wept openly now, her lower lip fluttering as she continued. "We picked up the glasses. He drank his right away. I took a pretend sip, and I promised I would finish it later, when I was thirsty."

"And then?"

"When I came back later, David was asleep." Theresa smeared her tears on her sleeve. "He never woke up."

Ethan shuddered. He felt rage and sympathy, resentment and compassion. That David had attempted to poison Theresa sickened him. Still, her caregiver must have realized that alone she would fall victim to either starvation or madness. Faced with this tragic decision, Ethan believed that David had shown courage and strength of will by taking a course of action that would otherwise have been considered criminal and immoral.

"Where to, guys?" Lamar called out, startling them both. He had walked up along side the SUV, tapping on Ethan's window. "Sun's down, and it's just gonna get darker. Better find a place to rest our heads, right?"

"Yeah," Ethan said, fiddling with the button panel on his door until the window sank. Cold air rushed into the vehicle. Theresa shivered, pressed her head against her window and stared at the ground. "Sign says there're three or four motels at the next exit. Let's pull off and have a look."

"Sounds good. Let me lead — I've got a searchlight on that thing. May as well put it to use."

"I'll follow."

As Lamar walked back to the ambulance, Ethan rolled up his window. His eyes scanned the darkened metropolis that had been Kansas City. It had outlived its builders and its most recent residents. Its vacant streets no longer surged with streaming rush hour traffic; its homes no longer lit up each evening as families gathered for meals or seceded into various rooms to watch television, complete homework assignments or surf the web. Church bells had been silenced. In libraries, the collected wisdom of humanity gathered dust.

"Why didn't you drink it," Ethan abruptly asked. He doubted she realized what David had attempted to do, even now. "Why didn't you drink the magic potion, Theresa?"

"Because there's no such thing as magic."

JOURNAL ENTRY, FRIDAY, OCT. 27, 0001 AE:

Only the dead know what really happened in Denver — but having spent the better part of a day searching the ruins for survivors, I think we have a pretty good idea. Unlike other cities, Denver appears to have somehow avoided the original outbreak. While most places were failing, while the federal government was collapsing, at least a portion of Denver continued to function and remained untouched by the pandemic. Something happened, though, in late July, if the final newspaper accounts can be trusted. Martial law had been declared. Paranoia ran rampant. A self-appointed tyrant adopted a policy of "preservation through elimination," identifying prospective plague victims and targeting them for eradication. Death squads swept the streets, rounding up those members of society perceived to be a threat. When we went through the city, we saw hundreds of bodies strung up on streetlamps, victims butchered by machine gun fire in their vehicles as they tried to flee. We found the centre of operations in a shelter beneath the airport, where a small group of the elite apparently tried to find sanctuary from the plague. They tried to create a buffer zone by commanding paramilitary groups wearing biohazard gear to commit genocide on the surrounding community. Their plan evidently failed. We found no survivors. If we had, I cannot honestly say what we would have done with them.

Ethan sat in a secluded booth in an abandoned Reno casino bar room plucking roasted peanuts from a bowl on the table. One by one, he chucked the emptied shells onto the carpeted floor. With no cleaning crew to sweep up after the establishment's infrequent and unexpected patrons, Ethan wondered if mice would pickup the slack.

Lamar stood behind the bar, marveling at the variety of liquors. Like a kid in a candy store, he harvested bottles from their shelves, lining them up neatly along the bar.

Each booth in the lounge featured a high-resolution plasma screen and surround sound system. When the place had been crowded, Ethan imagined music videos ran nonstop while guests frittered away their modest winnings on exotic drinks. He prodded the controls unsuccessfully, not expecting a response.

Ethan had sent Theresa off with Alice, a 62-year-old widow they discovered in Cheyenne. The casino boasted several clothing stores, and Theresa only had the clothes she had been wearing when they found her. She needed a new wardrobe, and Ethan thought Alice could help her make the appropriate selections.

"Not far now, my friend." Lamar sat down across from Ethan, cradling a bottle of whisky and two shot glasses. "We'll be in Sacramento tomorrow night. Only another half day from there."

"It will be weird to stop; we've been going for so long." Ethan downed his first shot solemnly, winced as the whisky burned the back of his throat and settled in his gut. "So many desolate cities behind us, so many nightmares. I've been so focused on reaching Grants Pass; everything else seems like a blur."

"Keep drinking this and things will get even blurrier."

"I'm serious, Lamar," Ethan said, running his finger along the rim of the glass. "We've been so preoccupied with getting there; we haven't stopped to ask if it's what we really want."

"Of course it's what we want." Lamar lit a cigarette, pushed the pack across the table toward Ethan. Ethan shook his head. "If there's only a handful of people left, don't you think that it's to their benefit to band together? There's safety in numbers, right?"

"Sure," Ethan agreed, pouring himself a second shot. "But what if these people are something other than we expect?"

"What do you mean?"

"I don't know." Ethan rubbed his eyes. In his head, a dull ache that had taken root days earlier now burgeoned. "What if they have expectations...beliefs that differ from ours?"

"You've just gotten use to being alone, kid. When you see all those smiling faces welcoming us home for the first time,

I'm sure all your worries will evaporate." Lamar waved, his gaze redirected to the far side of the room where Theresa and Alice had appeared. The two of them had evidently cleaned out every sales floor in the place. They each carried bulging bags overflowing with designer clothes. "Leave the stuff there and join us for a drink," Lamar said, howling across the sprawling nightclub.

"We'll be right there," Alice said. Brimming with maternal instincts, she had taken an instant liking to Theresa, and Theresa seemed to enjoy the attention. "We need to make a pit stop, first."

"We'll be here." Lamar's broad smile momentarily displaced Ethan's anxiety. To possess such blind optimism in the face of catastrophic adversity and terrifying uncertainty seemed an enviable gift. If ignorance substituted for bliss, Lamar's unsubstantiated confidence and childlike hopefulness might well bring them all much-deserved peace and security. "Don't you worry about Grants Pass," Lamar said, reassuring his companion. He poured two more shots and held up his glass to Ethan. "I'm sure they'll take us in, especially you young folks. If we're going to rebuild society, there'll have to be plenty of young women able to bear children."

As Ethan's fleeting delusion of contentment faded, he downed one last shot of whisky.

❦

JOURNAL ENTRY, TUESDAY, OCT. 31, 0001 AE:

Civilization is winding down. The species has survived previous bottlenecks, but from what I've seen, there's far too few of us left now to reorganize, to rebuild and to repopulate the planet. Even if pockets of survivors manage to establish small colonies, they probably won't last for more than a few generations. Too much has been lost, too much sacrificed. Some of those left behind will assign spiritual significance to this event, chalk it up to God's will. Some may believe earth and the environment conspired to eliminate humanity before humanity managed to destroy the planet. Maybe mankind simply outstayed its moment in the spotlight. No matter what, whether our endangered species manages to avoid extinction or not, one this is certain: Life will go on.

"Do you want to stay with us while Lamar and the boys go check things out?" Ethan sat perched on the edge of a picnic table at a rest stop along Interstate 5 south of Grants Pass. Lamar and the two teenage boys who had joined their convoy in Sacramento busied themselves ransacking a vending machine. Theresa sat next to Ethan and Alice paced back and forth beneath a sycamore. "You're welcome to wait here until we see what they find."

"No, sweetie, I think I'll tag along with Lamar," Alice said. She stopped, leaned forward and kissed Ethan's cheek. "Thank you for the offer though. You're a good man."

"I just want to do what's best."

"I know, sweetie. Lamar is doing what he thinks is best, too." The terminally gray skies overhead and the arctic winds left little doubt that rain would soon be falling. By this evening, snow would dust the mountains. "He wants to find utopia down there, you know."

"Maybe that's just what you'll find."

"Maybe. But one person's paradise might be another's prison. He doesn't see that." Alice opened her arms and

Theresa hugged her tightly. "You be a good girl, now, all right?"

"Yes ma'am," Theresa nodded.

"You take good care of her Ethan."

Lamar and the boys wandered up with armfuls of snack chips and pretzels and candy bars.

"Let's move out," Lamar said, beaming. "We'll have a look around and be back for you before sunset."

"We'll be waiting," Ethan said, lying. Alice knew his intentions. Deep down, Lamar probably did, too. Ethan stood, extended his arm and shook hands with the first man he had met after the end of the world. "You be careful."

"We will," Lamar said. He hesitated, and then embraced Ethan. "Thanks for getting me this far. I think we can manage from here."

Minutes later the caravan pulled out of the rest stop on the last leg of its journey, leaving Ethan and Theresa sitting beneath the sycamore.

"We won't see them again, will we?"

"No."

"Where will we go now?"

"Well," Ethan said, watching the icy breeze tease her hair. "We can go just about anywhere. Have you ever heard of the Appalachians?"

JOURNAL ENTRY, SUNDAY, JUNE 10, 0002 AE:

Alice and Lamar left this morning, heading north toward Chicago. It was their third visit since they brought Hannah back to Newfound Gap from Grants Pass. Lamar helped put the finishing touches on the new cabin near Oconaluftee. I don't know how I'll ever repay him. Theresa decided to join them on their trip to Canada looking for lone survivors and settlements. They'll all be swinging back this way in October, when Hannah is due. Alice promised to stay until the baby comes, and hinted she might spend the winter here. Hannah would like that. Between our weekly runs to Cherokee, my hunting and Hannah's garden, we have plenty of food. Still, we live day to day, knowing we're both on borrowed time. Everyone is on borrowed time, now. Civilization may be extinct, but humanity might yet endure if it can learn to face hardships and harsh conditions as it struggles to persevere. Paradise is neither Grants Pass nor Newfound Gap; but living either place is far better than the alternative.

BIOGRAPHY

LEE CLARK ZUMPE

Lee Clark Zumpe is prone to fits of creativity between 2 and 6 a.m. During these seizures, he locks himself in a room in a remote corner of the house and writes. His work has appeared in *Weird Tales, Book of Dark Wisdom* and *Horror Express* as well as the anthologies *Horrors Beyond* and *Corpse Blossoms*. As a reviewer for *Tampa Bay Newspapers,* Lee was honored with a Florida Press Award in 0001 AE. Lee and wife Tracey enjoy scouring antique festivals for vintage toys, Victorian ephemera and linens.

Contact Lee at leeclarkzumpe@yahoo.com.

AFTERWORD

The latter half of the 20th century is rife with post-apocalyptic fiction. One of my favorite selections in this subgenre is George R. Stewart's *Earth Abides*; it paints what I believe to be an accurate picture of what might happen should humanity suffer a population bottleneck due to some form of natural or manmade catastrophe.

While archaeologists and paleontologists have shown that the species has managed to claw its way back from the brink of extinction several times, one must wonder if an advanced civilization, ill-equipped to face the day-to-day tribulations of survival, could replicate past recoveries.

Post-apocalyptic fiction often asks whether humanity — in its quest for technology — has sacrificed the very survival instincts that allowed it to flourish. In 'Newfound Gap', I strived to portray Ethan as pragmatic, but cautiously optimistic as he observes the transformation of an advanced society into a more primitive one.

INK BLOTS

"Specialists estimate that only one in 10,000 people will survive the genetically altered viruses that have been released across the world in an act of terror."

— The Age Newspaper

Margie put the paper down and ran a hand across the crinkled surface. The faded date read August 29th — that was eleven months ago. She traced the date again and again, absorbing the ink, feeling it soak into her skin. It flooded through her; the words branding themselves into her mind.

Leaning across the kitchen bench, she scanned the headlines of the other papers scattered across the black granite surface. The bench top felt smooth to touch, cool against the indeterminate flavor of the newspapers. Their words swam lazily through her vision, some dominating, others slinking into the background. Pinching the bridge of her nose with her index finger and thumb, she fought to stay focused, but lost. Images swam behind her closed eyelids, colors, bodies...text.

She opened her eyes and looked at the pile of black and white sheets. The letters continued to backstroke through her vision and she shivered. They were taunting her.

The thin sunlight that crept in through the windows slowly sunk into her; washed through her onto the paper. The words seemed to crystallize, deciding to obey the light. "Cure Found" was followed by "More Die". A sense of defeat surged through her body, dimming the meager warmth of the sun.

Initially, she'd collected the papers as a way of keeping the hope alive. Margie hadn't believed that the viruses were going to kill everyone. But hope began to fade, much like the ink on her papers. During the riots that had followed the Prime Minister's 'Speech of Doom', she'd spotted *"Kayley's Dream: Grants Pass"* printed in bold across the front of a newspaper's first page. Apparently, some important analyst in the States had announced that the people of Australia needed plans like Kayley's.

Her post had been quoted underneath.

That had been the last paper she had ever bought. Probably one of the last ever printed.

Kayley's dream had been an escape. Not a physical one; Grants Pass, Oregon, was 13,280 kilometers from Melbourne. She'd looked it up in the atlas. It had meant that more ink was absorbed by her fingers, but she'd had to do it. Kayley's words had become a symbol of something — action, she supposed. But so far, she hadn't managed to do anything about the inspired hope. Margie knew she was trapped, isolated as Australia was. Even crossing to Tasmania was out of the question. The only part of her dream left was the papers.

Margie was dying from the truth of ink stained pages.

Listlessly, she flicked through the sheets, her fingers touching only the white edges, avoiding the text. Her soul — that shrunken, withered pulse inside her — wanted to find something new; something she hadn't read before. But there was nothing new. There never was. Useless dreams, that's all it was.

Her soul ran from the ink.

"You can't keep doing this!"

The sound shattered her reverie, and she turned around, startled. Her heart was pounding, and she could feel her hands shaking. Was someone there?

Margie called out into the silent house, but there was no answer, just a sick sense of *déjà vu*. It had been her own voice yelling at her. Feeling hollow, she brought a shaking hand to her forehead. She hadn't even recognized the sound of her voice; it had been so long since she'd spoken to anyone.

"I'm all alone." The tasteless words seemed to solidify the statement; what it meant. She was the only human for miles.

Standing, she pushed back the chair and walked towards the floor to ceiling windows of her dining room. Her feet felt heavy, like reality was weighing them down. Unconsciously, her hands kept rubbing themselves together; the dry skin rough to touch — different to the papers. Both ink stained.

Looking out the windows she stared at the backyard, at the overgrown swath of colors that varied from dead brown to misty, wishful, green. She felt cornered — cheated by past ambitions. Her pride, her tidy home, her gloriously shallow existence; they made her a prisoner now, stuck between four walls, too afraid to leave for good. Before, her prison, the bricks and mortar, had been a statement of her success. She had felt superior to her friends, family. *Look at me*, the two million dollar mansion had cried, *I'm going to save the world from crime*. Save it from what? Stupidity? Selfishness? Greed?

The world hadn't needed saving.

It was doing just fine without humanity.

Now the house meant nothing; it was just shelter, keeping her safe from the yowls and cries of starving animals; the ones that had survived SVHF, that is.

Margie watched through the window as a fur covered bundle of bones prowled through the yard. Light flashed, distracting her, drawing her eyes away from the garden and focusing them on her reflection in the glass. She winced.

Shaggy brown hair, tired blue eyes and a face that was all angles. She turned away.

She didn't like going outside; hated it. There, the watery sunlight was real — the rays tangible, weighty. The cold air battered her and the scents stung her nostrils; potent reminders that nature didn't care about her. Not about anyone.

"You can't stay in here."

This time, she would have liked to pretend that there was someone else; that she hadn't finally hit the point where she had absorbed so much ink that she was talking to herself. But she couldn't lie; not to the scrawny cat outside, not to the windows, not to her shrunken soul.

Margie went back to the papers.

Margie was driving. She was wearing sunglasses against the weak light. The skeletons on the side of the road, in the front yards, took on an almost watery appearance through her lenses. It made them less real. Some of the bones were scattered across the road, but it didn't matter. It wasn't like there was anyone else driving. She could dodge them as she pleased.

She owned the road.

She owned the world.

She owned nothing.

Margie didn't know where she was going; there wasn't really any point in heading anywhere specific. She blinked to find herself driving down the Nepean Highway, on the way out of Melbourne, towards the south-east. She'd driven there before, of course. Not long after all the power and gas went. She'd driven everywhere soon after it had all stopped for good.

Her hands hadn't absorbed so much ink then. Her blood had still been hers. Not that that had done her any good.

Back then, she'd thought of being another Kayley. Of making the world work. But there'd been no one else to work with.

She'd done the math. Her papers had told her there would be one in 10,000 people left. That meant there would only be around 400 people left in all of Melbourne. Her atlas said Melbourne was 8,806 kilometers squared. More ink had to be absorbed by her skin for this information, but she'd had to know. The polluting of her blood had told her that there was one person per 22 kilometers squared. She rubbed her fingers together. You couldn't see the stains, but they were there.

Margie drove slowly. "There ain't no peak hour anymore," she muttered. Animals, once shy of the roads and the painful deaths they meant, tended to cross whenever they felt like it. Margie had never thought to see large cats roaming the streets of suburbia, but then, her papers had told her that people had campaigned for the zoo animals to be let free.

Free.

What did that mean, exactly?

Free to die from SVHF? Free to roam the streets, starving for lack of food?

It had been crazy. *They* had been crazy with their ideas. People had died on the side of the road, in their beds, hospitals. People had died on her manicured lawn. Margie had locked her doors, stayed inside. Hoarded the canned food she'd bought out of panic. And look where she was. Alive. And they were all dead.

They were lucky.

She was 'free'.

What would Kayley do?

Margie sat in the front seat of her car. She had the best parking spot, high on a cliff face, staring out at Port Phillip

Bay. Its surface barely rippled. It was a mirror, showing the world above it; distorted and yet pure. It held no lies, no illusions. Not like her ink stained hands. They held lies upon lies from all the papers she had touched.

She turned on the radio, randomly flicking channels. She'd wait a few seconds, trying to find a pattern in the chaotic sound, but there was none. Inevitably, she moved on. At first, she'd hated the radio. Couldn't stand the static. Now it was the only sound she heard, apart from her CDs.

Her fingers hit the dial again, paused at the next former station and moved on.

"Hello—"

Margie froze.

No, it was just her mind.

She dialed the radio back, but there was only static. Maybe it was further? No, she should stop. She was taunting herself. But her fingers — those ink stained liars — moved the dial of their own accord.

"—if anyone can hear me, please keep the radio on." Margie bit her lip so hard she could taste the tainted copper of blood and ink.

"It's not real," she whispered to herself. It had finally happened. She was insane. The ink had done it, filtered through her until it had eaten away at her brain.

"I live in Melbourne, Australia. I survived the plagues. If you're interested in meeting me, come to Flinders Street Station. I'll be underneath the clocks at 4:30pm every day."

Margie's fingers tightened on the wheel. Her lying fingers. She was insane. This wasn't real, it wasn't happening. She was imagining it. She breathed in the scent of the car; the metallic smell of tin cans and the gas bottles she'd raided from a store on her way to the beach.

What if it is true?

♦

"You can't tell me that some survivor (probably male), wouldn't get it in their head to become some sort of warlord and try to rule their own little bit of land. You know it would happen. Personally, I'd rather band together with people I already know than some random tough guy who has figured out how to rule through strength and fear."

More words on paper. More ink.

Margie stared at Kayley's letter, waited for the sentences to burn themselves into her mind. Now, it was more than just ink running through her veins, mixing with her blood. The dream had started again; hope was back.

Part of her, the part of her that knew she was lying to herself, said she should give up. That there was nothing there; it was all a figment of her imagination. That it was all an elaborate ploy by the light and ink to give hope to her withered soul. But the shadowy part, the part that had watched as people died on the streets, said that it was worth it.

So what if the man was one of Kayley's warlords? Would it really be that bad? Margie knew that she didn't have much time left. All the words on all her pieces of paper were eating her alive. The diseases may not have killed her, but solitude would.

Margie had to go.

She sat staring at Flinders Street Station. It didn't look how she remembered; the beautiful yellow of the building was stained with rust colored smears and graffiti. Maybe it wasn't safe to leave the car. Maybe she was being stupid.

Her fingers itched. The ink was telling her to stay.

Margie left the car. *I hope he doesn't have a gun.* Guns had been illegal; Australians didn't have the right to bear arms.

But that didn't mean that they weren't available. Especially now.

She walked across the road, towards the clocks that were situated under the tower at the station. Most of them were shattered. Crossing over the out of use tram tracks, her eyes rested on the building ahead. Her breath seemed to be coming faster in her chest; dots began dancing in front of her eyes. Ink blots. They'd gotten into her vision.

Feeling a new kind of desperation, Margie hurried her pace; almost panting by the time she reached the bottom of the stairs. *Hurry, hurry, hurry.* It was a chant in her mind. If she took too long, it would all be over. The words would win. She would be alone. Insane.

"Hello," a deep voice said.

Margie jumped, feeling shaken. Frantically, she looked around. Federation Square with its ugly buildings — a work of art, they'd said, but not to her — the Young and Jackson pub; St Paul's Cathedral: No one. *No, no, no.* She really was insane. Tears prickled her eyes, and she felt her hollowness expand; like a maw ready to close.

Margie looked at the top of the stairs, started walking towards them. There was a man-shaped inkblot standing there. Tears welled in her eyes, bleeding the ink from her soul. It had all been an illusion. It wasn't real, nothing was real. Her hope — the ink — was toying with her mind.

"Whoa, lady, are you all right?"

A strong hand touched her shoulder, and Margie froze. The ink wasn't physical. Looking up, she gasped. There was a man, with the sun behind him. *He was real.*

But he didn't say anything.

"I thought I was insane; that you were a figment of my imagination."

"I'm real all right," he said.

He turned her around, towards the station, out of the sun. He had a weathered face, with dark hair and prominent, thick eyebrows. Dark, like ink. But his eyes were safe; they didn't hold lies, they weren't blue or red or black. They were brown, honest brown.

Something seemed to bloom within her chest, "I'm not crazy?"

He grinned and the world seemed to brighten. Margie brushed her tears — the poisoning ink — away and felt alive. The ink was fleeing from the new light in her soul.

"I can't vouch for that," he chuckled.

"And you're willing to extend that invite I heard on the radio? Knowing I'm a possible nutter?"

"Don't stress about it now. We'll learn if you're really crazy in time." He gently put a hand on her shoulder and began leading her down the steps.

His hand was warm, warmer than the sun's teasing light. "Have you ever heard of a girl called Kayley? She made this Internet post about what she'd do if the end of the world came. Gave me the idea to set up a community where we could try and rebuild the world..."

AFTERWORD

I've always been a fan of post-apocalyptic novels and stories. What would the world be like, if humanity was all but destroyed? How would we survive?

Then Jennifer came to Morrígan Books with the *Grants Pass* anthology. I fell in love with the concept immediately. I'd just seen *I am Legend,* and quite a few of these stories really evoked that sense of isolation and fear from the movie (despite the very different scenarios).

Both concepts got me thinking.

When I wrote *Ink Blots*, I couldn't help but remember those two situations. I wanted to show what solitude can do to a person. Especially someone trapped in a rather poorly populated country, one that is incredibly isolated and very far from the candle flame of hope.

Humans often crave 'quiet time' (I know I do); but what if that was all you had? How would you cope?

BLACK HEART,
WHITE MOURNING

JAY LAKE

DAY ZERO

I tried to write this all before. I know I done that. More than
once. Every time, I am wrong wrong wrong wrong wrong
wrong wrong wrong.

~~Stupid stupid stupid stupid stupid stupid stupid.~~

Everybody's dead. I don't mind so much. They're quiet
now. At first, I thought zombies were going to get me. How
many dead people can fit into a Cap Metro bus anyway?
They all died like they got somewhere to go. Rushing, afraid.

I live like I got nowhere to go. Rushing, afraid.

Dr. Macushla told me to write it all down. That was back
before everybody died. She's dead, too. Her phone stopped
ringing a long time ago. When I call I just get a quiet noise,
clickie-click like when the CIA is listening in.

I still phone her up sometimes and talk to the clickie-click.
Like it was her. I always used to think therapy was stupid. I
know what Grams said, I know what the judge said, but it
was always stupid. "How do you feel about that, Louella?"
"And how does *that* make you feel, Louella?" "What did the
fires heal, Louella?"

These days I know therapy ain't stupid. Now that I ain't
got it no more. But Dr. Macushla's clickie-click is there when
I call her number, so I tell it all about the things I seen and
done. Like the little white dog I saw in the street yesterday. I
ain't seen a dog in two months, on account of they all died or
ate each other or run off or something. So I seen this little
white dog all shaggy and muddy which goes running

through the gutter like it has somewhere to go and I follow it.

I got food, never will run out with all of Austin dead so fast people didn't have time to burn the grocery stores. (Beef jerky and Hostess snowballs last forever). Maybe it wants food. Finally it stops and lets me come close, then I whisper sweet things like I used to whisper to the matches before Dr. Macushla cured me, then I show it some jerky then it bites me then I kick the little fucker then it cries and bites me again, then I stomp it.

Ok, I lied. I didn't stomp the dog. I just cried til it ran away.

I know you ain't supposed to hurt people or animals or nothing. Except the Black Death hurt us all, so bad we'll never get better, so those rules don't matter no more.

Once someone told me white is the color of mourning in China. Like they wear white to funerals and black to weddings, I guess. So maybe the dog was in mourning or a ghost or something.

~~It took me a while to clean my boots good after.~~

Stupid stupid stupid stupid stupid stupid stupid.

Dr. Macushla's clickie-click tells me all nice how I ain't stupid. Like she used to tell me herself in that little office with the flowered carpet. I tell her about this dog and lie about what I done to the dog, then I lie about lying about the dog. I can hear her nose wrinkling like she does when she knows I ain't being all truthful, then she asks me about the fire again.

People say fire is red, or orange, but fire is black. Really. Go look at a burned up house. You don't see no red, do you? Black char, black ash, black smoke. It's just red for a minute, the way people are just pink for a minute, then when they're dead they're all gray and black and blue and that's how they stay. When fire is gone it's all black, too.

Ashes are the ghosts of fire.

So I'm going to try to write this down again. Maybe this time it won't get lost or the fire won't sneak up on my pages. I'm pasting ruled copy paper inside an old phone book so no one will know it's a journal. 'Cause an old phone book is so useful, I guess.

Tonight I'm going to drive a Porsche. I found a good one with not too many stains on the driver seat after I dumped the crusty, mummified woman out. And cars burn so nice when you're done with them.

DAY ZERO PLUS ONE

I saw the Guy again today. I think he checks out my burning cars. I put them all in a row on the overpass from Mopac to 183, so they are already in the sky before I set them on fire. I'm like an Indian with smoke signals. And you can see halfway across town from up there, when the weather's good.

So the Guy comes and watches sometimes. He leaves me presents along the line of burned up cars. Well, someone does, but the Guy is the only person I run into more than once. I know there's some church people living down by the river in the old Magnolia Cafe. They put notes around town, painted on bed sheets and tablecloths to hang from bridges and power lines.

"JOIN US. FOOD, SAFETY, MEDECINE."

I don't believe that stuff. I don't need it anyway. I ain't afraid of coyotes, and there's nothing bigger here that can bite me. The other stuff that bothers me a lot I tell to Dr. Macushla's clickie-click, and her ghost makes it go away.

Plus I don't trust no one who can't spell. I keep a dictionary with my phone book on account of wanting to keep trusting myself.

They got other notes, too.

"JESUS STILL LOVES YOU."
"THE WORLD IS NOT OVER."

Which just proves they're idiots. Of course the world is over. God just ain't turned out the lights yet.

The Guy ain't one of them. He's about my age, maybe he was in college when the Black Death came. He always wears this Longhorn hoodie, and I'll bet he found a store full of them because he's always clean when I see him. And finding a store full of Longhorn hoodies in Austin wouldn't take a ~~genieus~~ genius.

~~Stupid stupid stupid stupid stupid stupid stupid.~~

That's how I know the presents come from him. They're always stuck inside some Longhorn bullshit. Like who cares about a football team that's all dead and got no one to play but other dead football teams?

Sometimes he leaves me food, like something special maybe he found around town. Hershey bars. A jar of runny peanut butter that I finally reckoned was foreign food sauce. Sometimes he leaves me a nice hat, or gloves. It's coming on the fall here, and even Texas can be cold.

Not that I can't find this stuff for myself easy enough. Austin's a big, empty place, and even I couldn't burn it all down. He's cute about the gifts, though.

Today I see the Guy and he's kind of leaning on the bridge rail down by my second BMW. That was 2010 750il, a big blue one that went real fast and the inside smelled like a shoe store with all the leather and oil smells. No one had died in it, but the keys were in a purse on the ground beside it, which I figured meant someone had dragged the lady away a long time before I found the car.

It went up in flames good, too. I opened one hundred and forty four cans of Sterno from the H.E.B. grocery store and set them around the inside of the car in puddles of camping gas. I always set fire to them with the engine running. That seems fair, like they have a fighting chance. Cars with pop-up headlights are best, because they wink at you while they're dying, but it's also lot of fun to burn a big pile of some yuppie's money.

There's the Guy by my 750il, and he smiles at me all shy like.

I ain't dangerous, everybody knows that. Long as you don't get under my boots, and there's no fire talking to me. I'm a big pussy otherwise. In high school the guys knew this. About my pussy, I mean. I'd let them ~~fuck~~ do me if they'd let me put out cigarettes on their backs and stuff. You'd be amazed how many guys go for that.

But now I take better care of myself. I don't smoke no more, I burn cars instead of jocks, and there's no one touches me but me. Dr. Macushla is proud.

Still, sometimes it's good to see another person who ain't got a shotgun or a Bible ready to come after me with. So I give him a little smile, the kind that says "hey" even if I don't mean it. I swipe a glance at my boots to see if there's no white fur or nothing on them. Then I hunker down by my gold Cadillac Escalade pickup to see what he's going to do.

After a few minutes, he kind of waddles toward me, coming halfway between my 750il and my special edition Saab. "Hey," he says.

The wind is all chilly and plucking at me with a whining sound, but his words carry just fine. I had just talked to Dr. Macushla the day before, so my voice is still ok, even in the weather. "Hey," I say back. I rock on my heels and wish I had a pack of cigarettes.

He'd better not bite me, that's all I am thinking.

The Guy reaches into the belly pocket of his hoodie and real careful takes something out. I ain't afraid of no guns, either. If my time comes, I can't stop it. And who'd kill me? No one owns these cars any more, and there's plenty of everything for everyone. It will all rot and rust and blow away long before we can use it up.

It don't matter. I ~~appreciete~~ appreciate his being careful.

He's got something skinny wrapped in a pale green paper. He skitters it hard toward me, to get the package going up the slope of the highway deck between us. It's wrapped in twine, and the paper is clean, like he just been looting an Office Depot or something.

I crabwalk toward his present and pick it up carefully. It takes me a moment to get the twine off. When I look up again, he's jogging down the ramp toward Mopac. With the old highway behind him, the Guy turns and waves. I can see his smile, even from fifty yards away.

Fuck him if he brings a present and doesn't want to stay for the date. Not like I had any cigarettes to use on him anyway.

Then I realize the present he has given me.

It's a stick of dynamite, wrapped in detonator cord. A little box of blasting caps is duct taped to one end.

Oh, man.

Fire talks to me, not explosions. It's the flames, and the ashes, and the power to transform. I am whole inside where everything else withers. That's what Dr. Macushla says.

But blowing shit up is *COOL*.

The paper's about to blow away. I don't like to litter, so I grab at it. The inside part has a little poster on it, with a headline reading, "The Grants Pass Hoax!!!"

I tucked the scrap inside the ruins of the Escalade and begin the serious business of thinking through what to blow up. Gas station? Bridge pillar? Shopping mall entrance? I'll have to hit a book store and read up on blasting safety, so I don't take off my hand or something.

The Guy is my new boyfriend. I know this now. Pretty soon I'll get a chance to show him what that really means.

DAY ZERO PLUS FOUR

Still keeping the journal. It's only a phone book. Those are everywhere. No more Internet, you want to look something up, it's the best way. Maybe this one will stick. Not like Dr. Macushla or my social worker is going to read it this time around.

I ain't seen the Guy since he gave me the dynamite. Dr. Macushla thinks this is good, that I need to take my time with strangers. She reminds me about the dog.

I'm feeling kind of bad about that, so I've started raiding white sheets and table cloths — there's plenty up here in north Austin, so the church people must get theirs for banners from some other part of town — and whenever I find a body in my way, I cover it with white. I like to think of it as a Chinese funeral.

I've burned three more cars, but didn't want to use the dynamite on them. That would be wrong. Destructive.

Most cars won't start anyway, unless they're a stick and you can get them going along a hill. A lot of them have bad tires now. When I really want a car that ain't in the right place or is an automatic, I have a battery rig bungeed to a hand truck. I keep it charged up from other cars before I burn them up on the bridge, so I can use it to jump a new car. But that thing is a pain in the ass to haul around.

And when I do, they don't always catch. I figure after another wet winter, there will be too much water in the gas tanks, and the gas will be too stale. Already is, half the time. Maybe I'll set wildfires next summer.

For now, I'm not done with my bridge of cars. These three latest were a Dodge Viper — I can't never tell the year on those without looking at the plate under the hood — along with a really sweet 1975 Cadillac Eldorado convertible, and a pimped out 2009 Mercedes SL550. Each of them was a pleasure in their own way. There's a couple of stretches of Mopac where I can hit well over a hundred before I have to slow down to weave through the wrecks and abandoned cars.

There were two dead ladies in the back of the Eldorado, their dried-up bodies gray haired with rotting silk Sunday-go-to-church dresses on, curled together like they'd climbed in there to die. Them I laid out side by side and did a Chinese funeral on. Maybe I'll burn bodies when I run out of cars, but people smell funny when they go up.

Well, live people do. I don't suppose everybody who's been dead for a year and half will. I never did tell Dr. Macushla how I know that about burning people, and the judge didn't have enough evidence to blame me for certain, or it would have been a lot worse than therapy for me, back before the Black Plague.

The end of the world was the best thing that ever happened to me.

I decide to have a picnic along my bridge of cars. Spam, Twinkies, diet cherry Dr Pepper, some wild onions I found in the bar ditch alongside the highway. Good eating. Getting everything spread out, I see the Guy has left me another present, tucked under a pebbled paving stone shaped like Texas.

I check it out.

A map of Oregon.

This confuses me. Like, he's always come by with practical stuff before. As if he cared. And the dynamite was a real gift, from the heart. But Oregon's thousands of miles away in Canada or someplace. Nearly foreign.

I look the map over anyway, to see if there's something written on it. I used to know a kid who could read secret messages in the way the freight trains ran. The order and color of the box cars was a CIA way of telling things to spy satellites, secrets too powerful to be put on the radio or Craigslist, even in special codes. It always sounded kind of weird to me, but the messages he could read made *sense*. At least when he read them.

So I scan for codes. What I find is a pink highlight circle drawn around a town called Grants Pass.

Home of the hoax.

Which makes me wonder what the Grants Pass hoax is, exactly.

I go to the Escalade and find the green paper. It had been rained on a little, and was smeared with black ash, but it isn't ruined yet. I read all the tiny crazy person handwriting at the bottom. Somehow I don't think it was the Guy's. He seemed like he was passing it on, not preaching to me.

It's all about some crazy girl and her plan to rebuild civilization without warlords or taxes or whatever, in this little town in Oregon with her friends with stupid names, and the scribbled writing says how this is really a plot devised by Satan to trap anyone unlucky enough to survive the plagues and destruction, which had swept this mortal Earth free of the stain of sin blah blah blah.

I quit reading after I got to the "stain of sin" part. I don't believe in Satan anyway, he's just a way the Bible Belters have of pretending it's not their fault when they fuck their kids in the ass or rip off people too poor to go to the cops or hire a lawyer. And I'm *lucky* to survive the plagues, not unlucky.

The thing probably wasn't a hoax, on account of whoever wrote the little poster was so crazy I want to believe the opposite just on principle. Even so, who wants to go to Oregon anyway? It's cold there, and full of moss and mold and bigfoots and shit.

I tuck the green paper back in the Escalade, along with the map, and weigh them both down with the Texas-shaped stone so the wind won't take them away in case I want them again. Then I go back to my feast.

Oregon.

Why?

Who cares?

Plenty of cars here in Texas, anyway.

DAY ZERO PLUS SIX

Stupid stupid stupid stupid stupid stupid stupid.

~~Cunt cunt cunt cunt cunt cunt cunt.~~

Dr. Macushla says I'm not supposed to say that word. Not about myself. But sometimes I deserve it. I have stubbed some lit matches on the inside of my forearm to punish myself, but I deserve worse. Far, far worse.

I scored a 2010 Bentley Arnage today. A sweet, sweet ride, I'm telling you. It went 140 like it was in the driveway. Quietest car I ever drove. No one dead inside, as clean as the 750il had been. I got it up my ramp finally, set it in place to burn, filled it with crumpled Christmas paper from Walgreen's, all soaked in lamp oil.

When the Bentley went up, this kid finally comes bailing out of the trunk. I never knew she was in there. Hell, I never knew she was around at all. You don't see a lot of people these days. Her hair is smoldering, and she is screaming, ~~and she surprises me so bad that I stomp her like I'd stomped the white dog.~~

I let her go. There's some things you don't do. You don't even think about ~~having done~~ doing them.

Stupid stupid stupid stupid stupid stupid stupid.

I can't do nothing else, so I give her a Chinese funeral, and push her body into the flames. That's a kind of letting go, isn't it? The sick, sweet, crispy pork smell is so familiar it makes me cry and puke, and I stumble to the edge of the bridge and throw up over the rail.

Then I see the Guy watching me. He's got a funny look on him, like he thinks I'm crazy.

Now, on top of everything else, I'm scaring off my boyfriend.

"Hey," I say, and start toward him, but his face gets real twisted and he runs off. I turn around, and my boot prints are bloody dark.

I got to go call Dr. Macushla, real bad.

Stupid stupid stupid stupid stupid stupid stupid.

DAY ZERO PLUS SIX AGAIN

Down at the Circle K off Mesa Hills Drive, I talk to the clickie-click on the phone behind the clerk's counter. I'm not crazy, I know Dr. Macushla's been dead long as everybody else, but it is her phone and her phone number. It's almost like talking to her. And it helps me. So shut up, if you're reading this.

She's real sad with me. Says my heart is black as night. Says she's tired of me, and can't work with me no more. Says I've used up my welcome here in Austin, that I'm a danger to myself and others.

Or maybe it was the judge who said that. When I'm real stressed out I don't remember so good.

Maybe the end of the world isn't as hot as I like to think it is. Maybe I made some mistakes. Maybe I'm not as good at all this as I like to pretend.

I whisper to her how sorry I am. I tell her I'm going to make amends. The social workers always like those written apologies. I can use my journal, make this entire thing an apology.

Maybe everybody's dead and nobody cares what I do. Maybe I'm crazy. Except I can't be, because I still remember everyone and everything.

It's coming on a storm outside. The sky is the color of an old bruise, swollen and leaky. The wind has that crackle smell like it was lightning's cousin. I put down the phone and go outside and apologize to the raindrops.

Rain.

It rains in Oregon, I realize. Like, all the time. As if God meant the place to be the world's drain.

My heart might be black as night, but that can be washed away in water. That's what the Bible Belters say with their ~~baptisums~~ baptisms. And water is the opposite of fire, right?

Right?

I make a big space in my journal, and use really giant letters:

WATER IS THE OPPOSITE OF FIRE

For the first time since the nurses got sick on the psych ward, back when this all started, I feel hope.

DAY ZERO PLUS TEN

I'm ready now.

I found a nice little 1985 Geo Metro. Old, so I might be able to fix it if it breaks. Here's what I got in the car:

> My journal
> My dictionary
> A box of ball-point pens
> A 24-pack of sanitary napkins in case this takes weeks
> Forty gallons of siphoned gas in the back seat in five gallon plastic containers
> A full tank
> My stupid battery stand in case the Geo dies and I need to start another car.

Cables to charge the batteries every night when I stop

A toolbox I got from a Midas Muffler shop

The green sheet and the map of Oregon from the Escalade

A trucker's atlas of the United States from the Circle K

More Hostess snowballs and Twinkies than I can keep track of

Four cases of Slim Jims

Ten gallons of water

A blanket

A dozen white sheets in case of Chinese funerals

Matches, lots of matches

There's just enough room for the Guy in the front seat, if he don't mind all the food stuck under where his legs will go. If I don't find him, I'll just burn cars along the way so he can follow my pillars of fire and smoke through the wilderness. My heart might be black, but I'll cover it in white mourning until I get to Grants Pass. That girl Kayley will take me in.

And if she doesn't, well, fire is the devil's only friend.

There's a lot of miles between here and there. Lot of cars to burn.

Last thing I do before I go cruising for the Guy is drive up to my bridge of cars and say good-bye to the kid I ~~killed~~ didn't kill.

"I didn't mean to be stupid," I tell her charred bones all quiet like, where she lies under the Bentley's back bumper. "And I'll make it up to you by being a better person."

That's what I have to tell the world, I guess, and all of everyone in it that's died and rotted away.

I'm leaving this journal with her. I'll start another one on the road. I won't need an Austin phone book on the way to Oregon anyway.

If you're reading this, good-bye. And if you're not reading this, good-bye anyway. Watch for the fires. You'll recognize me because I'll be the only living person wrapped in a white sheet.

I'll make it up to all of you by being a better person.

BIOGRAPHY

JAY LAKE

Jay Lake lives in Portland, Oregon, where he works on numerous writing and editing projects. His 2008 novels are *Escapement* from Tor Books and *Madness of Flowers* from Night Shade Books, while his short fiction appears regularly in literary and genre markets worldwide. Jay is a winner of the John W. Campbell Award for Best New Writer, and a multiple nominee for the Hugo and World Fantasy Awards.

AFTERWORD

I lived in Austin for 18 years, from the time I moved there to go to college until I left to move to Oregon, not terribly far from Grants Pass, at least as seen from Texas.

When I heard about this anthology, I really wanted to write about the story of my relocation, through the lens of this concept. I've written a couple of my old cars into it, and a former workplace of mine, so you could say the piece is autobiographical. Except for all the parts which aren't, of course. Differentiating the two is left as an exercise for the reader. Hint: I am male, and have never killed anything more neurologically complex than a cockroach. I have, however, messed up a few cars in my day.

BY THE SEA

SHANNON PAGE

Elizabeth Barnett stood on the veranda, lifting a wiry hand to shade her eyes as she watched Christos sail away. The sun gleaming off the Mediterranean assaulted her, but the light was beautiful all the same. Sometimes the loveliness here made it hard to remember how thoroughly everything had gone wrong.

Or maybe she was just being an old fool. Sunlight, kilometers of pale beaches thrust against bright blue water, hills covered with scrubby brush, khaki-colored rocks, and the occasional dark green cypress tree — it was not enough to hide the fact that she was very likely the last person left on the island. The last living person, anyway.

She snorted and turned away from the sea before Christos, in his little white sailboat, had moved out of sight. No point in watching him go. He wouldn't be back. She'd seen to that — they'd fought for weeks like rabid dogs. Or plague-infested weasels, more like. In the end, she'd set her teeth and scratched his lovely face with her long fingernails until the blood touched his chin. And still he stood, pleading.

"Beth, come to Grants Pass, I know it's real."

"It's a lie, and you're never going to get there on that damn fool thing anyway."

"This is our only chance."

"We have no chance."

He'd simply stood there, looking at her.

"*I* have no chance," she'd finally added, her voice bitter and dry. "I'm seventy-eight years old, and you know my health. I'll die out on the water."

"You'll die here." He'd leaned forward, almost touching her, but holding back.

That was when she'd scratched him, digging in with every last shred of strength she had. It was either that or touch him in a different way, and she'd held on to at least that much dignity, through it all.

Now she would not watch him go. The world had died; what difference would one more person make?

❧

"Kayley's journal," Beth said out loud as she heated a slab of halloumi over a wood fire she'd built in the stove. Bitter as it still was, at least her voice had lost its edge of testy near-panic, she thought. Three days Christos had been gone, and although she was growing accustomed to the terrible silence, she still felt the need to speak to the air from time to time.

She'd made this batch of the cheese herself, and she was proud of it, even if it didn't have the tenacity of the stuff she'd been able to find at the market when she'd first bought this property, fifteen years ago. Or even the weaker but still salty-sweet cheese that Christos had come up with, using the thin milk they'd managed to glean from the last goat.

"Bunch of adolescent fantasies."

She might as well talk aloud. There was no one to hear, no one to judge. No one to answer.

...No one to brush her thinning grey hair, to stroke her hard and ropy shoulder muscles, to clear the weeds from her front walk. No one to argue back to her. To bring her a drink when the sun went down. To glance up from his work in what passed for her garden, his dark eyes smoldering at her as he...

"Stop it, you stroppy old cow," she muttered to herself. She finished toasting the cheese and then stood over the stove, eating it with callused fingers that hardly felt the heat of it.

Then she stood, staring unseeing out the window as she remembered.

❦

Elizabeth Barnett, international best-selling author of *The Caged Sword* series of dark and twisted romantic fantasy novels. Elizabeth Barnett, the toast of London, New York, and Prague literary circles — at least, those circles civilized enough to consider the genre of romantic fantasy. Elizabeth Barnett, who shocked the world by retiring at the height of her fame and purchasing a three-million-pound estate in the hills outside Larnaka, Cyprus, with her third husband, James — seventeen years her junior and famous in his own right as the developer of those ridiculous computer games that children played, instead of reading decent fantasy novels.

"The writing was on the wall," she said to the window. The sea shimmered far below her, and Christos was not coming back.

❦

James had been one of the first to die. Maybe he had even brought the plague back with him, on his last trip to France...but if he hadn't, someone else would have. The plane had been full of people, and there had been ten more flights after that, before all air traffic had stopped. Beth had sat with him in the Apollonion Hospital on the Greek side of Nicosia — even then, with the wall down, the city was still deeply divided between Turk and Greek — holding his hand as he coughed blood, sobbed, and finally choked out his last breath. The sad-eyed doctors had searched their stub of what remained of the Internet, pumped him full of expired antibiotics, anti-inflammatories, and steroids, and mopped up the effluent that had poured from her beautiful husband. He had died all the same.

"You filthy bastards! You swine, you cowards, you Mediterranean cretins!" she had shrieked at them, wailing and beating at the chest of the infuriatingly calm chief resident. He'd stood and listened to her, blinking his large dark eyes, waiting for her to wind down.

It was those Greek eyes that had prompted her to move here in the first place, when she could finally afford it. Not this doctor's eyes per se, of course; but dark Greek eyes in general, remembered from some long-ago junket she'd taken with her editor and her agent. Three middle-aged British women on holiday, slumming in a sea of sweet Greek manflesh. Beth had always remembered that trip, long after she'd married reedy blond James. She'd always intended to end her life here.

Just not like this.

Beth shook her head, still standing at the window, the fire gone cold in the stove, the uneaten bits of halloumi sticking to her fingers, cloying. She felt sick to her stomach, and wondered for the thousandth time if the plague had finally found her as well.

"No, nothing can kill you, old loon," she said aloud, half-affectionately. She turned away from the window, taking the greasy pan from the stove. She set it in the sink without rinsing it. There wasn't much water left in the bucket anyway; she'd have to go to the stinking well for more.

Instead she went to the basement, or what passed for one. It was a low space half-dug into the rocky hillside, intended for a wine cellar. But Cypriot wine was harsh and sour, and her English palate had never adapted.

She stood blinking in the dim space, waiting for her old eyes to adjust, and pulled down a fresh bottle of Bombay gin. She stocked the large bottles — 1.75 liters — even though they were hard to maneuver above her glass, especially as the evening progressed. Before leaving the cellar, Beth counted the bottles. There were eighteen, not including the one she had in her hand.

"That's all you've got," she said. "After that, it's all over." Her words were swallowed by the earthen walls.

Seven weeks after Christos sailed away, Elizabeth Barnett sat in a leather chair with one of her own books in her lap — book seven of *The Caged Sword* series, and her personal favorite: *Man and His Weaknesses*. She could hardly stand to read books written by anyone else. They were never written as she would have done; they were over too soon, or too late; the relationship between the hero and heroine never rang true; and the endings were always contrived, seemingly invented merely for the purpose of making a good story.

Well, of course they were, she knew that. But other people's imaginations, to Beth, just seemed...inferior.

So she read her own work. And certainly there was plenty of it. When twilight fell, she lit a fire in the hearth and a small candle by her chair, refilled the glass of gin, and picked up the book again, chuckling to herself as Larion prepared to storm the Fair Castle Rhuligel and save Marleena. Naturally, Marleena would refuse to be saved; that was when the fireworks would start. "Oh, you minx, you little vixen," she murmured.

That was when she heard the crash from the back yard.

Beth froze, holding the heavy hardcover on her lap. What was it? Definitely something large. Another goat?

She heard another noise, not a crash this time, more like a bump. It was closer to the house.

She slowly got to her feet, leaving the book on the chair. A goat would be good news: it would mean milk, or at least meat. She walked over to the doorway and peered down the hall, craning to see the back of the house, but it was too dark inside. A small window was set high on the back wall of the living room for cross-ventilation.

She sidled over to the window and stood on tiptoes, but could not reach to see out.

She could hear, though. She heard footsteps.

"Who's there?" she called, making her voice strong, projecting to the rear of the audience as she had done for years.

The footsteps stopped.

A goat would have kept on, ignoring her in its desperate search for food. What other animal could it be? The dogs were all long dead, eaten mostly by one another, and then by the remaining people.

And the people were long dead as well. Most of them, anyway. If one in ten thousand humans had survived the plagues, that would have left Cyprus with a population of eighty. Not counting tourists, of course...but the tourist trade had slowed greatly before the final plagues. The last ten flights in had been matched by as many flights out before the planes were grounded for good.

Moving quietly, Beth left the living room and went into the hallway that led to the back door. It was darker here, and there was still a little light outside. She made her way to the window in the door, staying back a bit so as not to be seen.

A man stood in her back yard. He was staring at the house, the roof. The chimney. He must have smelled the smoke from her fire.

Ignoring the clutch of fear in her chest, Beth studied the man. He looked terrible; he was clearly starving, and filthy. But he didn't seem plague-bit. He was about fifty, maybe, though it was hard to tell in his condition — no, she corrected herself. It was impossible to tell. He could be thirty or seventy, who knew?

Anyway, he appeared weak. Frail as Beth was, he was likely not a significant threat.

By the looks of him, he was not Greek or Turk or Armenian or any of the other more customary inhabitants of the island. He could be at least as English as she was.

What were the odds?

As she watched, the man suddenly became animated. She sucked in her breath and pulled back farther from the window. He took a step toward the house, then stumbled and pitched forward.

"Oh," Beth said, as the man landed on his face on her cobblestones.

He lay on a narrow bed in the guest room, still unconscious. Beth cleaned and bandaged his bloody forehead, and had brought in some more halloumi — the last she had, it would be canned food after this unless she found more milk — in case he woke up. He was breathing, but unsteadily; his temperature seemed high, but she was no doctor. Beth had never been a mother either, had never wiped a fevered brow as people did in her novels. Maybe he was plague-bit. But no, there were no buboes, there was no swelling. And the only blood was from his cut.

She sat in a hard chair beside him, biting her lip. It had taken much of her strength to drag him here, and lift him up onto the bed. She wouldn't have been able to do it at all if he hadn't been so emaciated.

The man's eyelids flickered and he gave a small moan.

Beth leaned forward, peering into his face. "Are you awake?"

"Ah..." One eye fluttered open, then shut. He gave a long, sour exhale.

Beth touched his shoulder, giving him a light shake, and touched his forehead again, next to the bandage. "Wake up."

He was silent a moment, then both eyes opened. "Wh...mou...uh..."

"Do you speak English?" she asked.

Now his eyes opened wider. "Yes."

"That's good." Beth stared into his face before looking away. "But then of course you do, everyone does."

The man blinked, staring at her. He asked, "Where...where is everyone?" His accent was flat, broad — American, perhaps.

"What do you mean?"

He swallowed and glanced around the room. His face filled with fear. Terror, even. "Nobody's here, are they?"

"I'm here." Was the man a fool? Quite likely. Most people were fools, and if they hadn't been before the world fell apart, they certainly were now. Or, rather, they were dead now, the vast majority of them. And the fools like Christos had sailed off to follow a dream, a computer hoax, a cruel fantasy someone had written, about a place called Grants Pass, where society would begin again. As if there was any chance of that.

"You..." The man struggled to sit up, and Beth didn't stop him. He leaned against the pillows and shivered in the heat. "Who are you?"

"Elizabeth Barnett." She watched his eyes as she said her name, but he gave no flicker of recognition. "Who are you?"

"Tyler." He blinked and swallowed, and she stared at his throat, but saw no swelling. "Tyler Anderson."

"I am pleased to meet you, Tyler Anderson," Beth said, slipping into the tone she would use when greeting over-eager fans.

Tyler closed his eyes, leaned against the headboard, then opened them again. He had already smeared the white coverlet with his filthy, stained hands. But without water, she'd have no way of washing them. Everything was just going to get dirtier and dirtier from here on out, until everything was the color of the sun-baked earth. Including herself.

"Is it true that California...?" His eyes appealed to her as he broke off, then started again. "Is San Diego really ruined?"

Now Beth stared at him. "That was two years ago."

She was not a nurse, she told herself that she didn't care if he lived or died, but for some reason she fed him and cleaned him up a bit, and changed the bandage on his forehead. The bleeding slowed and stopped, and seemed like it would heal.

Once he was cleaner, she saw that he was even younger than she'd realized. Probably in his twenties, though he'd lived a hard life during those few years. Well, who hadn't, lately?

He slept a lot, and ate the halloumi she brought, and the canned foods. Beth began to wonder if she'd need to make another raid on the neighboring houses, or even — god forbid — venture down into Larnaka again. Christos had packed the small cellar full before he'd left, even as he'd continued to beg her to change her mind. But an old woman didn't eat nearly as much as a young man.

Within a week, Tyler was able to walk around a little, and a day or two later, he washed himself, using most of a bucket of brackish water. Beth brought him pants and a cotton shirt that had belonged to James, handing it to him without comment.

Tyler dressed himself, then came and found Beth in the living room.

"Drink?" she asked, indicating the bottle of Bombay on the sideboard.

"Oh my god," he said, his blue eyes glittering with a touch of madness. Or at least that's how she would have written it, as she thought about it later. In the moment, she only thought, *Now, there's a healthy young man who appreciates quality gin.*

He poured himself a full three fingers of the stuff, his arms shaking as he lifted the heavy bottle with both hands. Sitting in the second leather chair, he raised the glass and smiled at her.

She lifted her half-empty glass, and they clinked.

He took a generous swallow of the gin, closing his eyes as it went down, and turned to face Beth, grinning. "Oh, man. That's incredible."

She lifted an eyebrow. "I take it it's been a while?"

"Ha!" It wasn't a laugh; more like an ironic bark, and a bit too loud. "Yes, it has. I'd say two years, at least."

Beth leaned forward, holding him with her eyes. "So, Tyler, tell me: what do you know of what has gone on in our world these last few years?"

He took another drink, not quite as gulpish as his last, but she still noted it. *If he drinks like that, eighteen bottles won't be near enough,* she thought. "Not a whole hell of a lot, to tell you the truth."

"What's an American boy doing in Cyprus anyway, now, knowing nothing? If I didn't know better, I'd say you've been in prison."

Now he did laugh, though it was as bitter as before. "Why, yes, as a matter of fact, I was in prison." He finished the glass of gin, setting it quite deliberately on the table beside his chair, next to the cut-glass coaster.

It turned out to be the usual story — young tourist arrested for drugs in a country with little patience for such things, thrown into prison to teach him a lesson. It would have had the usual outcome — his parents sending money or coming to retrieve him, a whole lot of nuisance and no lasting ill effects — except for the unfortunate timing of the apocalypse.

Tyler spoke no Greek, no Turkish, nothing but English. His parents had presumably died in the initial earthquake, but he didn't know for sure, as communications went down almost immediately thereafter. The plagues had come then, sweeping across the world. He had known almost nothing of this as he languished in prison, waiting for rescue, for anything. His guards changed weekly, then daily, with no explanation. Then one died right in front of him, and he finally, belatedly, understood.

"How did you get out of the locked cell?" Beth asked him, swirling her drink.

He shrugged, looking down. "Reached out, took the keys from him. I thought for sure I'd get the plague then, but I guess not." His words were casual, but his face was bleak. There was more to the story. If he wanted to tell her, he would.

He was vague on the timing — how long he had been out of the prison, surviving on the rough countryside. But that was because he didn't know, Beth felt, not because he was trying to deceive. It had obviously been a while. He must have wandered the entire island before finding her. Christos had come to her in the first few weeks after the initial devastation, when the few survivors were banding together. And Christos had stayed with her when the others had left the island. Until he, too, could no longer resist the empty promise of a dream.

Tyler's strength grew, and soon enough he was poking around the place, exploring neighboring houses, trying to figure out ways to improve their lot. Just like Christos had done. Beth was pleased enough to have the help, although she'd been doing perfectly well on her own, thank you very much. Tyler began talking more, yammering on to her in the evenings about everything and nothing — his boyhood in California, girls he'd liked, his world travels on a shoestring. She took to retiring early, going to her room with a book and a candle where she could read in peace until she felt like sleeping.

"What's this?" he asked one day. Beth was in the kitchen, trying to decide whether to light a fire to heat up the canned lakerda or just eat it cold. She turned around at the sound of his voice. He was holding a sheaf of papers.

Beth recognized them at once. "Where did you get that?"

Tyler shrugged. "I was cleaning up, I found them. Is it true?"

"Give me those." Beth reached out for the papers, but Tyler held them away from her. "I asked you where you got that."

He stared at her, his eyes wide and needful. "We could find other people. We could go; we don't have to stay here!"

"Put that down. You're a goddamned fool, do you know that?"

He started to say something else, but she interrupted. "I said, *put that down*, and don't speak of it to me again."

He paled and set the papers on the counter, backing out of the kitchen.

Beth took the Grants Pass email hoax, intending to put it back in her bedroom, where Tyler had had no business snooping in the first place. She had made it perfectly clear that her room was off limits, yet where else had he gotten it? It was the only copy.

She stopped at the doorway, thinking for a moment, and then went back into the kitchen to light the fire.

But once he'd read it, he wouldn't let it go. He was worse than Christos. "We can be saved!"

"You go ahead if you like," she said. "I'm fine here."

"I can't leave you here. You're, um, you'll die." He was shaking his head, stubborn, desperate. "Please!"

She laughed in his face. "You were going to tell me I'm old. I *know* I'm old, and I know I'm going to die. And therefore, I'm not going anywhere."

"We can take a boat — there're plenty of boats left in the harbor."

"And petrol?" She sneered at his naiveté. "Do you know how many people already left the island? You don't think they left a lot of petrol lying around? That's why Christos sailed, you idiot American. And now he sleeps with the sharks."

He bristled. "You don't know that for sure. And yes, I am American — what of it? Why shouldn't I want to go home?"

She waved at the harbor. "I am not stopping you."

That night, she heard him sobbing in his bedroom, long after she'd gone to her own. "Mom...oh, Mom..."

So that was it: he missed his mommy. And he'd fixated on Beth, in some sort of perverse mother-complex way. She snorted to herself. "More like a grandmother."

But the next morning he was at her again. She had to shout at him again to get him to stop. He stormed out without eating breakfast, and spent the day somewhere else. Down at the water, if she was any judge.

He returned at twilight, calm, not mentioning where he'd been. She offered him a glass of gin, and they sat on the veranda, drinking together.

After two drinks, he said, "I found a boat. I think it could make it across the ocean. And it's got a full tank of gas. So I know I could find more."

"I'm not leaving," she said, without turning her head. The sun glimmered red on the water as it sank. "I hate America.

SHANNON PAGE

And I forbade you to speak of this." She set her glass down, got up, and went inside.

She walked all the way to her bedroom, then through it into her small private bathroom. Of course she didn't use it as a bathroom any more — the septic tank was overfull, and there was nobody to call to come clean it out — but it had other uses. She opened the medicine cabinet, first looking, then rummaging, then yanking everything out. But they weren't there.

He'd not only stolen the email from her bedroom. He'd also raided her stash of narcotics, carefully hoarded from James' final illness.

Beth stood before the ransacked medicine cabinet, shaking with anger. She had to make him leave. He was not like Christos — he was worse, far worse. Bad enough that he would harangue her, try to control her. But that he should steal from her — that he should steal *drugs* from her — a man who had already gone to prison for drugs — oh, this was not good. A man whose life she'd saved.

"Not good," she whispered.

She felt a prickle on the back of her neck and wheeled around. He was standing in the doorway of the small bathroom. She hadn't even heard him come in.

He was pale, and shaking. Now that she knew, she recognized the signs easily. He must have taken several pills, and then two — at least two — glasses of gin on top of that. "Beth," he started, taking a step towards her. The name was a bit slurred, the consonants softer than they should be.

"Get out of here," she said.

He took another step, and now he was right in front of her. He reached up and took her shoulders in his hands, hard, and shook her. It hurt. She pushed back against his chest, trying to twist out of his grip, but he was decades younger than she, and very strong. "We...have...to...go," he

270

said, staring at her even as he rattled her thin bones. His eyes were too liquid, too glossy. "I'll *make* you go."

She pushed harder, and he abruptly let go, staggering back and bumping into the wall behind him. He didn't seem to notice. "You're drunk," she said. "Go and lie down. We'll talk about this in the morning."

He looked at her, wary. "You mean it? We'll talk about it?"

She shrugged, resisting the urge to rub her throbbing shoulders. "You are in no condition to talk now."

He kept staring at her, then turned and went to his own bedroom. She stood in the bathroom a long time, shaking, listening as he fell onto his bed. He was snoring within a few minutes. Only then did she pull her shirt open and examine the bruises, peering into the mirror. He'd crushed her shoulders so hard she could almost see the imprint of his fingerprints.

Beth re-buttoned her shirt and left the bathroom. She knew what she had to do.

She stood over his bed as he snored. He looked so helpless and frail, lying there. Almost innocent. Though she'd never had children, sometimes she could understand the appeal. Having someone to love, someone to take care of.... Of course, she'd had James for that.

Tyler was somebody's son. His mother and father had loved him and raised him, and had let him go, had watched as he had flown the nest. He'd flown far — all the way across the world, where he'd gotten in trouble and caught up in the terrible things that humanity had done to itself. Maybe he'd deserved better. Maybe not. Who knew anymore?

But it was too late now. There was no better to be had, and if he was going to refuse to understand that, there was nothing she could do about it.

She raised the knife, leaning over him to reach the far side of his neck. In book 8 of *The Caged Sword* series, *A Clutch of Posies*, Marleena finds she must murder the Lord of Terror, using only a dull kitchen knife. In her fear and hesitation, she botches the job at first, and he awakens and threatens her, but in a stroke of luck, as he is leaping onto her, the knife nicks his jugular and he dies. Then all the Sisters are freed, and the land rejoices.

Tyler's white, exposed neck was surprisingly tough at first, despite Beth's knife being as sharp as it could be. She remembered slaughtering the goats, and pushed harder. When she thought of it as butchering meat, it came easily. She even knew to step back so as not to get soaked with his blood.

The covers, of course — that was another story. Tyler's blood spurted at first, another rush with every beat of his heart. Impossible to believe there could be so much; but the goats had been even worse. Soon it ebbed out more slowly, flowing down his body as he twitched, gurgled, and stilled. It spread across the white cotton coverlet, pooling and sinking in, threading fanlike out along the folds of the fabric. Beth watched it for a long time, unmoving, and finally turned to go.

She shut the door of the guest bedroom behind her, turning the latch that would keep it fast. The corpse would smell at first, but she knew that in this hot, dry climate, it would soon desiccate, even mummify. In any event, she could put a towel under the door if she had to. She wouldn't need that room any time soon.

She walked down the hall to the kitchen, washed the knife, and laid it on the counter to dry. Then, she went to her bookshelf and pulled down the final book in her series: *Alone at Heart*.

Night fell as Elizabeth Barnett sat on the veranda with a tumbler of warm gin, the book unopened beside her, and waited for her world to finish ending.

BIOGRAPHY

SHANNON PAGE

Shannon Page was born on Halloween night and spent her early years on a commune in northern California's backwoods. A childhood without television gave her a great love of books and the worlds she found in them. She wrote her first book, an adventure story starring her cat, at the age of seven. Sadly, that work is currently out of print. Her stories have appeared in *Interzone* and *Black Static* and she has several forthcoming short-story publications from Morrígan Books, Gilgamesh Press, and Three Crows Press. Shannon is a longtime practitioner of Ashtanga yoga, has no tattoos, and lives in San Francisco with nineteen orchids.

AFTERWORD

About ten years ago, I went to Cyprus. The stark beauty of the place has stayed with me ever since, along with a sense of how incredibly isolated it would be without modern transportation and communication. When I was sent the call for submissions for *Grants Pass*, I loved the idea, and the character of Beth came to me at once.

REMEMBRANCE

JAMES M. SULLIVAN

Dr. Bhanu Daswani,

I have sent along the following transcript, which was recovered from a dig site in Oregon. Dr. Crystal Jefferson was the archaeologist who made the discovery.

This evidence is fascinating and if further tests prove conclusive, it could be the first personal account of the Collapse on record. Of course, we know Kayley Allard's fate, but this early information is incredible.

Please send me your opinions; your historical expertise will be invaluable with this project.

Dr. Mary Tillinghaust

The fresh scent of wet grass fills the air. I feel cleansed by the recent downpour. The crispness and the rain-speckled flora provide a sense of newness; a feeling that all is right with the world and that what has come to pass did not. I know that there will be many others who will record what has taken place with much more skill than I, not to mention with more information of what actually happened and where. Please forgive me, I'm no author, poet, or historian, but I do think what I know should be written down.

I do not have specifics, at least not about anything that happened outside of San Francisco. I suppose I should start at the beginning. That is always where they say to start — though I never figured out who 'they' were.

JAMES A. SULLIVAN

I was in San Francisco on business, leading a training class for an in-house product database. I had been there three days and I was already beginning to miss the greenness of Seattle, where I had lived for the past seven years. I guess none of this matters; it is strange how that even after the world rebooted (at least that's how I've come to think about the devastation that has happened to us), I still lapse into thinking in terms of my old life. I'll never train another class on how to use computer programs. I'll never again go to my office. I'll never see Seattle again, most likely, and even if I do, it will not be the Seattle I remember. I hope that my family shares the same immunities that I seem to possess. I'm rambling; I suppose I should get to the point.

It was the third of June. I was unwinding in my hotel room after a frustratingly long day of training people who shouldn't be let near computers. I'd crawled into bed and clicked on the television. I remember the comforter was splashed with bright colors vaguely reminiscent of tropical flowers. It's funny, the details that stick in your mind. As I recall, I had to turn the television up to compete with the noise of the rain. There had been off and on drizzle all day, but now it was pounding against the thick glass of the hotel window. So much for sunny California, eh?

I returned my attention to the broadcast with its neatly pressed and coifed news anchors who proceeded to inform viewers about the strange and fierce strain of SVHF — Severe Viral Hemorrhagic Fever — that was quickly becoming an epidemic in southern California and Sydney, Australia. They cut to highlights of an interview with a doctor who claimed to be an expert on communicable diseases. I do not recall if he was from the Centers for Disease Control or not. His theory was that SVHF was related to the Ebola virus. He prattled on about how the two could be connected. Frankly, he was talking over my head.

Somewhere during his dissertation the national news interrupted the local.

There was yet another malady at work. I could not believe what I was hearing. A Super Flu had overtaken Washington D.C. The flu was also appearing in other cities; the capitals of all the countries belonging to the United Nations. I was dumbfounded. Did the conspiracy theorists have it correct? I'm certain that I would have sat there for hours taking in the varied hypotheses of experts, ignoring the world outside, but the world outside had other plans.

I barely registered the first roll of the earthquake, but soon enough it was clear that it was a big one. I was born in California and had lived there until I was twelve. I knew I had to get out of the building. I grabbed my shoes and laptop, and dashed for the door as a major jolt thrust me forward, stumbling. The television came crashing to the floor, its screen exploding. Everything happened so fast. I was in the hall, the floor pulling down and away from my feet as I ran; there was the cracking of wood and breaking of cement. My eyes stung from plaster dust. The conditioning of growing up in earthquake country kicked in and I quickly moved towards a sturdy doorway; the emergency exit.

I was nearly there when a loud crack dominated the rest of the bedlam and I was thrown to the floor as the entire corridor heaved forward. I've no idea how I got up again, but I did, and now survival instinct overrode any conditioning. I was determined to get out. I started down the stairwell — half running, half tumbling.

I was only on the second floor, yet it seemed like all the distance in world at that moment. What happened next is just a blur and I can't really tell you exactly what occurred.

I do know that I came to on my chest. The first thing that registered was the pain. I ached. Certainly worse than when Mikey O'Connell had beaten me up after school. It hurt more than the only car accident I had been in. Just trying to shift my weight resulted in spasms of agony; I was sure that I was bruised head to toe and that more than one bone was broken. The smell of ozone and copper was stinging my nostrils, and just beyond that was the wretched combination of fetid garbage and piss. I choked back the bile rising in my throat.

Finally, I opened my eyes and saw only darkness. My legs were caught under something. I could feel them, and even wiggle my toes, but I couldn't move them. Then I heard the sounds from outside. It was a dreadful cacophony: people screaming for help, ambulance sirens and wailing children; all of it a distorted echo reverberating around me.

I don't know how long I was there in the dark, trapped with my own thoughts of various worst case scenarios and wondering if I had even made it out of the hotel. I remember reading a website that had said that earthquake training — to get to a doorway — made it easier for those who survived to find the bodies.

Would anyone find my body?

For hours I contemplated a myriad of fates, each worse than the next. Was I going to be crushed from debris in an aftershock? Was I going to die from blood loss? Was I going to starve to death? You get the idea.

I eventually braved the pain and stretched my arms to begin exploring my surroundings by touch. I discovered there was open space above me and a metal structure to my right. I was fairly certain I was lying on my laptop case. To my right I felt debris: brick, glass, plaster, and an assortment of things I couldn't identify. I brought my right arm back and down my side to see if I could detect what had pinned my legs. This was difficult and painful, but yielded an unexpected discovery; light. I had shifted rubble next to me and it revealed a faint glow. I began clawing at the small opening in earnest. Soon, I could pass my hand through the hole. I began flailing it about, doing my best to shout for help, hoping someone outside would notice.

I found myself silently praying to a God I had long ignored, because we had a few disagreements about what was said in His book. Luck, or perhaps God had not been so offended by my absence, came through for me that night. Someone noticed and people began digging me out, which as it turns out was not a difficult task. Luck, or again God, was on my side.

I had made it.

I'd actually gotten free of the hotel, but had become trapped under a dumpster that had fallen sideways. It was holding the weight of some of the collateral wreckage of the hotel, part of which had spilled down onto my legs.

My injuries were fairly minor considering all I had been through: a few cracked ribs, a fractured wrist (which still stings a little when it snows), a concussion, and of course, bruises just about everywhere. It was a miracle that my legs were fine, that I had lived.

The next few days were hell. I found a Red Cross shelter and ended up volunteering. At first I couldn't do much in my injured condition, but as I healed I was able to be of more help. After a week, volunteering had become my life. Everything that had come before was like a dream. I connected with two people there: Connie Van Den Poole and Miss Ruby Divine.

Connie was a nurse, Ruby a drag queen. They were a combination that injured people needed. Connie would tend to aliments of the body and Ruby those of the spirit. They complimented each other well and both kept my spirits high. When Ruby and I were alone she would share what news she had gleaned from gossiping with those in charge.

The Super Flu that had appeared was moving rapidly through the country, and the fatality rate was high. Way too high. When we were alone, she would cry on my shoulder, wracking sobs that shook her whole body. With me, she was able to let herself go, feel her grief, her fear, her frustration. I comforted her the best way I knew, cooing and wiping away her wet raccoon eyes. It was the least I could do for her and everyone else she made smile. She did so much to keep everyone happy with her saucy wit, painted face and bright red wig. I prayed that she would not get sick, or Connie.

By the eighth day, three people had died of SVHF. That number had more than doubled by the second week. I can't recall when the first flu case came in, but it was not long after that our fate was clear to me.

I sat with Connie. The rain coming down was cleaning away the noxious smell of the funeral pyres. We talked about what was to come. I tried to change the subject, to make light of things, poking fun at the medical masks we all wore now. She finally confessed that she had a fever. There was no question in her mind that she was as good as dead. Connie would not cry and she never did. She asked that I be there at the end. I was and held her hand as she slipped away. That was almost the end of July. By August, Ruby and I were the only ones left. We got drunk that night in the darkness of a once popular watering hole.

She ranted about how help was not coming, how the end was indeed nigh. Her voice reverberated throughout the abandoned pub, giving it the sound of some powerful goddesses from Greek Myth; prophesying doom and destruction. In my drunkenness, I remembered something, a memory of my life from before. I can't tell you why I remembered it then, but I did. At first, it was just a wisp dancing at the edge of my recollection. As she raged, I recalled more of the moment. A silly one to be sure, but in the haze of my inebriation I was convinced it could offer a ray of hope. I interrupted the drag queen to share my news.

I explained it to Ruby, as I will explain to you. The first thing I should mention is blogs, as I imagine they will not be part of the new world. Blogs, short for web logs, are diaries, or logs, which are maintained on the Internet, sometimes called the World Wide Web. The Internet was an interconnection of computers which allowed for almost infinite data to be shared with whoever owned a computer with access to the Internet.

Shannon is my partner, and while many things, just happens to be a bit of an enthusiast of all things apocalyptic, like zombie movies and nuclear winter. It's a little quirky, but I don't mind. Our friend Karl also shares this odd hobby and it was really him that set this in motion. A couple of weeks before I left for my trip, Shannon had invited Karl over for a night of "end of the world movies" and typically, it dissolved into a good natured debate over what locations in Seattle would be highly defensible and well equipped should the apocalypse come. Shannon always came back to this fancy retreat spa in the mountains we frequented, because it has its own water source and hydroelectric capabilities. That's when Karl jumped in with this idea he had read about in a blog of a woman named Kayley.

She was musing, rambling really. She had dreamt about a man, a friend of hers, Monte. He represented survival to her and after speaking of what she had dreamt, they agreed to meet in Grants Pass, Oregon, if the apocalypse ever came. Shannon had found the idea amusing and after researching the place online, we all agreed that should the world end, we would meet there. It was silly and not serious at all. We laughed about it and soon it was forgotten. Who ever really thinks the world is going to end?

Ruby laughed at me. She laughed long and hard; so hard that tears streamed down her cheeks like black rivers. As she collected herself, tucking her false crimson hair behind her ear, she smiled. It was a large, full smile. That moment is forever burned into my memory.

"My dear, the fucking world has ended and you are still a geek. You plan to find salvation in an online journal. Javier, you still tote that damn computer around, as if you are ever going to be able to connect to the Internet again. It's all gone now." She gestured with her slight wrist, rolling it as she swept her arm, indicating the world.

"It is all gone, Javier." She sashayed towards me, her black scarf trailing behind her. "You should go, find Shannon. You deserve to be together." She kissed me then, gently on the mouth. It was slow and sweet. I could smell her perfume, rich and heady. It suited her well. I asked her if she would come with me. She smiled a slight smile, but her eyes were sad and reminded me of Connie's eyes when she had come clean that she had contracted the Super Flu. "That is very sweet of you to ask. However, San Francisco is my home. I was born here. I came out here. I was fabulous here...and, Javier, I shall die here."

She sauntered away from me, glancing back over her shoulder; a performer until the end. She knelt down to her purse, wavering just a bit. She removed something from within, stood, pivoted flawlessly on her spiked heels and tossed me what was in her hand. I caught it despite my intoxication. It was a prescription bottle for valium. It was empty.

Ruby looked me in the eyes, tears once again trickling down her cheeks. "Dance with me until I'm gone, Javier, then lay me out with candles on Hibernia Beach." I nodded and we embraced, slowly dancing in the silence of the pub.

That night I laid her out, surrounded by red and white candles. She was like Sleeping Beauty, if the princess had been a trollop. Ruby looked good tarted up. I stayed there and watched over her until dawn. I then returned to my bed at the Red Cross station. I woke in the afternoon and started packing provisions. I was going to make it to Grants Pass and if there was nobody there, I would continue on to Seattle to see, if by a miracle, Shannon had survived.

I met a few people on the way; Lindsey Porter and her daughter Sam were the first two I met. They had had a run in with an unsavory man. I helped them out. Thankfully, I had taken a gun with me on my trip north. This man — Walter was his name — had apparently decided that the end of civilization entitled him to anything he wanted; and Lindsey was something he had wanted. He had been keeping her daughter near him at all times with her hands bound. He had threatened to kill Sam if Lindsey didn't comply with his demands, which were all sexual. I shudder when I think of what the two had to endure at the hands of that man.

I met Lindsey as she was gathering berries for Walter. She had a wild look in her eyes; disheveled and dirty. I smiled at her and she just stared at me for a minute.

"Are you a good man?" she asked.

"I couldn't say," I replied. "I try to be, I guess. Do you need help?" She nodded, tears trickling down her face as she explained to me about Walter and her daughter. I believe I did what any decent person would have done. I took the gun from my pack and followed Lindsey back to their camp, such as it was.

Before Walter could even grab for Sam, I had the gun trained on him and ordered him to step away from the girl. Mother and daughter ran to each other. Lindsey removed the rope and as they were coming back to me, Walter made a jump for his gun. I shot him. I wasn't sure if I had hit my mark at first. Everything slowed down. Walter's body slowly twisted and fell, crimson seeping across his chest. It was comedic and horrific as his face twisted with surprise and what I would imagine was pain. Time returned to normal when his body hit the ground.

I remember that I couldn't catch my breath; my heart was pounding in my ears. I absently dropped the gun at my side. I sunk to my knees and vomited. The women rushed over to me, thanking me, and looking for assurances that I was alright, but I just waved them away.

They gave me a few minutes, but soon Lindsey's mothering took hold. First she insisted that we move away from Walter's body and soon after that she had me eating berries and drinking water. I didn't talk much for the next few days and most of that was asking them to stop thanking me.

Even now I have a hard time accepting that I killed another human being, even one as wretched as Walter. I still have nightmares about it, his twisted grimace accusing me; mocking me. I stand before God — who is sort of back in my life — desperately trying to hide my bloodied hands from him. I can justify it every which way, but still it haunts me.

Sometimes I wonder if Lindsey hadn't seen me vomiting — hadn't seen the glazed horror that turned my skin white and made my hands shake — would she have accepted my invitation for her and her daughter to travel to Grants Pass with me?

Somewhere near the border to Oregon we found a little boy, seven years old. He had been living in a gas station, eating the food from the snack mart. His name was Oswaldo Fuentes. He spoke no English, but I had learned Spanish years ago. Strangely, he seemed to have adapted quite well. I think mostly because he couldn't comprehend what had happened. We took him with us too.

We are all now in Grants Pass. As are many people, nearly a hundred and more arrive each day. The town is becoming a real refuge. We have no way of knowing if there are other places where survivors are gathering, but we here in Grants Pass are doing our best to build a future out of what has been left to us, which sadly is not much.

Monte, the friend mentioned in the journal is here, but everyone is still waiting for Kayley — I hope she makes it. It's the one thing that is preventing this community from moving forward. Nobody wants to go beyond what she started without her. Many here believe she is destined to be our leader; a couple even think of her as our messiah. I believe she's just an insightful girl with a brilliant idea. I hope she's safe.

As for me? Well, a friend from Seattle made it here, Annie Nguyen. She told me that Shannon died in his sleep. The Super Flu. She burned his body, as he would have wanted. My gut clenches every time I think of it, but I know it's time to let go of the past, to embrace the future, grim as it may be. I have adopted Oswaldo. Not officially of course, but in my heart, where it matters. Ruby was right, I do cling to a world that once was.

In fact, I carried that damn laptop all the way from San Francisco to Grants Pass. After locating a battery for it here, I decided to start a new journal. So if you're reading this, then it means you've found my laptop — better yet, you have a power source for it.

I ask, whoever you are, to remember that Shannon Patrick Conner was loved. Please remember Miss Ruby Divine as the bright light that she was — raccoon eyes and all. I hope that I, and the others here, have been able to build something good for Oswaldo, Sam, and all the other children.

Farewell to the past, may the hope of Grants Pass be fulfilled someday soon.

With all regard,

Javier Antonio Gutierrez.

BIOGRAPHY

James M. Sullivan has been spinning tales since his formative years, entertaining his family with tape-recorded stories and skits. As he matured, so did his medium — from school book fairs to essays to short stories.

Then Jim discovered gaming. He did not settle long for the role of participant and was soon creating plots and his own worlds. Live Action Role-Playing (LARP) was his next step. He has co-run a four-year fantasy LARP and a five-year vampire LARP. When a player asked Jim why he did not write stories and pointed out the plots he created were stories, he returned to writing short fiction.

He is a student now, pursuing a graduate degree in psychology, choosing to leave behind such jobs as network engineer, operator, and fundraiser. Jim enjoys volunteering at sci-fi/fantasy conventions, role-playing, cooking, reading, movie viewing, and spending time with friends and family.

AFTERWORD

When Jennifer Brozek asked me to write a story for her *Grants Pass* project, I was more than happy to write for the anthology. Not only was it an opportunity to work creatively with a friend, but I found the concept of *Grants Pass* a fresh and original idea for an anthology. I knew immediately I wanted to have my story take the form of an artifact discovered in the far future, and that I wanted to represent average people dropped into chaos.

To show characters forced to make the hard decisions, responding to internal and external stimuli, such as Ruby's choosing her own fate and our narrator's decision in dealing with Walter — but I did not want the characters to become subsumed by the need for survival and lose who they are as people.

This story was also personal therapy, as it allowed me to explore my feelings about my own move from California to Washington, even if in an abstract way. I am pleased that Jennifer asked me to write for *Grants Pass* and I hope everyone enjoys reading it as much as I enjoyed contributing to it.

EPILOGUE: Journal Entry

KAYLEY ALLARD

JULY 1: OBLIGATIONS

Twenty days ago was the last time I saw anyone alive in Redmond, Washington. That was June 11th. I had been at the small family grocery store, picking up supplies. Only two people had been in the shop: another customer and a checker. Both were very sick but both had the same grim determination that they — above all — would survive this.

This. This being the end of the world as we know it. I made a mark on the calendar to signify the day. Today, Thursday, the first of July. Just days before the holiday of getting drunk and setting off explosives, while someone burns slabs of meat over an open fire and everyone hopes that the injuries from the celebration of freedom happen to someone else. Only there will be no one to celebrate Independence Day this year. Nor any other holiday for that matter. Between the three plagues, global warming and the earthquake, the End, with a capital E, had come.

Now that it arrived and it seemed that I had survived, I felt a weird sense of obligation to write down what happened. I don't really know what took place except for what I read, heard and saw. People got sick and they died. Storms came and people died. The riots started, the city was put under martial law and more folks died. People died and there wasn't a damn thing I could do about it.

Some say I was lucky. My family was three thousand miles away, so I didn't have to watch them slip away. No. Instead, I got to watch my chosen family die. Cheryl, then her kids and, finally, her husband, Rory. Keane, Jim, Jeff and Robert. The last was Hans, three weeks ago. I had gone over to his townhouse to force feed him chicken soup. He was in bed, hallucinating. I think it was a happy hallucination. He died with a smile on his face as I held his hand. All I could do was tuck him back into his bed and leave before I threw up on him. I just made it to the bathroom.

As far as I know, I'm the last person alive in Redmond, maybe Washington. Hell, maybe the whole damn world. I think that's the most fucked-up thing about this. I'm in the heart of Redmond, three miles from Microsoft and I haven't seen anyone in weeks. If anyone could have survived beyond me, it should have been a bunch of geeks. Geeks are smart. I should have seen someone by now.

Right now, the power is still on and I mean to take advantage of that for as long as it holds out. I have started making a "To Do" list. I think it's to help me keep calm. If I'm busy, I don't have to think about anything.

TO DO:

Move. Scout out areas close to the library and the grocery store. Some place on 160th Street. I'm getting tired of that hill of mine. I need to be closer to these things for safety and comfort.

Figure out what to do about the bodies of the dead people around the new home. This is both a cleanliness thing and a smell thing. I'm debating about finding a dump or burning them in a grand funeral pyre — sending them on their way to heaven if there is a God. Right now, I have my doubts.

Turn off excess lights and machines. Maybe that will help the electricity hold out longer.

Find a generator and learn how to work it.

This is just getting depressing and really is not helping me do what I want it to do. I know I'm trying to distract myself.

I can confess this here because no one is going to read it. If they do, I will probably be long dead. Just in case: Hello, alien or historian! Maybe that is: alien historian. Wouldn't that be a hoot? *"Dead planet, yellow star. Tell us where your children are..."*

Two days ago, while I was boxing up my 'essentials' to take to the new place — once I choose it — one of my diaries fell out of the pile. It was the print-out of last year's online journal. Being a narcissistic lass, I sat down and started reading. I would read two or three entries, then skip a few pages and start reading again. How simple life was. I had a wonderful boyfriend, a good job, a great house and my only problems were whether or not I was going to have time to clean before guests came over, what the office gossip was and who my cat was going to bite next. Petty, insignificant, marvelously human thoughts.

Then, I came to it. That journal entry in May before everything went to hell in a hand basket. 'Grants Pass.' I had totally forgotten about that entry, written in a fit of fancy after a conversation with my friend, Monte. "If an apocalypse comes and you survive, think of me and then head to Grants Pass. My whimsy could save your life."

I lie. I had *almost* forgotten about it, but I had not been ready or willing to remember it. Until now. It probably explains why I have been so productive in raiding REI to gather supplies for 'just in case'. I have enough stores of dried food to last a single person for a decade.

Grants Pass.

May 17th last year, I made a written promise to meet any survivors of the end of the world in Grants Pass, Oregon. Four hundred and some odd miles south of me down the I-5. I told the survivors to meet me there. That I would be there to help rebuild in the new post-apocalyptic world.

I never thought it would happen. But, here it is.

Why the hell would I want to leave my secure environment, to face who knows what, to go to a little town in Oregon to meet other survivors who may or may not be there and may or may not be friendly?

I've been wrangling with this question for two days now. It reminded me of a brief conversation I had with Thea. She had pretty much asked me the exact same thing, but added in "secure bolt holes, a known fresh water source and a well known enough city that surviving people would flock to it instead of her having to leave for some tiny town in the middle of the mountains." She was right. I was wrong. I wish I could tell her.

I can't decide if I should go or not. I know I wrote that entry, but what are the odds of another survivor having actually read it? Read it AND decided to go there? Practically none. The only people I know who would have done so I lost touch with over three weeks ago. Anyone else, there's no guarantee that I would like them. That would be just my luck. Stuck with an asshole as my only companion for the rest of my life.

But I digress.

I said I would meet them and I have always been a woman of my word. Always followed my promises. Does my obligation still hold? Do I *have* an obligation to them, total strangers? I'm comfortable and happy here. Happy enough. I have my plans. I have my books. I know what I need to do to fix up Redmond. What's waiting for me in Grants Pass? Much less, along the way?

I'm afraid. I can admit it. I'm scared shitless that there won't be anyone there. Even more scared of *who* might be there. What if they want me to lead them because I was the one who called them there? I'm good at making decisions. Just not always the right ones. What if they don't want me to lead? Maybe some know-it-all is there and has already taken charge? Worse yet, what if he or she is damn good at the job and should have it?

Christ! I'm insane! I don't even know if anyone is alive out there and I'm already making up enough drama to float a soap opera for at least two or three seasons!

Still. I have to wonder. What if Monte did make it through and is waiting for me, wondering where the hell I am? Or if anyone else did survive. It has been kind of lonely without anyone around. I could keep myself busy for a while with my list of tasks, but eventually, I would have time to think. Time is one of those things I have an abundance of now.

I miss everyone so much. I used to dream about a world where I could be by myself with no one around me. No one to tell me what to do or to cut me off in traffic. No one to yell at me or ask me about deadlines or to forget to invite me to a movie. A world where I could be left alone.

Oh, God! What if all this is my fault? I wrote about it in my journal. I secretly wished for it from time to time. I loved to watch *The Stand* by Stephen King and my favorite apocalyptic 80s film, *Night of the Comet*. What if I had wished for it and the universe decided, for some unknown reason, to grant my plea? I killed everyone with my own romanticized selfishness!

No. No. No. I'm getting myself worked up for nothing here. The apocalypse was not my fault. Talk about the ultimate in egomania. Global warming is a bitch and the three plagues were a terrorist plot.

I really need someone here to slap some sense into me. The world is not all about "I". It may seem like it right now, but that's not true.

You want to know how I know? Because, two days ago, I made a subconscious decision that I was going to take it on faith that there were other people out there and that by some miracle, not only had they survived, they had read my post

293

and are coming to meet me in Grants Pass. It has taken me until now to actually admit that to myself. Now that it has been written and acknowledged, my obligation is clear.

The question has become: Am I brave enough to make the trip?

JULY 12: THOUGHTS

It's been almost two weeks since I wrote in my journal. Writing longhand sucks. I have terrible penmanship. I haven't moved. I'm still in my condo. But, I have been thinking about Grants Pass. I think I am going to go. The silence is driving me insane.

I've been wondering about what I should bring. Books mostly. Specific books on keeping a community going. I've got a lot of my own in my apocalyptic cabinet. I never thought I would have to actually use it. I suppose that's one of the reasons the *Zombie Survival Guide* was in there next to *When there are No Doctors.*

Seriously though, if I'm going, I've got to be prepared. I've got to prove that my thoughts of meeting in Grants Pass were valid and not random happenstance. I've got to make sure that if there are people there, waiting for me, depending on me, that it was not in vain.

I've got to prove it to myself if no one else.

Beyond the books are the emergency supplies, batteries, crop seed and medicine. And weapons. I can't pretend that everyone is going to be nice and happy and polite. The old rules of order and society are gone.

I wonder if Monte made it. I hope to God — if there is a God — that there is at least one friendly, familiar face waiting for me.

JULY 31: JOURNEY

I'm ready to go. This is it. Everything is packed. Tomorrow, I will leave at 9am. That should put me there by 4pm, barring any unexpected nastiness. August 1st has always been my personal New Year's Day. It is an appropriate time to start a new life.

I decided to take a jeep instead of my car because it has four wheel drive, more room and can navigate rough terrain better. My neighbors had one and it's not like they are going to be using it. They decided to drink a nice batch of special Kool-Aid instead of fighting to survive. But that is neither here nor there. I am going to let the cat out of the house to fend for herself. I hate doing this, but it is better than a slow death of starvation if I don't make it back.

That's if I don't decide to take her with me. I might. I probably will. We'll see.

The jeep is packed with gas, food, water, medical supplies and weapons. I think I'm prepared. I have driven to the San Francisco Bay Area and back several times before. At 430 miles, I should make it within five to six hours. Barring any major mishaps.

My plan is to drive directly there and to stay for ten days. Then, I will put up signs with directions and return home to Redmond. Or, I will continue on towards the Bay Area, to my old stomping grounds and see if there are people there. It's damn hot in the summer, but you don't have to deal with snow in the winter.

I still can't decide whether I want to meet people at Grants Pass or along the way, or not. The idea excites and terrifies me. I think I'm leaning towards the former. It would be nice to hear a voice other than my own.

I'm leaving this journal, along with all of my other journals, here in the library, in case I don't make it back and someone else comes along. I know I'm vain. I want to be remembered. I want someone to know that I was here and that I had survived the end of the world.

I'm leaving a map to Grants Pass as well. Maybe it will turn out that Grants Pass is the right place to go and whoever finds this journal will meet me there.

Over a year ago, I made a promise to six billion strangers. I guess it's time for me to go see how many of them took me up on it.

Please don't forget me.

Love,

Kayley Allard

ABOUT THE EDITORS

JENNIFER BROZEK, the creator and co-editor for the *Grants Pass* anthology, is a freelance author for Margaret Weis Productions and OtherWorld Creations, as well as a technical writer for Amazon.com. She is a contributor to multiple RPG sourcebooks (Dragonlance, Castlemourn, Cortex) and has co-authored three books (*A Player's Guide to Castlemourn* with Ed Greenwood, 2006; *Chill*, 3rd Edition with Mike Callahan, 2008; and *Dragonvarld Adventures* with Margaret Weis, 2008).

She is published in several anthologies and is the creator and editor of the semi-pro webzine, *The Edge of Propinquity*. When she is not writing her heart out, she is a loving wife to her husband, Jeff, and an indulgent 'mother' to their three cats.

AMANDA PILLAR is a speculative fiction author and editor who lives in Victoria, Australia, with her partner and two children, Saxon and Lilith — Burmese cats.

Amanda has had numerous short stories in print, with more awaiting publication. She is also the co-editor of the anthologies, *Voices* (2008), and *The Phantom Queen Awakes* (2009), both published by Morrigan Books and is working on *Scenes from the Second Storey*.

You can read about her adventures at her livejournal, located at http://amandapillar.livejournal.com or you can visit her website: www.amandapillar.com.

ABOUT THE COVER ARTIST

I don't have a bio. I just lived. I never took notes! NO ONE TOLD ME I HAD TO TAKE FRICKING NOTES!

Sheesh.

Fine. I'll use the one from Three Crow Press.

REECE NOTLEY was born and raised in Hawai'i then, in her late teens, her feet grew itchy and she wandered off to see the world. After chewing through a pile of books, a lot of odd food and a stray boyfriend or two she eventually landed in San Diego, which she believes to be a very nice place but seriously needs more rain.

She currently has a day job that she mostly enjoys, herding pixels for the marketing department of a nice company with a fantastic view of the seashore from many floors up. As of this moment, she admits to sharing the house with three cats, a black Pomeranian puffball, a bonsai wolfhound and a ginger cairn terrorist.

Reece is also enslaved to the upkeep of a 1969 Ford Mustang Grand Coupe, a 1979 Pontiac Firebird and a Toshiba laptop. Her next published piece of writing will be in *Dead Souls* in 2009. She also rides herd on *Three Crow Press*, a horror, fantasy, sci-fi and speculative fiction e-zine (www.threecrowpress.com).

AVAILABLE NOW:

"In this grim fable, the stakes are suicide by Apocalypse, and the question is what can endure, and what refuses to end."

— Elaine Cunningham

THE EVEN by T.A. MOORE

In the Even — a city built in the intersection between the real and the not —ruled by the iron whim of the demon Yekum where treachery brewed amidst the ever-changing streets. Ancients dwell in the city who have out-lived their purpose and grown jaded with their immortality. They want only to die and they will take the whole world with them if they have to: suicide by Apocalypse.

Only Faceless Lenith, goddess, cynic and gambler, stands in their way. The fate of the world rests on her shoulders and mankind did not conceive her to be wise.

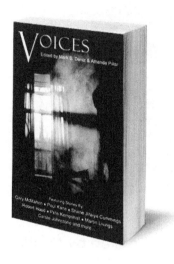

AVAILABLE NOW:

DEAD SOULS edited by MARK S. DENIZ

Before God created light, there was darkness. Even after He illuminated the world, there were shadows — shadows that allowed the darkness to fester and infect the unwary.

The tales found within *Dead Souls* explore the recesses of the soul; those people and creatures that could not escape the shadows. From the inherent cruelness of humanity to malevolent forces, *Dead Souls* explores the depths of humanity as a lesson to the ignorant, the naive and the unsuspecting.

God created light, but it is a temporary grace that will ultimately fail us, for the darkness is stronger and our souls...are truly dead.

COMING SOON:

THE PHANTOM QUEEN AWAKES
edited by MARK S. DENIZ & AMANDA PILLAR

The Phantom Queen, goddess of death, love and war, returns to strike fear into the hearts of mortals in the anthology, *The Phantom Queen Awakes*.

Meet a washerwoman on the shores of the river; cleaning the clothes of the soon-to-be-dead; try to bargain with the capricious goddess of war; hear the songs of the dead as they cry for justice; walk with heroes of the past

Revisit the world of the Celts; a land of mystical beauty, avarice, lust and war through stories told by Katharine Kerr, C.E. Murphy, Elaine Cunningham and Anya Bast, among many other talented authors.

www.morriganbooks.com

THREE CROW PRESS
MORRÍGAN BOOKS' E-ZINE

Editors
J. LEE. MOFFATT, T.A. MOORE & REECE NOTLEY

Three Crow Press is an online magazine specializing in quality speculative fiction, fantasy (urban, dark and gothic), horror and steampunk as well as non-fiction pieces and articles.

Well written young adult will be considered if the piece is within the 16+ market.

We are prepared to consider all forms of dark fiction works and are looking for stories that capture the imagination of the Three Crow staff. Please check submissions guides prior to submitting.

www.threecrowpress.com
www.morriganezine.com

Made in the USA
Monee, IL
08 July 2022

99320391R00187